TRANSLATED ACCOUNTS

Also by James Kelman

'And the Judges Said . . .' Essays
The Burn
The Busconductor Hines
A Chancer
The Good Times
Greyhound for Breakfast
Not not while the giro
An Old Pub Near the Angel

TRANSLATED ACCOUNTS

James Kelman

First published in 2001 by Secker & Warburg.
This edition published in 2009 by Polygon,
an imprint of Birlinn Ltd

West Newington House
10 Newington Road
Edinburgh
EH9 1QS

www.birlinn.co.uk

9 8 7 6 5 4 3 2 1

ISBN 978 1 84697 056 6

British Library Cataloguing-in-Publication Data
A catalogue record for this book is available on request from
the British Library.

Typeset in Minion by Palimpsest Book Production Limited,
Grangemouth, Stirlingshire
Printed and bound by [PLEASE SUPPLY PRINTER]

Foreword to the New Edition

I was glad to proof this new edition of *Translated Accounts*. It allowed me to perform an editorial. If writers get the chance they must take it. I thank the publishers and editorial team for allowing the chance. I thank also the typsetting team for respecting the work.

James Kelman

Preface

These "translated accounts" are by three, four or more individuals domiciled in an occupied territory or land where a form of martial law appears in operation. Narrations of incidents and events are included; also reports, letter-fragments, states-of-mind and abstracts of interviews, some confessional. While all are "first hand" they have been transcribed and/or translated into English, not always by persons native to the tongue. In a very few cases translations have been modified by someone of a more senior office. The work was carried out prior to posting into the computing systems. If editorial control has been exercised evidence suggests inefficiency rather than design, whether wilful or otherwise. This is indicated by the retention of account Number 5 in the form it emerged from computative mediation. A disciplined arrangement of the accounts has been undertaken. Some arrived with titles already in place; others had none and were so assigned. Chronology is important but not to an overriding extent; variable ordering motions are integral to the process of mediation that occurs within computing systems and other factors were taken into consideration. It is confirmed that these accounts are by three, four or more anonymous individuals of a people whose identity is not available.

1

"bodies"

There were bodies strewn throughout the building. I had to reach other rooms and it was so very difficult to walk, having to step over them, and it was so very dark the shapes hardly visible, whether any of these were familiar I could not say, could not stop, but had to reach this one individual,

acquaintance, this man who was closer to enemy than friend, I was to save him. But perhaps he preferred not so to be saved, that I should leave him to die. I could not help him in that. I would do as so determined, only that. I was representative.

I considered the time, what time? When was it? I now saw him and my immediate thought was, No, he never was my friend. Did they say that he was? They lied, as he also, he was a liar, this man. I knew him as a liar and it came to me this was a progression. We progress. I also would progress. A comfort came from this. I again was aware of the bodies but as in a dream, or dream-like, my own state. One by my feet, a woman. She had been dead for many years but her face and kind were familiar. If I had known her, her family, I thought I had done so, thus her sister now into my thoughts, what of her, who was to become my lover. How could it be? Niece, granddaughter. She too lived by the bridge. It was far to the harbour, north-east of there, and a river also there, families lived by it. It was an encampment, when in transit, they made a dwelling of that place, evil place, some said so. I knew dripping water, sewage, the dampness into our bones, and cold, of course cold.

Whose head is with the children? Who said that the children always are in discomfort, someone did say it.

Dreams, not nightmares. I would have had nightmares. I did not shirk. I do not. Her sister was a woman of strength. There is that strength. I could speak of this, and at an earlier time. Women came from here. I knew them. She was taller. She met me that morning, early, it was cold and the dampness, chilling. We came from our section. I said of the bodies, how securitys came, gripping their rifle weapons, herding us. We knew they had knocked the brains out of the heads of children and said so. Yes, if it was so, we said it. And they asked us things, certainly they did so. And saw in us our contempt, that we could not hide and could not, could not hide it, they were asking myself, had I found this man?

What man?

You know.

I know. No, I said, I do not know, if it is his body, is it his head, and if it is so it is not now recognisable, if it is one of those. Who it is, whom do you speak? There is the group, see the group, and I pointed to the main group.

I was not boastful. I told them I did not know why this building was a home but that it was and I was going through there and could not step but for bodies, everywhere. Now I see, yes, that I recognised many among them, friends yes intimates, intimates. I said it, familiars. I said that they were. If misrepresentation, there has been so, I have been exhausted and the times, evil. For they herded us. I am not an animal. Some may be, I am not. We make decisions, each among us. I told them too about the woman but that she had been dead for many years. One stepped to me and said, I too have read these stories. These times were evil, men severed from sisters, daughters, rapacious.

Yes rapacious, I know the word.

But not me, I would not be trapped. This was a dream.

Yes I saw the bodies. Yes I did know many of them. Of course not all, I did not say all. I could not have said all for this was not reality that it was all, I could not have said this but had it been reality, holding to be true, if so it had been then I would not shirk, not from it, truth, why should we, shirking from it.

I could say if this was reality. It is over. No charges were laid against me.

I came to that building, house or home to many and inside were the bodies. I went to another and this was a man who was the son of a man. He had been insolent, had not the wit to grasp of security how serious a business it had become and I said to his father what had happened to him. They killed him. He knew it.

The mist clung to us, we were herded, the chill, children. Yes we had heard the stories. I knew the stories, if one does not, who it is. There were the women here, these women were strong and of course stronger than the men as is said in their manner. It is to be remembered of our section and that encampment how at that time, feeling that those who dwell there cannot survive this other winter. I cannot, each of us thinking it.

And so we continued, I also. I was not a fantasist as many were among us. I saw former acquaintances, colleagues, who themselves were dead, now with these bodies, others alive, seeing them on the streets there, if I can say streets. I could say friends if it were true. They were no friends.

I was to recover him. He preferred that I leave him to die. I could not save such a man if the judgment was my own but it was not, this course was determined. What I could do, nothing. My regret also nothing, I regret nothing, nothing. This was a dream, not a nightmare. These were evil times, they say, now is not like then. But no matter that they say this it is not so, and those of us who then were we know it is not so. I could not save him. Those days were at an end.

3

2

"the elderly woman died"

The woman discovered early on the road, I know who she was. When she was living I visited her. I would talk and she would lie back on her pillows and listen not listen. My talk was stories, they followed patterns and within the pattern was space for dreams, her dreams my dreams, as of weaving, the story-web, spiders. She stared at the ceiling as though her attention wandered but also as to settle herself that she might concentrate. She wished me there as long as possible. But her gaze could shift to the window, was it open or closed. Had they, previous visitors, neglected to lock up afterwards. She believed some had methods of tormenting her. These visitors might not lock the door, the window, allowing the devils to enter from beyond. This was such a method. She trusted no one. I would say to her, Look, your window is closed. She was pretending not to hear. But look! and stepping across I pushed and pulled, the window not shifting. See, no one is playing tricks, this window cannot be shifted but by explosives, greater explosives.

She did not believe it. I would see agitation in her. I could not be trusted. In her eyes I saw it, she mocked at me, the spirit of me, hiding within me, it was a devil, spirit of a devil, a demon. Or if I was so speaking she might turn from me and to the wall, remaining silent, staying that way and I wondered if she was sleeping.

There were no people from earlier times, they did not come to her. This was not her homeplace. If she said that it was, it was not. Her mind was mistaken. Neighbours. What neighbours. What is neighbours. If visitors to her, there were visitors and she only cried at them, thieves, murderers! And with her stick, yes, lashing at them. At myself, also, neighbours may testify, if they so have said, yes. One might sit by her and she lashed with it, suddenly.

A religious man did visit her. I am not the religious man. She was not murdered, neither killed. She died.

If she would think of herself as having been murdered. None may ask her opinion. But the devils were responsible, evil ones, bringing her from behind the locked door to outside, outside as to the perimeter, they were dragging her, jeering at her, your breasts are withered and shrunken, old skin and bone, you are nothing, jeering also at her stick, it is a great weapon, oh greater, greater! and her agitation, everything, her clothing, what clothing.

She was of an age that to die is natural but she died on the road. Natural unnatural, unnatural natural. She died, it was on the road. She was an elderly woman whom I had known, had been acquainted. I spoke with her, she allowed my presence. If she did not consider me likeable. Yes, I accept this and accepted this, that she did not like me. I can say it as others might. They have done. I know that they have done. Why should they not if it is the case, as so, it was the case, certainly. If she liked anyone, did she, I do not think so.

I do not care. She is dead.

I had become familiar to her. From when I was in that area. The work had taken me to there and so I lived there. I lived in many areas, becoming familiar to some, as they to myself, many people, so it was with the elderly woman. She had nothing, no treasures, trinkets, no jewellery, no, not anything that I saw. Yet there may have been, she may have secreted such items. People do it, women. I did not look. These might have existed. I cannot answer. If she had a horde, treasure-trove, who is to say. Relations. She had a niece.

She had not been ill that I know. I had not visited with her but that last occasion. Not recently, other than the occasion referred. People have memories but in substance these may be false, not biased, not necessarily.

The religious man certainly had been visiting. I said about the religious man. If I am thought to be so, mistaken so, I am not religious, having none such belief. But this man did visit her, certainly, if from charitables, organisations. He neglected to close over the door. If not him, another. I came along and found it so. It lay open. People could have entered, children are here.

Elderly people, religious men, children, who is to say.

The door was open. I came along and saw it and so entered. It was not then, she was here, and sleeping. If I was not suspicious, I had to be so, of course. How this place had become and a door open, of course I entered. Perhaps she might be sleeping. She had her own manners, her customs. It would not have been his fault that now she was dead. She died on the road. I have no suspicions of the religious man. I have no knowledge of the niece. The elderly woman would blame no one not herself, would blame everyone, cared for none, only herself.

I have seen him, as they say religious man, I do not know him, have no recourse. He had been with her. I cannot say had his visit been requested. By whom? by her, I do not think so. Yet I cannot say what may be possible, anything. She was dozing when I entered but soon had raised herself, was sitting up,

of course on the bed, gripping the handle of the cane that she kept by the side. Stick, cane, a cane, she kept it by her, to herself. She had been waiting for me so was not frightened. She always was waiting for me. If I had made no plans, still she was waiting. Her memory was not good. If I entered she would expect me so to enter.

I did not correspond with her. If I was not in that area there was no communication. If I had travelled then was returning to the district, I visited. I had not visited for a long period of time and she would have expected that I come to see her. If I had not visited. She would have waited. I am saying it.

Her health was not good, she did not go walking. Not to the countryside, what countryside. Not beyond the walls of her home, where is the perimeter, she would not have known. Her life was there only in that place.

I took food. If I stole it from her, she thought so, food from herself. I have said it. But it was food I took to her, to herself. If visiting I took her food and ate with her, we two, I took food and with herself, we shared it.

Old people, elderly woman, we take food to them, if they will take it, some do not take it, they take nothing, eat nothing. How do they live, fresh air. There is no fresh air. I would say it, There is no fresh air. She did not answer, only looked to me and in her eyes she was mocking.

Also other of her possessions, all were stealing, all who came to visit with her. Thieves, murderers, everyone, all visitors. We took her possessions. That is what she said. Everyone comes into my house, they steal from me. Yet had I been doing such as she charged would she have suffered my visit. Perhaps having need of me, if she so had that. Yes, for she had need of visitors otherwise how she might live, she would have no food. Have you a book, she would say, give me a book, or have you a story, tell it to me, what songs are there? And if I would talk she would lie back on her pillows. I could not sing to her.

Of the niece, none knows what happened to her, if she disappeared. She did. I can say she will be dead. She is dead. If none says it I say it, am saying it.

I understand as much.

It is no prediction. I do not care. It is stated, I have so stated. Recorded, so, that the niece now is dead.

When the old woman saw me at her bedside she soon was talking, railing against all that she knew in the world. Myself also,

7

diatribes, against everyone. Neighbours may testify. Myself, whomever. And the religious man, yes, also. He is evil! He is a devil. Murderer!

If there is anyone else, who it might be. Everyone. Yes her niece, everyone, I have said. Also how her contempt for the people of this section, I have said it, she scorned them. She might refer to them as evil, yes, children, evil children, idiot children, she spoke so of them. Of the young, she spoke of them also as devils. I heard her say it. Devils. Spirits from the wall, young people of the district. I cannot say. Two kinds of spirits, real and not real, some came from the wall. I do not know.

Elderly people.

If the religious man said something, what he might have said, how I may know, I am not myself religious, if in God, yes, I do believe so, supreme creator. If without God, what kind of world that could be, if such a world could exist, no, I do not think so.

Where is the boy.

Yes, she would say this. Boy. She was referring not to her son but to myself. I know of no son. Nor daughter, if there is a daughter, neither son, I know nothing of them. It is myself whom she referred. I was the boy. I was that one.

If she had regard for me, perhaps. I do not know. To myself I was not likeable, not from her. I saw she did not like me, I thought so. If she had regard for me, no, if it is said so, I did not think so, do not.

I spoke to her, told stories to her. I can tell stories. She settled to listen, listen not listen, her mind moving by itself, fired by myself. I spoke to her of my life and her life, drawing stories from there, inventions. We do it, all stories.

I did not know her life.

She thought of me. I think of me. What is I think of me? She thought of me. The elderly woman. I do not believe it.

Then ranting about the devils on the staircase, their

screaming and shrieking against her, thieves and murderers, battering on her door, the walls of her room and too her roof, attempting to invade her room in what way any way to kill her in her own bed where she lay, dragging her out, twisting her limbs and her hair all out from her head, torturers. This was how she would cry out. She often did so. I would be there and suddenly awake she would be striking out with her stick. Often, she did so.

There was the staircase. I cannot say if she walked to there, upwards not down. If to the top of these stairs, that smell, always.

Striking out, yes, screaming and shrieking, ranting, to be murdered in her bed. It was her greater fear, more great, greater, murdered as she lay, as powerless, devils entering, coming upon her, demon spirits to drag her away. She had the stick, no weapon. But these were spirits, devil-spirits. She was at the mercy of these things. I would be calming to her, my hand to her brow. She would not be touched but I would touch her, yes her brow, one moment only. Old people, this elderly woman, I could calm her. She allowed it for one moment then might strike at me, to hit myself. No, I am your friend. But now she would mock me in her eyes, seeing myself, yes, I was a devil, spirit, spirit of a devil.

Until recognising it is myself, I am visiting. And into watchfulness she would stare to me, if she might speak it was of how they had stolen from her. Might I know where her goods had been taken. What goods. The goods stolen from her. No goods have been stolen from you, do not worry. But she would worry, she would cry out, goods are stolen! You are the thief! Yes, she would scream this. Murderer. These are my treasures.

What treasures there are no treasures.

I cannot say of treasures. Jewellery, trinkets. Articles held by women. These are precious. They so give to their family, daughters and granddaughters.

I had not known of any daughter. I can say this. I did not know of any daughter. But of her niece, I can say that she did not like her niece, holding her in suspicion. She told me so. This niece was a sly one. She said it. This niece also played tricks. The elderly woman said it to myself. I now am saying it, yes, that she played tricks, so may have done.

I did not meet with this niece. She may have cleaned, may have nursed, may have done all such things, cooked for her, other matters, nursing matters. If she spoke of myself, she did not know myself but if she said something, I do not know. I cannot say. I did not. When at my last visit the old woman was sleeping then was waking and her eyes opening, she saw that I was there by her, and she knew me, looking to me as to frighten me. Yes, sternly looking to myself. I knew of her suspicions, all who everyone might be and who I might be, I only was another man there thief and murderer. This was not new. I was seeking treasures and trinkets and had come to her house. It was not a house but a room, yes, in that section, by that staircase, that staircase. She had nothing. What someone would do. She was elderly. Elderly people also have courage. I could not be elderly. It is an opinion. I hold this opinion of myself.

3

"endplace"

No matter the outcome I would discover something of it, more of it, and here it is of the future. So, we had moved one from another. He now would know that this distance was between us. He had not the power to outwit me, it could not be done, not by him.

This place that we were inside had been a town building of a kind, building with people, seeming so also to have been offices. Many of us were there but myself and the one were finding the route of entry. The others did not help. The work I thought of interest, also physical, but excitement lay in its mystery, that this building as formerly was unknown to all, it was such a venture and if I should have been worried then no, the one with me I did not care about. His selection was by others, himself but by others and his enthusiasm was survival. Mine was not.

I had detractors. Who does not. They had no grounds. Not all were detractors, those who spoke against me.

It is not important.

Where we would begin. The others fifty metres off, the brick wall by there also dilapidated, over that which we would travel, climb upon and would it not crumble, would we pass there safely. Questions questions, those and others. Some would sleep, some talk, some only lying. All regaining strength. At first the one was by me, keeping there as if a team, we two. I ignored him. The building in length, horizontal, was twenty metres.

And so from the outside immediate impenetrability, we two there standing. In silence, I could not talk with himself, nor to myself, he to myself. If there is significance, I do not know, for myself it is nothing. He was to my left side. He had been on my right side and I did manoeuvre and now that he saw he said something but I did not respond, but moving then, yes, time and onwards. The approach itself was to be solved, I could solve it. The lower wall was ahead. Intact. Three metres in height and with the circular top to reach, hoisting upwards quickly, quickly. And the further wall now a greater test, but over it also and inside lay wood, beams of wood and concrete, iron rods, masonry. It lay in its mass, its mass. The impenetrability of this, seeking the entry and if this entry was to be discovered I could not discover it it was outside myself beyond myself, it was, I not discover it, could not. And he now was in sight, moving up and across the second wall, thirty metres from me, climbing. How could I push, it is not sensible.

But the mass lacked entry. It lacked entry.

If entry was there, if I was in error.

Routes existed. I only could seek them, dislodging the first beams, looking that I so might find. I could force entry and would force entry, I can say it.

He also was here. It was an irritation to me. Only that. I then had gained balance. He also. Where he had come from in seconds, I did not know, having been on the lower wall. If he was a capable man, it is certain that he was. Yet neither was there physical power in his body. Why that was. Yet he had none. What his life had been I cannot say, tall man but thin, thin. If power had been there I do not know of the form, perhaps endurance tests, as of the dancer in strength, lifting women. If so and he had this it was concealed, this could not be distinguished, nor when we began, swinging onto the uppermost wall, myself being first onto there but with an entry in a bad location, worse location, and I had selected it myself when from the ground seeing upwards, the mass from there, how I could make a way for myself. It could not be. I saw that it lay impossible. This was as confirmation. How I could succeed, I could not, and if I failed, I would not fail. I heard laughter. The laughter was to me. I saw the one now with a weight of concrete, wielding this as hammer against something inside, his attempt to force entry, bulwark to his entry, but he forced, was forcing, yes he had a strength. Yes, and I also, seeking the iron rods yes and finding one, breaking one, yes loosening and in my grip at that time it felt strongly to me my knuckles, gripping. I too had the strength, my arms with power, and I might do it, so would do it, yes. It came free, thus to be laughed at by those others, yes they may laugh, all may so laugh. What I may do. No, I do not think so

I would be inside very very quickly, squeezing entry into where it might be. But, too, caution. I could be trapped. I had strength, unlike the other, a chest strong, with power, my upper arms also and if we were to fight no advantage would be to him through physique, only than height. But height, what is height, reach, but to what, reach to something. I had strength, he had none to myself, what he could do, nothing, he could do nothing, not to myself, I do not sneer, I am saying it, simply, it was as that.

I was at this time near to one ceiling, walking quickly to see where I should be and some way along there I saw a place that had this possible way. I said it I was not so tall as the one in opposition but above the lower wall here was a further tanglement of wood, concrete, iron bars, more rods, and I could grasp these latter with my left hand, retaining my own weapon, and they held for me. I also was not heavy in weight, so to be tossed by the wind, if not by this other, if as nothing, not so to him.

No bitterness was in me. Others may do so what they will do, feeling such, yes, all their lives, themselves themselves, there is no bitterness to myself, in myself. I have none, I can say it, am saying it.

I looked to him, hearing the knocking, he was wielding the iron bar. What had happened to his concrete piece, yes, had it smashed into fragments and looking at him my bar might crunch into the shell that was his head, it would come not long from there.

I had not selected him, not myself selected. Securitys were there. If I am to say more, what it might be, that is not yet known. I was to move to him, so moving, he now was in retreat. What is not known. All is known or may be predicted and at any time. This man had no power, not to myself, and I move swiftly, so may do it, swiftly

4

"one of many"

Yes, this was the redhaired woman. She was coming from outside. She had a large bundle, parcel. Where do things come into existence? She hurried into our section. I listened, the door shutting. It was quietly done by her, not wanting one sound. She has a child, a baby, was carried on her back, its face was tiny.

The face of the baby, any baby

This woman did not have a companion. I did not know of one with her, if accompanying her. This companion was not seen. None saw him, her. I did not, no other. How I can say it, if I may.

I also have a child.

The wind blew. She wore a wide top, clothing piece, and so her body was revealed. She would wear clothes that are not her own, seeming as such, as in an effort to conceal herself, wide clothes, wider.

But if she did not care, it is possible.

She never would look to me. I smiled now but again, not, why not look to me like this? Yes she was afraid but not of me. Why? There is no reason. I had an attraction to her and did want her if I did so, sexually, yes, as this is man to woman, not a horrible and terrible thing. She saw me, yes watching her I did so. Often. Yes, I do not deny it. But I would do nothing that might be unwanted. Thus, I studied her. She saw me, myself, I also as seeing myself, watching. This for her too was something, if she thought of it, what she did think, as I watched her, studying herself, what she did think, it is man to woman, if she was fearful.

This place where we were, horrible things, events, leaving their sign. Yes, these then are signs of existence. Their existence. Some are material.

Its effect on us, myself, as on anyone, human beings, lowering our strength, lowering our resolve, weakening our spirits, yes, we were weakened spirits, this is how I can say it.

What history may be.

She had her baby, it was with her.

I said I have a child, so thoughts of my child, one other life, one to another.

I do speak of spirit. Something may reach out. It is no recourse, I was comfortable with such thinking, am comfortable now, comfortable with it now too, also, yes.

What is there to enumerate, essence of human being, our strength alone, this thing, what it is, more than resolve. I was unable to avoid these descriptions of my state, reaching to what was, if what it may be, that I in becoming. What happened would not become clear until I was out from my own self, away from there but when that could be, and how were we to live through this until it, if it should come.

None explains this to us. None ever does so.

I cannot say either what happened to the redhaired woman but she was one of many, if she was, I think that she was. She had a large bundle, a parcel, if something was inside it. I also, having a child, I have said it.

5

"¿FODocument"

vvvvvvvvvvvvvvvvvvvvvvvvvvvvvvvvvvvvvvvvvvvvvvvvvvvvvvvvvvvvvvvvvvv
vvvvvvvvvvvvvvvvvvvvvvvvvvvvvvvvvvvvvvvvvvvvvvvvvvvvvvvvvvvvvvvvvvv
vvvvvvvvvvvvvvvvvvvvvvvvvvvvvvvvvvvvvvvvvvvvvvvvvvvvvvvvvvvvvvvvvvv
vvvvvvvvvvvvvvvvvvvvvvvvvvvvvvvvvvvvvvvvvvvvvvvvvvvvvvvvvvvvvvvvvvv
vvvvvvvvvvvvvvvvvvvvvvvvvvvvvvvvvvvvvvvvvvvvvvvvvvvvvvvvvvvvvvvvvvv
vvvvvvvvvvvvvvvvvvvvvvvvvvvvvvvvvvvvvvvvvvvvvvvvvvvvvvvvvvvvvvvvvvv
vvvvvvvvvvvvvvvvvvvvvvvvvvvvvvvvvvvvvvvvvvvvvvvvvvvvvvvvvvvvvvvvvvv

vvvvvvvvvvvvvvvvvvvv¿F0Document₍ NB0Documentifwe may do so if
wemaysppeakvvvvvvvvvvvvvvvvvvvvvvvvvvvvvvvvvvvvvvvvvvvvvvvvvvvvvv
vvvvvvvvvvvvvvvvvvvvvvvvvvvvvvvvvvvvvvvvvvvvvvvvvvvvvvvvvvvvvvvvvvv
vvvvvvvvvvvvvvvvvvvvvvvvvvvvvvvvvvvvvvvvvvvvvvvvvvvvvvvvvvvvvvvvvvv
vvvvvvvvvvvvvvvvvvvvvvvvvvvvvvvvvvvvvvvvvvvvvvvvvvvvvvvvvvvvvvvvvvv
vvvvvvvvvvvvvvvvvvvvvvvvvvvvvvvvvvvvvvvvvvvvvvvvvvvvvvvvvvvvvvvvvvv
vvvvvvvvvvvvvvvvvvvvvvvvvvvvvvvvvvvvvvvvvvvvvvvvvvvvvvvvvvvvvvvvvvv
vvvvvvvvvvvvvvvvvvvvvvvvvvvvvvvvvvvvvvvvvvvvvvvvvvvvvvvvvvvvvvvvvvv

¿F0ocumentforwhichdept₍infanyNB0Documentifwe may do
so if wemaysppeaknocurfewanycurfewwhatforthatevening
Therewasnocurfewthatevening'@-œ‡°±·₍ˇR\onwhich perimeter
ifwe aretospeak how is it we may do so if we may speak
≤≤±≤Document"≠""'"''zz%z%%This also was early for myself,
he had come to this town, he had obligations!! ¿ F • • ˅ˇ
£§§§Ä0rcforwhichdept₍@ifdotcom ˅˅˅NB0Document tildnot-
tild æ forwhich deptiflangwhichlangifwespeakhabla @FO
@ifdotcom if what @ifdotcom Compus Obj††ü† ObjectPoo if
irreligiouslùùùúú°°† †ü†üüüûùùúú ööõõôö ˅˅ \ˉ æD o c u m e n

t for FO dept of r | hot:whatlanguage G º3G ‰5ˇˇˏˇÃÃ ÃÃ
ôôôô ôô ff ¨D commentarycommentary whosawfather"""art ffO
b j e c t P o o l in earlyto this town, hehadobligationsfo ff33
ff33ˇˇ 33ÃÃ33ôô33ˇˇˇ^$Y]æ^ $Y]æ33 ÓÓ"ˇˇˇ ˇˇˇ ˇˇˇ ˇˇˇ
65ˇˇˇˇˇˇˇˇˇˇˇˇˇˇˇˇˇˇˇˇˇˇˇˇˇˇˇˇˇˇˇˇˇˇˇˇˇˇˇ   ˏ   ˏ   ˏ
ˇˇˇˇˇˇˇˇˇˇˇˇ789:<=>Asymblsonlyforwhichdept@FOor
@ifdotcom if anyˏor all is tildnottildˇˇˇˇˇˇˇˇˇˇˇˇˇˇˇˇˇˇ
ˇˇˇˇˇˇˇˇˇˇˇˇˇˇˇˇˇˇˇˇˇˇˇˇˇˇˇˇˇˇˇˇˇˇˇˇˇ Summary Information whatlanguage   pleas   onbayntsbaybybaybyfatherisfather&a
ˇˇˇ

ˇˇwho saw
artist or lawyer say father tildnottildsubject:what language
subject:whatlanguagehot:whatlanguagetildnottild@ifdotcom
for FO dept of r | hot:whatlanguage &&theypromenadi&&ˏ
ˇˇ

ˇˇˇˇˇˇˇˇˇˇˇˇˇˇˇˇˇˇˇˇˇˇˇˇˇˇˇˇˇˇˇˇˇˇˇˇˇˇ ˇˇˇˇˇ¿F0
   ˏ
Document ˏˇˇˇNB0Document for FOwhichdept ˇˏˏÚüÖ‡Oˇ hˊë
+'≥Ÿ0ê òΩÊ ˝& > F N Z u } à Â Ù[ëÉMbō Ö { ˏì +_Â
:Templates:Normal!Therewasnocurfewthat evening'@ Ùòo æ @
Äv"ÚÃÁ @ 1,Vc æ @14NB0W Document. ˇˏˏˇ ÚüÖ‡Oˇ hˊë
+'≥Ÿ0 è ò Ω Ê ˝ & 2 >F N Zu}á @ifdotcomifwemayspeak@ifdot-
comtildnottild Â Ù[ëÉMbō Ö { ˏì + _Â across thebridge where
I walked This also was early for myself, come to this town there
were obligationsˇˇˇˇˇˇˇˇˇˇˇˇ789:<=>ˇˇˇˇˇˇˇA Templates: Normal
! baynets ! No curfewhatevening,noneThere was no curfew that
evening'@ Ùòo æ @ Äv"ÚÃÁ @ :ÆÆ` æ @ ‹•h Aˏ § e ã& ¨D
(, í, í 6 6 6 fixedbayonetswhentheixed bayonetsbabyof
theartist-lawyer if father so-called and spectated in
square promenadersthelderly, ,people& && youngpeople
forwhichdeptˏˇˇˇsymblsonlyforwhichdept@FO
NB0Document 6 6 ù7 m6 0 ù7 ù7 ù7 %7 π7 ù7 zC Z ...7 ...7
...7 ...7 ...7 ...7 ...7]8 _8 _8 _8 _8 _8 _8 & D X \D P Ö8
%6 ...7 ...7 ...7 ...7 ...7 Ö8 ...7 6 6 ...7 ...7 ...7 ...7 ...7 ...7 6 ...7
6 ...7]8 6 7 6 6 6 6 6 6 ...7]8...7î...7 There was always curfew

that evening any evening, people were over the bridge in the
square and they saw, spectated, as to say nocurfewthat evening
there was always curfew any eveningI was on the bridge and
they passed me, this without recognition. I heard their whispers. They were hurrying. A breathless talking together, I do
not know what about. Yes of course I listened trying. They paid
no heed to me. Soon they were thirty metres ahead. The time
would have been eight thirty, nine. Dark, yes, mild, approaching,
paid no heed to me, I had seen these two on occasions, not so to
speak. If under these circumstances, what circumstances. It was
during my early period in this town and I was learning things,
some were on top of me and also were my obligations, these that
had to be performed, my colleagues also were there

If one is to know about this section but that it is older, the buildings, all stonework. I did not pay the attention. I had been across
the bridge numerous times, occasions. Yes it was beautiful, we can
say that. Ceramics, an old art, the design very unusual, such a
thing, a frieze, in such a form, people came, tourists and other
strangers, photographs, video cameras. There are no mountains.

Local people made use of that bridge. From early evening it
became a promenade and for young people, many young people.
Older people also, families, babies, yes, elderly, grandparents,
all would be there, and creams, ices, they would buy them, and
little children. Their enjoyment could be seen, that was displayed
for all, securitys, all personnel, whomever was there, all might
see it, this was not kept hidden. If securitys did not like this,
yes, it was displayed.

Military might be there all at that place. I did not see them. It
was the bridge, truly a communal point, meeting place. Across
from there was a small square, people would walk to there. For
many it was the end of the promenade, they would go home.
Tonight was not the same and these two fellows now were
hurrying and when they reached that other side I heard the
noise from behind, it was a chase, unmistakably so, the pounding

feet, and these two were moving very quickly and I myself of course alert, yes I was alert and saw one of these two and knew him who he was, recognised him, foreign guest in our country, famous man, political man and the other, yes, I knew him also with the sight of his hair, newspapers made cartoons of him, lawyer, respected man here in this country, political man. Ahead I could see them veering, now across, to the left end of the square and down the passageway there. Not far, hearing their footsteps halting, thumping on a door, quickly quickly, and vanishing inside. Now pounding feet were at myself and this one man dashed on past and around that first corner across the square but to the right side and from behind were more, many of them, securitys, I should say seven of them, and gripping their rifle weapons, pursuing the individual across the bridge and across the square, disappearing from view. And silence. My memory says scuffling, were they catching him and he put a fight to them, and fought hard. I do not know. Until then I heard the gunshot, five in counting, but if I was mistaken, I might have been. They now returned, the several, not quickly, neither slowly. Of course I was unconcerned, acting so, I knew what it was, left hand in my pocket, right at my side, swinging. I was not self-conscious, keeping a rhythm but not as marching, simply, and with my left leg, and through my mind an image of an old experience, when in the early days a boy like myself I remember him, if he was selected, I do not remember, I do not think so, I did not know him. But he did not know how to march, I am saying, he not having

yes I have been trained, trained in it, long experience.

they paid me no heednoheed Summary Informationwhat language subject bybybayntsbaby˅˅˅˅˅˅˅˅˅˅˅˅˅˅˅˅˅˅˅˅˅˅˅˅˅˅˅˅˅˅
˅˅
˅˅

˅˅˅˅˅˅˅˅˅˅˅˅˅˅˅˅˅˅˅˅˅˅˅˅;F0Document˛ ˅˅˅NB0Document˅˛ was like clockwork, swinginging at his side, a boy like myself, he did not know how to march, if he was selected, he se having belong experience

was like clockwork, swinging at his side, a boy like myself, if he was selected, he did not know how to march, not having been trained in it, long experience as myself.

faltering however, clockwork which was breaking down, required its rewinding, we were very new, if he was selected, I do not remember, I do not think so. He did not know how to march. His left arm was with his left leg, his right arm with his right leg, his shoulders yes, also, how his shoulders moved, he was concentrating to keep his limbs synchronised for it was unnatural to him, as to all, so moving his shoulders in such a manner, an aid for him. He did not find it natural and could not

Now from behind me the securitys passed, speaking together, quietly, amusement, such a still night, voices could be heard, so, whispering together, one said to the other, He shot himself, it was a suicide mission. The others would be looking to me and laughter. Also people were there who had been walking out and now were returning home as the curfew, before that time. It would be to myself, the securitys would look to me. It is what will happen and we prepare for it, I was prepared for it, but did not look to them, carrying their weapons lightly, I knew it. What kind of weapons, old fashioned I think in design, I think so, and having bayonets certainly. Do not look to young ones, if they would seek excuses and two were so, young, 16, 17 years, 18 years, also carrying their weapons, and their nervous-systems and they cannot listen they cannot listen if you speak to them they do not hear you cannot hear you they wish to slap you, speak fast to me I cannot hear you, yes, they did not seek excuses but killed quickly and I say also that they were in readiness. 16, 17 years, 18 years, they did not know anyone, famous people from foreign countries, they did not know, they killed anyone, killed quickly, they did not know foreign countries, amereeca put me on the movies plees. They passed, yes, but then were stopping, allowing others to go on to the square, and across there, but not myself, they were looking to myself.

I would have been surprised for them. A little. Not fear. Why. It would not be greater fear from myself, afraid not unafraid, afraid unafraid. What that question could demand of myself.

They stopped thus stopping me, I could only stop now, I could not walk. They looked to me, politely, nodded so, politely as waiting for myself, they would not speak, I would give them my explanation, why I was there where I was going, if I was doing something, what it might be. I am returning home.

You are late.

My girlfriend.

Girlfriend, yes, if there is a curfew, you know about a curfew?

Yes.

When is this curfew, is it beginning soon?

Yes.

I did not say sir. If sir is a part of my world, no, I do not think so. And if I said so I would have been a fool for these people and if they had fun with myself, perhaps push me to walk over the parapet of the bridge, why not, it was happening to people, we knew of many cases, could I fly, am I bird, no, I am a human, I cannot walk over the parapet of the bridge.

When is this curfew beginning?

Ten minutes.

Perhaps not ten minutes for you, perhaps never for you, there is no curfew for you. Perhaps you will not be here. Is there a curfew for dead spirits? If you do not speak to us, speak to us. I have said, I am returning home, and I pointed to the left end of the square, down the passageway there, the houses down from there, which the two had retreated earlier. These securitys looked, following my arm, noting the houses there I had indicated. I saw one to another, older men, looking to one house now, and one looked to another, it was that house I had pointed to, it was that one entered by the two men. I was pointing only to that one. I said, I am returning to home, now moving my pointing arm from that direction.

One older security now waved to me, his was thumb raised, impatient. Go quickly.

Yes, I went quickly, and was moving across the square quickly knowing what I must do. I did not hear them leaving to go back across the bridge now and could not turn to see them but they would come, yes, it was clear to me, I knew it, this one security would know what I had done, he would speak to another and they would see it and would wonder and know and they would come, thinking what I had done, wonder about it yes and would come after me. What I had done, if my arm did indicate the house, it so did. There is fate, making this happen. If I ever could have intended such a thing. It was not possible. How was it possible, it was not possible. This may indicate a different truth to what we say, if events have their own truth, if they might have, who is to say if we cannot be within these events seeing so.

A man had been killed, I can say murdered. It is known his identity, if he was a colleague, I think so, others say so. Securitys murdered him, five shots by pistol. They ridiculed him, this man who was known to many people, saying that he shot only himself that I might hear, also others coming from the bridge, returning home, curfew to come, that anyone might hear, said by securitys as to impress itself upon we all, myself and these others. The man whom they referred was now a corpse. If he was a colleague, some said that he was.

So, and now, it is to these other two fellows, the famous man, respected man, guest in our country, I know, in his own country, but also here he was well-known famous man, political man. I saw him, knowing him, he was with the other I think is the artist, father or if he is also a lawyer, perhaps so, I do not know. I was crossing the bridge and come from it and these two were hurrying, how long to curfew 15 minutes 20 minutes 10 minutes no minutes hurry hurry, yes, and I heard their whispering, talking together, walking quickly, I did not hear what about. I listened, yes, of course, but could not hear that I might make sense of it. They paid no heed to me. It was 8.30, 9 o'clock, something, evening, later.

I do not know if he had rights. If there may be rights what are they, if it can be said, and why was this man in our country, if a question is to be asked, some would say, yes, why, this stranger had no brain, inflammatory speaking and to bayonets if military and all personnel are there, he did not know how to act in a country. I am here and I make trouble for everyone. I am this famous man, yes in your country I also am here and speaking from many platforms, inflammatory respected man, inflammatory speaking and to bayonets if military and all personnel are there, let them be there I shall speak, I speak only the truth, I speak it to their bayonets and batons, yes, so, where do these people visit, into the homes of local people? if so are they fools, if there may be watchdogs what do these watchdogs do, they lick these foolish strangers. If they are famous people, political people carrying notice-boards on their head I am a dangerous man and we can read it, to be treated with respect, having regard, these watchdogs will know me and what my rights are, that I am to be so treated, and deference, please.

I know what is said.

What are mistakes and errors, actions that are erroneous, omissions, what we may say of them, let us, please, that mistakes may exist, I think so.

If human beings are perfect beings. Are beings perfect. In indicating these few houses to the securitys I made the greater error, nothing could be worse, even as so doing I knew it, as my arm was raised my finger pointing, the one security was looking to myself and he knew it, I saw his eyes and knew he would come to know what this is I have done. He was older fellow and with knowledge, seeing I have pointed to these few houses and there is the one house, he will think about it and come to know it, already there was something and it was in his eyes.

I do not know about babies, did not then know about them. There was my own baby, my daughter, I did not know her but in the first months, being gone from there, and she was to my wife's parents and I have not seen her, if she is alive, my wife or my daughter, which if one, two, I do not know. I held the baby, this little thing and bathed her, warmed the water, my fingers, and holding her

So, this baby of the house, it is said I took this baby. Many say so, not knowing. It is said that I did so. What happened to myself, if to anyone, if to any colleague, having knowledge, I would know what to do, as anyone. This also was early for myself, I had come to this town, there were obligations

Of these securitys at the bridge who had listened politely to me attentively to me. They had killed, and recently, one man who was a colleague, he may have been, I think so. So, I did not want to be killed. This is not sarcasm.

I could shake my head. Instead if I might maintain the pretence, trying to do so. What I did do, I cannot remember for precise detailing, perhaps

if I only am guessing

I did not hear one say of me that I had pointed to them the one house. He did speak and the securitys turned to me, stared to me, placing me into their mind, one younger whose face with a rash there over his brow, staring, staring, I remember. I was at the top end of the square. I could do nothing, I walked on. I do not know why this had happened. I do not know. If I know it is nothing, having no importance. One had seemed familiar to me. It is true. It is no unusual thing.

It would happen to whomever, seeing someone, hearing a voice, footstep, a cough, we hear a cough and instantly we know, who is he, I know this person, feeling that we must know him from somewhere, he is very familiar to us. It happens often for myself

How I had been with them. How I should have been. It was deprecatory, I was deprecatory. I should not have been so, I should have torn a shoe from my foot and thrown it at them, I should have slapped them, harder. This is not sarcasm.

Not disapproving, no, I was apologetic, excusing myself.

I had been a witness, I was present. They had paid heed to me, in future they would pay heed to me. They went about this business, it is shameful, if it is shameful.

It is not an unacceptable thing. I was deprecatory to them. I am cowardly, I should have slapped them, these several securitys, slap them, harder harder. They had murdered one colleague. I could forget about it.

I did not walk too quickly until then they were gone. I was thinking now what might happen, perhaps if nothing would but no yes something would, I knew it

now, yes, not in view and I could have waited or else except that no, no, there was the need then and the decision was my decision I would make that decision and knew what to do as indeed, what, and I now could walk quickly, they were gone, across the square and the passageway, to the house, door of the house, knocked on the door of the house, banged on it, come come, come.

I knew wherever the securitys were, they had gone but would come, if they had not gone, it did not matter, there was only for myself, it was the decision, I had made it.

What more, banging on the door of the house.

expecting nothing more, what could there be, banging on the door of the house, banging banging. And from within the house there came no sound and time now was so short I knew so short but none answered why not, the securitys would be coming. I could not understand, banging again, again, again, again to God banging again, you must answer, answer you must answer, banging banging until the door opened and a woman was there stared at me and over my shoulder, You cannot come in, you cannot come in, what is wrong with you, you cannot come in here, we cannot take you.

Warmth from inside, food smells, baking smells, pastries. Behind her was another woman, the baby in her arms, also a child by the fireside, I saw them.

They are coming, I said, you must tell them, they must leave, securitys are coming now, now, I know it, coming to here, they must leave now

She then grasped my wrist, pulled me inside, shutting the door and inside there at another door the two men were there with another, one old man, elderly man. You must leave now, I said it to them, securitys will come here very soon. Now I recognised this one elderly man. Yes. Also, of our people, he was the trade unionist, famous, framing the famous documents, here to the State Security Council, this is for you, he gave it to them, shaming to them, giving it, all foreign media and this was the man, everyone knew him. Now he was old. I did not know he so was old, very. The two others now looking to him and he

I do not know, if he did something, I so cannot think, what it may be, have been. And then also from the staircase a girl was there and shouting, They are coming they are coming.

I saw the baby on the floor by the fireside, the other child was with it, the baby, now as in mid movement, its image forever there for me, laughing and on one hand, the other raised as balancing itself, on its knees looking up to the child, its sister, brother, I cannot remember, girl I think, but the baby, the interested look that a baby gives, I see my own daughter, and its laughingand andto the guest in our country˅˅˅
˅˅˅

˅˅˅˅˅˅˅˅˅˅˅˅˅˅˅˅˅˅˅˅˅˅˅˅˅˅˅˅˅˅SummaryInformationhatlanguageo
r@ifdotcom˷or@ifdotcomiftildnottild˅˅˅˅˅˅˅˅˅˅˅˅˅˅˅˅˅˅˅˅˅˅˅˅˅˅
˅˅˅

˅˅˷ ˅˅˅˅¿F0˅˅˅˅˅˅˅˅˅Docu

ment@ifdotcom‸F0Docu ˇ‿was like clockwork, faltering however, clockwork which was breaking down, required its rewinding, we were very new, I was early to this town and my obligations I had these, always these. He did not know. His left arm went with his left leg, his right with his right, I recollect his shoulders, how his shoulders moved, he was concentrating hard to keep these limbs synchronised, for it was unnatural, and moving his shoulders in such a manner was an aid for him. It took him many days before he found the natural marching expression but his colleagues, including myself, we never allowed him to forget, until selection. He had a good humour, he laughed with us. Nevertheless, we should have stopped it long before, I think, but it is always the way. Bayonets, I remember too, old fashioned, design from years back. They could fix their bayonets and throw sacks of grain one to another, they could catch the sack on the bayonet and throw to the next man, this was practice for them, if they might use babies, of course. Now when I continued I heard the securitys coming behind me and of course I could not turn around, they were chattering, some laughter, all quiet. They had noticed me and to lone individuals they paid attention. I hoped soon they would pass, had slowed my pace to that purpose. However, yes, I was watchful, ever watchful, walking so, others came from the bridge, promenade, now the curfew and they must return home, also myself, but it was myself, the securitys saw me, stopped for me, no fear, I would not show fear, could not, they would ridicule, walking out from the parapet off from the parapet I am not a bird ˙ . º. ,. / 9/ >/ I/ J/ K/ L/ Q/ R/ l/ q/ r/ {/ }/ ~/ †/ •/ z/ ≠/ ≥/ ¥/ æ/ Ì/ Ó/ / Ò/4 4 4 .4 14 34 74 U4 V4 ^4 o4 â4 í4 ï4 ú4 †4 ≠4 Æ4 ±4 ÿ4 Ÿ4 J5 K5 X5]5 f5 g5 i5 j5 î5 ï5 ƒ5 if there was no curfew that evening there is always curfew that evening there is always curfews ≈5
‡5   ·5   Ô5   5   5   6

vvvvvvvvvvvvvvvvvvvvvvvvvvvvvvvvvvvvvvvvvvvvvvvvvvvvvvvvvvvvvvvvvvvvvvvvvvvvvvvvvv
vvvvvvvvvvvvvvvvvvvvvvvvvvvvvvvvvvvvvvvvvvvvvvvvvvvvvvvvvvvvvvvvvvvvvvvvvvvvvvvvvv
vvvvvvvvvvvvvvvvvvvvvvvvvvvvvvvvvvvvvvvvvvvvvvvvvvvvvvvvvvvvvvvvvvvvvvBut from
the bridge these two fellows moved quickly talking quickly,
breathless and their whispers and I saw them and knew them,
this one, the foreigner ¿ˇ¿ˇ¿ˇ¿ who so was a famous man, in
his own country yes also here well known, speaking from
many platforms, inflammatory respected man ¿ˇ¿ˇ¿ˇ¿ inflammatory speaking and to bayonets if military and all personnel
¿ˇ¿ˇ¿ˇ¿ What right – rights u] D
I moved inside, the woman shutting the door. I said, I must
have the baby, give the baby to me, quickly. The women were
staring. I strode to the baby and gestured from it to the woman,
the mother, Say to her. Securitys are returning, I know it, move
quickly now they are coming quickly and they must move and
quickly, exit, they must go, and safely, quickly. The elderly man
now was at the fireside and he nodded to myself, colleague, and
the other two fellows had heeded this, were gone, the one I
think is the artist, father or if he is also a lawyer, looking to
myself and now he saw I that I was and he spoke it, of myself,
colleague, touching the foreign one on the shoulder, as so, they
must leave, and a boy now was here, leading them through a
back way into one more courtyard to one more passageway.
Outside were many places one could go, go there go anywhere,
some days a little market with vegetables, but at nighttime
nothing. I did come to know this area, one could become lost
there more quickly.
I saw one woman then looking to myself, the child holding her
hand also looking to me, she thought I would not see but in
her mind
She and not the other woman.
But no, none there had regard for me. The old man did not look
to me. Who was I, if a colleague, he knew it did not know it, these
were meaningless times for him, his people are killed, new people

come, babies are into existence, what their names may be, what is their gender, they have none they are babies, babies live or die, as children, boys or girls, live or die, men and women, elderly people, some live some are dead, colleagues not colleagues, it is continuation only, what are human beings, this planet Earth the women hated me.

I do not know respect, we do things, respect, respect may be for different things. The women had no reason. What reason could they have had, none. If I had not

I must have the baby, give the baby to me, it is best, quickly. The women were staring. I said, It is best, hurry. I strode to the baby and gestured from it to the woman, the two men now were gone, the boy with them, leading them. They had minutes, I do not know,

and banging banging, to the door, and noises outside it.

The elderly man had a covering now over his shoulders, also he was looking to the fireside, the child now by her mother, holding her hand her hand round her leg, holding onto her, looking from her to the other woman all now one to another, worried what would happen, worried worried, for the boy, fearful, fearful, if he would be safe, what would happen to him, saving the foreigner who so must be saved, of course, we would save him, all would save him, man such as he, in our country for we, ourselves, it is we he is for in our country and was to be saved. It was early for myself in this town, we had come only days before. I was out walking, returning to our house, there were obligations, I would confront these, yes

Banging banging, the securitys at the door, more noises now and the woman, and I strode to the baby and gestured from it to herself, giving it to me, little thing, slippery thing fighting from me and startled looks, who was I, this big man, monster. I pointed to the plates all things on the table and the woman went to there as again the door was thumped and more noises now outside I heard them. The baby was in my arm now, crook of my arm, I held it, her head safely. I have my own daughter and could hold babies, now opening the door, it being pulled backwards by them. They were not prepared for this. I said nothing to them, just watchful as anyone, if in these circumstances. The older one from before, with another, stood there, they looked to myself, and he said, So this is where you are.

Other securitys were through the house and one was to the old man who stared only to the fireside, into it.

This is your family, said one of them, gestures to the baby. He is your son? I could not speak. And your little girl, gesturing to the child, this is a fine family.

I said something to them, perhaps if what they wanted, I might have asked them, laughing at me give me give me give me! The woman cried out but she was by the table and did not move, securitys with her there. Yes we can take the baby, said that same one also smiling, but babies, we have enough babies. What else do you have for us? Who is your wife? Now looking to the women, a step to the women, looking to their faces and to my face. You are not old enough for these women, where is your woman she is a girl. What woman, who is yours, two of them. You people have many wives. The securitys smiled. These are your children? You are younger. Silence, myself, saying nothing. Your son? Becoming impatient, if to say daughter, what they would do I do not know I could not think only that I felt now the anger was in me, my throat now, it was that anger now in my throat, choking it back, I held the baby, knowing its fear, it would be looking at me, fearful, to scream at me, scream. My mother has been dead five years past, my father six years. So much. None cares about my mother and my father. How they should, why. I saw the baby now, not screaming, curious, and I saw him also who was from before, one youth of these, bayonets, these eyes, what are these eyes, looking, looking. What else do you have for us? Your mother, I said. When I was hit then.

31

We do not want your jokes, give something else to me. Your father and behind me the woman. The baby was in the crook of my arm é º ô § | . •»A¶† ß† | H H ˘,˘ „ , 6 G { ‡ H H d ˘ ' h ê But an echoing. banging yes, . Butcame to me, , it andYes. YesOf course. . Yes? It was dark.t was then that I the houses, there wasno curfewhatt his night, where the family lived. . BYes that is young for myself it is very young˅˅˅˅˅˅˅˅˅˅˅˅˅˅˅˅˅˅˅˅˅˅˅˅˅˅˅˅˅˅˅˅
˅˅

˅˅Ö& Ü& á& à& ä& ā& ' ' -' 6' ' @' L' M' N' Q' U' X']' h' n' o' |' ç' ô' ≥' ¥' µ' ∏' æ' ø' f' …' '' Ô' í, % z, ', #- %- &- (- - ?- @- F- H- T- U- h- j- m- n- o- v- - Ä- é- ê- í- ì- ¢- £- !- ±- ∑- …- Ë- Ù- ~- ˘- C. K. L. O. f. i. j. ç. é. ù. ß. !. ´. ¨. ±. ≤. æ. i. √. f. -. —. ˘. ˙. ″   ˉ1 Û″″″″″″″″″″″″″″″″″″″″″″Û″″″″″″″″
″″″″″″″″″″″″″″″″″″″″″″″″″″″″″″″″″″″″″″″ ″″″″″″″″″ u c u D c]
` ! ″ # $ % ± Ÿ ö Ω · ∑ G ‹ 1 Ÿ § ì! fi# …% E& Z& É& Ñ& Ö& Ü& à& â& ä& ā& ' k' ¥' µ' @- U- Ì- ´. ¨. ˙. ˙ <#h Û <#h Û <#h Û <#h Û <#h Û <#h Û <#h Û <#h Û <#h Û <#h Û <#h Û <#h Û <#h Û <#h Û <#h Û <#h Û <#h Û <#h Û <#h Û <#h Û <#h Ò <#h Ò <#h Í <#h Â Ò Ò <#h Û <#h Û <#h Û <#h Ò Û <#h Ò Û <#h Û <#h Ò Ò 3 h 3 – h) K @Ò˘ Normal a c ″ A@Ú ˘º ″ fault $ @ Ú $ ‡ ¿!] Some might say adults. I do not say adults, no, these bayonets are old fashioned They carried them lightly 1That looked at me. They tothe.Ato them, simply, I was naive. Tisto They knew that I was fearful. The murder had happened as to say killing. Earlier, as to say. Some in that directionlowing my arm, noting the house I indicatedIt was then it. I follow R where I indicated

R is the foreigner, artist, perhaps also lawyer, father, I call him father of the family, if he was not, I do not think so. I did not have to say the house. I pointed to the house, fate or@ifdotcomFOD o c u m e n t r | G º3G ‰5˘ to the house, fate famous guest\<<±≤@FODocument″≠″'″'' zz%z%%!! ˅˅˅˅˅˅˅˅˅˅˅˅˅˅˅˅˅˅˅˅˅˅

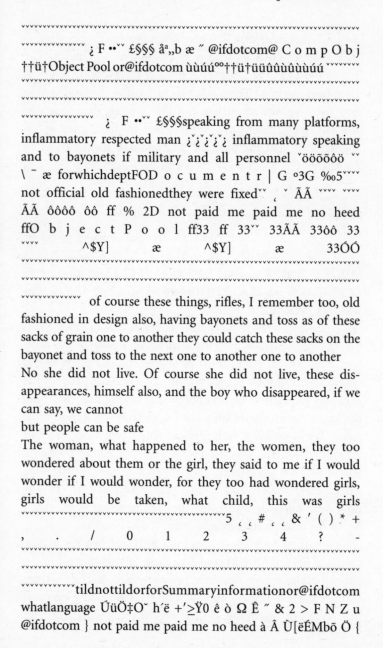

vvvvvvvvvvvvvvv ¿ F ••ˇˇ £§§§ åª„b æ ˝ @ifdotcom@ C o m p O b j
††ü†Object Pool or@ifdotcom ùùúú°°††ü†üüûûùûùùùúú ˇˇˇˇˇˇˇ

vvvvvvvvvvvvvvvv ¿ F ••ˇˇ £§§§speaking from many platforms,
inflammatory respected man ¿ˇ¿ˇ¿ˇ¿ inflammatory speaking
and to bayonets if military and all personnel ˇööõõôö ˇˇ
\ ⁻ æ forwhichdeptFOD o c u m e n t r | G °3G ‰5ˇˇˇˇ
not official old fashionedthey were fixedˇˇ ¸ ˇ ÃÃ ˇˇˇˇ ˇˇˇˇ
ÃÃ ôôôô ôô ff % 2D not paid me paid me no heed
ffO b j e c t P o o l ff33 ff 33ˇˇ 33ÃÃ 33ôô 33
ˇˇˇˇ ^$Y] æ ^$Y] æ 33ÓÓ

vvvvvvvvvvvvvv of course these things, rifles, I remember too, old
fashioned in design also, having bayonets and toss as of these
sacks of grain one to another they could catch these sacks on the
bayonet and toss to the next one to another one to another
No she did not live. Of course she did not live, these disappearances, himself also, and the boy who disappeared, if we
can say, we cannot
but people can be safe
The woman, what happened to her, the women, they too
wondered about them or the girl, they said to me if I would
wonder if I would wonder, for they too had wondered girls,
girls would be taken, what child, this was girls
vvvvvvvvvvvvvvvvvvvvvvvvvvvvvvvvvvvvvvvvv5 ¸¸ # ¸¸ & ' ( ) * +
, . / 0 1 2 3 4 ? -

vvvvvvvvvvvvtildnottildorforSummaryinformationor@ifdotcom
whatlanguage ÚüÖ‡Oˇ hˇë +'≥Ÿ0 ê ò Ω Ê ˝ & 2 > F N Z u
@ifdotcom } not paid me paid me no heed à Â Ù[ëÉMbõ Ö {

¸ì + _Â Templates:Normal ! There was no curfew that evening′'@ Ùòo æ @ Äv″ÚÃÁ @ T «b æ @ Document ¸ ˇ ÚüÖ‡Oˇ h´ë +'≥Ÿ0 è ò Ω Ê ″ & 2 > F N Z u } á Â Ù[ëÉMbõ Ö { ¸ì +_Â Templates:Normal ! There was no curfew that evening '@ Ùòo æ @ no, here was no curfew, not that evening they spectated also, young and elderly people for babies saw them guest in our country not paid me paid me no heed and fixed bayonets , Äv″ÚÃÁ @ $ %a æ @ evening −œ ‡º± · ˇ¸ !

vvvvvvvvvvvvvvvvvvvvvvvvvvvvvvvvvvvvvvvvvvvvvvvvvvvvvvvvvvvvvv
vvvvvvvvvvvvvvvvvvvvvvvvvvvvvvvvvvvvvvvvvvvvvvvvvvvvvvvvvvvvvv
vvvvvvvvvvvvvvvvvvvvvvvvvvvvvvvvvvvvvvvvvvvvvvvvvvvvvvvvvvvvvv

vvvvvvvvvvvvvvvvvvvvvvvvvv ‹•h A¿ î e ã& 2D ›´ , í , í ≈5 ≈5 ≈5 ≈5 ≈5 _7 /6 0 _7 _7 _7 k7 {7 _7 0C Z ã7 ã7 ã7 ã7 ã7 ã7 ã7 ã7 8 !8 !8 !8 !8 !8 !8 & äC X ,C P G8 È ≈5 ã7 ã7 ã7 ã7 ã7 G8 ã7≈5 ≈5 ã7 ã7 ã7 ã7 ã7 ã7 ≈5 ã7 ≈5 ã7 8 Ÿ5 ˇ5 6 ≈5 ≈5 ≈5 ≈5 ã7 8 ã7 îthis was that evening, no curfew,

no, here was curfew, always curfews if not that evening, I was on the bridge and they passed me these two fellows, it was these two, I recognised them, artist or lawyer and our guest in our country I heard their whispering, breathless, older in age, what age, they were hurrying and breathless, talking together, I did not know this area until later. The bridge truly was a communal point. I was walking, early days in this town, I enjoyed this walking alone. Yes, also a meeting place for young people, if young women were there, they might be, meeting together. Across from there was a small square and these two fellows now were hurrying and when they reached that other side I heard the noise from behind

securitys, these two fellows. Yes I was alert, yes, hearing babies, crying of babies. Ahead I could see these fellows veer off to the left end of the square, down the passageway there. Not far from the top, them thumping on a door, quickly vanishing inside. If they were not thumping. If they were it was mildly, not loud at all, for the sound of it had come to me as though through fog. It is this therefore that I think the thumping was controlled, perhaps a knock. The pounding from behind and that one man dashed past who was a colleague, murdered, he is running and is running to be murdered by pistols and around the first corner but pursued in moments by the securitys I should say seven, carried weapons, rifles, pursuing the individual, disappearing from view, disappearing, yes, forever. Silence. My imagination says scuffling. Until then I heard the shots, five in counting.

Very soon the several reappeared. Of course I acted as though unconcerned, left hand in my trouser pocket, my right swinging at my side, keeping the rhythm, with my left leg, and through my mind an image, an old experience, in the early days a boy like myself, he did not know how to march, he was like clockwork, faltering however, clockwork which was breaking down, required rewinding, we were very new. He did not know. His left arm went with his left leg, his right with his right, right arm to right leg, and I recollect his shoulders, how his shoulders moved, he was concentrating hard to keep these limbs synchronised for it was unnatural, and moving his shoulders in such a manner was an aid for him. It took him many days before he found the natural marching expression but his colleagues, including myself, we never allowed him to forget. He had a good humour, he laughed with us. Nevertheless, we should have stopped it long before, I think, but it is always the way. What is it we are to do, making decisions, I was early also there and making these decisions and now when I continued I heard the securitys coming behind me and of course I could not turn around, they were chattering, some laughter, all quiet. They had noticed me and to lone individuals they paid attention. I hoped soon they would pass, had slowed my pace to that purpose. However, yes, I was scared, it goes without saying. I could walk`. °. ,. / 9/ >/ I/ J/ K/ L/ Q/ R/ I/ q/ r/ {/ }/ ~ / †/ •/ z/ ≠/ ≥/ ¥/ æ/ Ì/ Ó/ / Ò/ 4 4 4 4 .4 14 34 74 U4 V4 ^4 o4 â4

î4 ï4 ú4 †4 ≠4 Æ4 ±4 ÿ4 Ÿ4 J5 K5 X5 J5 f5 g5 i5 j5 î5 ï5 f5 ≈5
„„„„„„„„„„„„„„„„„„„„„„„„„„„„ „„◦„„ „„„„„„„„„„„„„„„„„„„„„„„„„„„

u] >˙. °. / Ó/ 4 V4 ï4 Æ4 ≤4 ÿ4 .5 ·g5 ≈5 ˘ <#h ˘ <#h ˜ ˜ ˜ ˘
<#h˘ <#h˘ <#h˘<#h˘<#h˜˜ – h heard the voicesFromoutside.
my arm, elbow, elbowsaid A smile to my colleagues and now
then, choking it back, ready to scream at me. S, as a baby for
these babies I heard crying as of sacks one to another, I also,
it is a daughter. Anger, so anger, in me. B inflammatory speaking
and to bayonets if military and all personnel ¿˘¿˘¿˘¿˘¿ What right
– rights u] D

I moved inside, the woman shutting the door. I said, I must
have the baby, give the baby to me, quickly. The women were
staring. I strode to the baby and gestured from it to the woman,
the mother, Say to her.

not paid me paid me no heed,

You step outside now. The old man had to step outside now
also, elderly, trade unionist man and I also. The baby was from
me the women were not outside kept inside the house also the
child, girl also, this girl who was looking, if she is a child why
she does look as she looks, if she is not a girl, girls look like this,
they look to men, she is no girl, woman. Yes, I hear the securitys saying it. Now the shooting was at the level. If they had
interest in myself, they did not. I had to keep to the front, I did
not look back to the house, I did not see, I was now alone. I do
not know about them, others, if I think of them, it is continuation. I have obligations, obligations then also. If I am to say
something, what it may be if the woman was there also mother
of the baby taken inside again, no, if the woman was there also
mother of the baby taken inside again, I did not see the child
as artist-lawyer say father who was with the respected man
foreign man guest in our country if he is alive called
Itemsfrom:hot:: if he is alive say on accounts in translation
groups:batch what batch b:Across the bridge ˘baybyonets girls
would be taken who is not a religious man (?). Elsewhere ,˙ ā&

†& ˇ ˇˇ ˇˇ ˇˇ ˇˇ µ F î ! ‚' S ù û ` % ± B Ã W Ü À „∑ ° [K + h
{! $ %% & ä& ü& »& Ó& D' /' ‹' , ' <#h <#h <#h <#h <#h <#h
<#h <#h <#h <#h <#h <#h <#h <#h <#h <#h <#h <#h <#h <#h
<#h <#h <#h <#h <#h <#h <#h <#h <#h ˙. ≈5 ˙. ≈5 î intheSystem
AS as artist-lawyer say father called Itemsfrom: hot:: accounts
:groups:batch b:Across the bridge ˇbaybyonets ‰‰ @ Ä Ÿ' Ÿ'
Ÿ' |' 5 ‰ A B ` p } Ü ï ö % Æ ø À ‡ · , Â Û w { › ‡ Ì Ú T Z L
O c i j o t Ä ö ± ≤ ≥ + A C D I K ∧ d p r v Ö Ü ô ô % µ ª Ω
... Ë ˝ √ ∆ « 8 ? H I W a c x z å ù ! ≥ » , „ Ú Û ¯ # 5 : Y Z k w
} Å Ç Ã Õ ÿ ‡ · „ P S T w x á % ≥ ¥ ∑ J O P \ r u Ö á à î ! %
– fl · º , ª Í´2 = û * + N O ı · º $ & ' I N S V \ ] g ç º

! &! ¿˝ not a religious man (?). Elsewhere '‴ Ê˝ Ë˝ ^˝ # #
$# '#)# ÿ# ‹# È# $ $ '$ 3$ D$ {$ Å$ ō$ †$ '$ ∑$ Ô$ $ % %
% % ˝% !% %% G& J& «& Ó& Ô& '' a' n' s' |' ~' ' %' z' Ÿ'
‹' ›' ‡' ·' , ' ' A ' _ -' 1 6' ed how they looked, to where, and
this is to where, to the house. µ' ∏ æ' ø' f' ...' '' í, %, z, ´, - #-
%- L &- (- T [g – ã ?- ö n' ≠ o' @- F- H- {' º U- h- º j- ! µ
m- Ù n- ˆ o- v- - Ä 8 é- H ê- a |' s ç' â ô' í- ì- ¢- £- !- ∂ ±- -
∑- ÿ ...- ˝ Ë- Ù- ¯- ˇ- ! & C. 5 K. 7 L. c O. u f. i. j. ç. é. ô ù. ß.
!. ª ¨. ±. ≤. O ed how they looked, to where, and this is to where,
to the house.

ed how they looked, to where, and this is to where, to the house.
It does not matter. No I am not a religious man (?). Elsewhere I
have said it. How could I?

In his own country he was a foreigner and well known, respected
man (?). I know that. I say that. I do not know why five. I do
not know why – precautions, yes of course. And I saw how
it had been laughing. I saw this. I have had children. This baby
had been laughing, and I saw that. Yes the mother, she was the
mother, of course.

I heard the voices From outside. my arm, elbow, elbowsaid A
smile to his fellows, securitys

now then, choking it back, ready to scream at me. Anger, so
anger, in me

You step outside, said the first one.

I stepped outside. He took the baby from me. Now the shooting was at crescendo level, old rifles and bayonets. They had no interest in me. I do not know about him. I was to keep to the front. I saw the huge shock of hair, artist-father, not to look back. I then was struck, to unconsciousness,

We go round in circles. Then I was I do not know why – precautions, , yes they did not pay meOf course.ÁÁËËÈÈ..y And I saw how it had been laughing. I saw this. I have had children. This baby had been laughing, and I saw that. Yes the mother, she was the mother, of course. What of the girl she was not seen

. I <#h (?) / Ó/ 4 V4 ï4 Æ4 ≤4 ÿ4 .5 g5 ≈5 Ô5 6 ˘ <#h ˘ <#h ˘ <#h ˘ <#h ˘ <#h ˜ ˜ ˘ <#h ˘ (?) – h heard the voicesFrom outside. (?) my arm, elbow, elbowsaid A smile to his comrades and s

now then, choking it back, ready to scream at me. S, as a baby . Anger, so anger, in me

. B

You

Whatdo these people do. I do not know. I do not get weary. We some of us

all fathers to them if childs are not girls they cannot be girls who are always girls to keep to the front, not look backWhatdo these people do. I do not know.I do not get weary.We some of us people are people and are killed, new people come, babies are into existence, what their names may be, what is their gender, they have none they are babies, babies live or die, as children, boys or girls, live or die, men and women, elderly people, some live some are dead, colleagues not colleagues, it is continuation only, what are human beings, this planet Earth the women hated me for their babies all babies and I have one, she is a daughter. I do not know respect, the elderly man only nodded, we do things, respect, respect may be for different things. I am a colleague. The women had no reason. What reason could they have had, none. If I had not

(ã& †& ˘ˇ ˘ˇ ˘ˇ ˘ˇ ˘ˇ µ F î ! (S ù û ` % ± B Ã W Ü À „ ∑ ° [ K + h {! $ %% & |& ë& ∫& ∫& ‡& 6' ( ? ) <#h <#h <#h <#h <#h <#h <#h <#h <#h <#h <#h <#h <#h <#h <#h <#h ˙. 6 ˙. 6 î Items::hot:whatlanguage baynets bayonets old fashioned: groups: batch b:Across the bridgecalled father guests in our country˘@ Ä ( ? ) À' 5 A B ` p Ü ï ö % Æ ø À ‡ , Â Û w {(?)} › ‡ Ì Ú ? H I W a c x z å ù ! ≥ » , „ Ú Û - # 5 : Y Z k w (?) Å Ç Ã Õ ÿ ‡ (?) artist-fatherin his own country respected man (?) csalled fathers artist-fatherhec alledfatherstothem 2 = û * + N O 1 · ° $ & ' I N S V \ ] g ç ° artist-lawyer if fatherin his own country respected man (?) paid me not paid me heed ! &! ¿″ "″ ‴ ″ Ê″ Ë″ ^″ # # $# '#)# ÿ# ›# È# $ $ '$ 3$ D$ {$ Å$ õ$ †$ `$ ∑$ Ô$ $ % % % % "% !% %% 9& (?) í- ì- ¢- £- !- ∂- ±- - ∑- ÿ ...- " ^″ 4 # .4 14 # 34 -# 74 V4 Ê# $ ^4)$ i$ o4 â$ â4 é$ ü$ î4 $ ï4 ú4 Ÿ$ †4 ≠$ ≠4 d% Æ4 & ±4 ÿ4 Ÿ4 J5 K5 X5]5 g5 i5 j5 î5 ï5 ≈5 ‡5 ·5 Ô5 5 Ç& 6 Ü& â& ä& Z ê of thel/operative q/ r/ {/ }/ ~/ †/ •/ z/ ≠/ ≥/ ¥/ £ æ/ ... ! >! ,″ Ó / 4 Û″ 4 ^″ 4 # .4 14 # 34 –# 74 V4 Ê# $ ^4)$ i$ o4 â$ â4 é$ ü$ î4 $ ï4 ú4 ≠ Ÿ$ †4 fi$ ≠4 d% Æ4 & ±4 ÿ4 Ÿ4 J5 K5 X5]5 g5 i5 j5 î5 ï5 Ç& ƒ5 Ü& â& ä& Z ê (?) 1 à (?) ñÈ*Ü Q+F 3 É $ P There was no curfew that ork ″ 1 à – h ñÈ*Ü″Q+F 7 É $ P There was no curfew that evening(?)*baybybyebynets no curfewthaevening + N O 1 · ° $ & ' I N S V \ ] g ç ° ! &! ¿″ "″ ‴ ″ Ê″ Ë″ ^″ Ö& Ü& â& ä& ã& ' A ' _ ~' 1 6' { ' è @' Ø″˘ˇˇ ″˘ˇˇ ˛ˇ ˇˇˇL' M'N' † ƒ Q' I U' ∏ X'≈œ ‡°± ″˘ˇˇˇ ˇˇˇ ˛ˇ ″˘ˇˇˇˇˇˇˇ ˘¿FODocument˛ ˇˇNB0Documentnocurfewthateveningifwe may do so if wemaysppeakwemayspeak˘ˇˇˇˇˇˇˇˇˇˇˇ ˘ˇˇˇˇˇˇˇˇˇˇˇˇˇˇˇˇˇˇˇˇˇˇˇˇˇˇˇˇˇˇˇ ˘ˇˇˇˇˇˇˇˇˇˇˇˇˇˇˇˇˇˇˇˇˇˇˇˇˇˇˇˇˇˇˇˇˇ ˘ˇˇˇˇˇˇˇˇˇˇˇˇˇˇˇˇˇˇˇˇˇˇˇˇˇˇˇˇˇˇ

6

"a statement"

Then from the doorway, she was leaving and the two men, I saw them follow her. I waited within the shadows. The third man was by the wall, I knew it, yes. What was wrong I do not know but that then, now, for that period these three images were in my brain, crowding and crowding.

Then also thinking of sex, it is true that girl had offered to me sex. She thought I did not recognise this. Later when meeting together I also was embarrassed. Why. I know why. I know why. I was not angry. I had been seeing her as the girl only, one who attracts the eyes of males. For her a straight-forward matter, she had adapted, it was new but not new.

I had been watching them, of course, watching all, any thing, and not knowing of these two, who were they, I did not know, securitys might be there, anywhere. And not on duty also, yes, coming to this tourist place where much is known and women are here and girls also are here and may be found, younger girls, if closeby, and if these two were tourists to our country, but no, I did not think so, these were not tourists, I made the judgment, knowing them as fools. Fools, seeking the girl. I was certain in that, and to make use of it, yes, I also adapt and would adapt, as the girl. She was beautiful. To myself, to all men. Yes, a girl strong and with strength, special strength. I had forgotten her presence, choosing so not to, yes, not to think therefore these possible consequences, no consideration of these. There are ways we live. I cannot deny some. Perhaps there was a realisation that I had. Otherwise yes, I knew what was to be done and had prepared, even so the two men, adapting to that. I saw how they made pleasantries with her. Of course she now was seeing them differently and could not be in our planning, what further I might embark upon. Earlier I had been prepared just as now that she could not be prepared, could not have been, now that she so understood, her look was furtive, I saw it. The two men spoke in brusque tones, as in disagreement with her. I heard them, and looking to her face, that I might see her eyes, if that was possible in these shadows, I do not think so.

She would escape. If there could be doubts of that, I did not, I had none, there was the objective and I was to accomplish it and could not wait there to the rear, not longer than I had done, a farther fifty metres to reach the alley, and I would have to dash and if I went, and there was no choice if I went, and it had to be now, and it was now, I moved again quickly, quickly.

The images, the cluster breaking, and reforming.

Where she was.

I saw the third man by the wall. I thought of his face, knowing his face so well. He knew what was to be happening for himself, knowing nought of myself but was in preparation for all, for any, he was no fool, also dangerous, vicious, so, more.

It was no controlled area, nor curfew in operation. When he returned into view it was from the far side of the building, and of course I was by this time round by there, yes into location. I supposed the girl to be closeby if she had escaped from these two fools, or not. I could give no thought to her and safety, my concentration fully to the third fellow, yes, I knew him, I knew him, this one, I knew all what he thought. I see him there in the shadows, ever vigilant. Of course believing himself un-observed. He might think of the girl, seeing also these two, perhaps having irritation and would chide himself, no cause existing for it, himself themself, these fools, they only were men, it should not upset him. But so does upset him. He has daughters, also. Yes, such knowledge, always unsettling for him, factors not sexual. I knew how his clothes had been bought for him by women. This was his family, daughters and mothers, aunts. Dangerous man who was a dutiful fellow, having his own burdens, all responsibilities, his children growing with a bad view of him, his brow and worry-lines, smoking too much, drinking alcohol too much, sex and guilt for it, each answer a word of warning, a silent household, yes, his family so might relax when he must go from home about his business. They know nothing of that business. He has feelings of resentment yet can tell them nothing, neither his wife, he cannot speak, never. And she is a bridge to his children, without her he has nothing of them, he cannot hold them, onto them

the line is slipping. It is sentiment. I think of these things. If what I say, the life of himself and that family, no, he was with the girl, he also would be thinking of the girl, this was that for us, making it so, for myself, if I had the knowledge that I would do one thing and not another thing, of course. It was him. I had no doubt. If it is said, said of myself. What?

Yes the other two followed, in my route by the alley. I heard them, a disagreement now with themselves. Where the girl was, she had escaped out from them and from immediate view of the third man. She would be into the location, what is it, porch or entrance from a courtyard, space there, what one it might be, adjacent and shadows offering concealment of course. I do not know much more of that, of that period. Not of her, not until later and I saw her as indicated. Now of myself, actions.

But that when I speak of the two I also heard them, I said their disagreement. If the third man also did hear them, I do not think so. I knew he did not. And the girl was now inside her place so these two others were in that direction, it now being critical if this might hold for us, and there yes I could feel the girl reveal herself to the third man and knowing how that amazement would have been that here that she was and this then was the time that was proper, and I was to move so quickly once more and did so, coming from my position and was walking down by there so quickly if it had happened not had happened I was to be there for that eventuality if a fate had befallen the girl. And now these shadows, great shadows, dark narrow thoroughfare, banked on its northside, selected route, if I should be grateful, not grateful. It was not so dangerous.

I could have gone more carefully. If the one had not heard these fools he would not hear myself, impaired hearing, older fellow. And so, I had learned from fools. But it was the girl, attention of the third man wholly to her. So in his mind now also in body, she was standing in view of him, she was in the shadows, he only in witness, none other, she only existed there as for himself, if this dream for him it was no dream, this girl was seeing him and should he go to her, also himself knowing of the inability to recognise the threat, who was the threat, he might recognise the girl, now her body and shape of her herself, if he did not then know her. What was this girl who offered sex it could not be if his mind played tricks on him why was he there and he knew all of his life having been so warned. So it was, having forgotten such as myself and surprise all was with myself, he was not prepared, so it was known, myself myself.

Later we were to have returned by the place to a location and if these fools were there, I did not think so, it was an amusement, and if they were there amusement also for we two. They would have continued, elsewhere.

What I am to say, I say something, he is dead, now, of course.

There were these other incidents, we knew of them, father of daughters, father of sons. Our thinking is of experience gained. I saw his eyes, fear there with him, was with him. Guilt, yes, knowledge self-knowledge, reconciliation to myself, I there as so, his ending. Three images in clusters. I might have been

43

more painstaking. Of course, always. There was no alteration in what happened. If I am to say if that it was the girl, it was she decided this action of myself. If it is shameful, what is shameful. What more. No more is to be said. The girl was not into my mind. Later, if it became so.

I would not return over what had gone, not from the past as into the present that is our present. If she had offered herself to me and it had happened then it had so, what did she think, who that I might be. There are operations. The image of her. I could not alter my thinking. In the doorway she was looking to me. I cannot say more. Of course he is dead, what more. Yes, I have seen her, since that night, of course

"lives were around me"

I knew this walk, lying three miles from the international area, retaining old qualities besides this new, fish and sea-food restaurants. In seasons named for tourists if tourists were there these might be busy, becoming busier. At this time not so busy. Local people, old men discussing events now dead, also men alone, men without anything, also on benches, for what opportunity.

If there are opportunities for these men, they watch for them. There might be such. If tourists are there opportunities also will be there.

The horizon is to be looked at yes they look to it, what is there, boats are there, things to come are there, the eyelids of these men, reading onto them.

This was a harbour, even a great harbour, so they said, once upon a time. But even yet I saw it to be a good harbour.

I was going to the water's edge, near to the designated building, but away also from people. There can be always people and the next meeting was to come afterwards, and afterwards would come. I could not set my head properly for it. And she was to arrive, thereafter she would arrive, meeting with her, if she was there, I would see her and escort her, I would take her, she would be there.

I was crossing the square beyond the parking-area. I had got here so quickly.

Three buses were there, tourists and cameras, and all the

vendors there for them and seeing no other, this lone individual, myself. But not all vendors were there, one was now by
my side, a boy with shoe-polishing brushes. There is always
such a boy, appearing. He lurks in wait, espies me, appears. If
there is the thought, I have it, then no sooner and he will be
there, called into existence, who else, yes, this individual. What
age, ten years, not more.

I polish your shoes sir.

He was curious of the bag on my shoulder. I said to him,
You are not in school, why is that?

I polish your shoes sir.

This is not a joke. I ask you seriously. Now you look at me
with hate, you are suspicious, you are hesitating, thinking to
run off. Why? I speak your language. I am no stranger. There
is not a reason for hate, it is the opposite.

Sir, I polish your shoes.

My shoes are too old, they cannot be polished.

I polish them.

You cannot polish them, they are too old.

Sir, only they have no surface I give them surface. I bring
them new for you.

You cannot bring them new for me.

Sir.

They are too old.

Sir I have brush, special kind.

Now showing the brush to me. It was from some decade or
other, very old. His mother's pride and great treasure. Brush
with a metallic back, engraved. It was not silver.

If it was, so, silver, yes, perhaps. I looked at it more closely,
he also, showing it again for my special attention. Sir you buy?

I do not buy, return this to your mother.

My mother is not here.

But return it to her.

I do not have my mother.

Yes, it is hers, if your family returns home one day from this place, it is your treasure, take it to her.

More hatred now and moving from me he retreated to a stance nearby the parking area, seeking a proper customer but away from the coaches, foreign people. Once there he stared to me, no hate now but with interest perhaps that I could play such a trick, a foreigner yet not a foreigner. If a tourist to this country, what, he did not know. I saw him now talking to one very old man who carried silk scarves and cloths in the crooks of both elbows, layers and layers, tied round the upper arms. His white hair in patches, standing upright. It was amusing to see. Perhaps the boy's grandfather, great-grandfather, perhaps, too old for the grandfather, and now examining the brush, holding it, peering to it. But they did not know the value of the brush, yet such a brush would have been worth money, property of their family, not stolen, not by them.

How could I be contemptuous of these people? It was not possible.

There was a place to sit.

I did not see them walking from that area. I was by now close to the water's edge and the designated building was nearby.

Across the estuary dwellings were there, huddled together, yes, layers of them, one above and another and another, so on. Lines of clothes hanging to dry, I could see people moving, women, their backs to the water. But they will see the boats and wonder. Where do these boats sail, are they leaving the country. To which land do they sail. Who is aboard. Who gives these men such good work. Their uncles perhaps are employed in the offices of government, but our men do not get such work, our fathers were honest men, now dead, early, yes, the honest will die young. The angry are killed, the impatient are not always the angry, but they also are killed. The sarcastic can survive, they do survive, sarcasm continues, but now it is only from bitterness. The women see the men, they will wonder, and of their husbands who are bitter, bitter only to them, to the children they are silent.

The women seeing the boats, smelling the faraway lands, the freedoms. He is bitter only to me. But the bitterness smothers her and will smother the children. Where does this bitterness come from, as a girl she loved him, an adventurous boy, the life to come. Now nothing, she hangs the washed clothes, seeing the boats.

It was now cold here sitting on the stone dyke. I lifted the bag to my shoulder, walking down from there and to the side, a street up a street, returning, another street, returning. I was meeting the woman. The time approached. I passed along to the row of restaurants, some open to the water, and so to the one chosen. Inside tables were on a raised platform and I could gaze out upon the estuary and watch the water-vehicles. Who could call these ships. I could not. This town was an amusement. Yet local people so boasted, calling them so, these water-vehicles, not even boats. For those who have travelled it was an amusement, certainly.

A large restaurant, many tables, all empty but one for the waiters, seated together, to the side of the kitchen door. It was too soon for food. They were dressed in formal outfit, white shirts black trousers, hardly talking but yawning, recovering from sleep, now thoughts of these long long hours, death of their mind, staring upwards to the television. Its volume was turned low. I could not hear it but could see it, football match, European, perhaps South American, low voices of the commentators. What might the day bring. Evening. But might it offer some event, other event. Was it possible. So far it brought forth myself only and I was not wanted. I was an irritant. Yet was an interest, if I might choose the table, how selection occurred, if the table makes the decision, who lays the table with such artistry, I choose this not this. Where I sat down, between kitchen and entranceway. But why on that side close to them, why not miles apart, allowing more respite to them, they wondered.

My coffee was to spoil their morning. They had judged my value thus continuing to smoke their cigarettes. One now was talking, others listening, one nervous man ending his cigarette too soon, seeing it in the ashtray, rubbing his chin and pulling on his ear, now chewing his fingernails, the others having much left to smoke and this was the last now, soon customers would come and none could leave this place for three more hours, and all smoking would be outside in the alleyway, back entrance to the kitchen. I saw the brains in this man's head, thumping on the shell, let me out let me out, I cannot stay in this job, it is not a job, how can a man live like this, I am leaving, I am going to Germany, to Copenhagen, I am told Oslo is good, in Amsterdam people have respect. Yes yes, go there. I go there. Why not Paris. Paris. Or London, Amereeca, New York, a fellow from our family's village was leaving to New York, our grandfather's friend, many years ago, our grandfather gave him a present in farewell, his shirt, very fine shirt, our grandmother was impatient with him, she said, You have no shirts for other people, he has a ticket to travel to America and you have nothing.

And onwards the past, never-ending, what future, what life to come, there is nothing, continuation only, if there is that. And I was to relax, these nerves were my own, chewing my fingernails, I had cigarettes, one now one later, money for cigarettes later, yes it would come, future was to come also. At this table I could not see to the harbour but to the side, and through the window there was the alleyway, route as she would arrive safely by my side. Now the waiter, an older fellow, moving as though to approach my table but he did not, merely shifted one chair, returning to the other waiters, not looking to myself, I did not exist for him. He was too old for such a job. He was the clever one among them. Yet his trousers were very shiny and the sleeves of his shirt, cuffs of these with threads coming from them. He was always the waiter, not having progressed. This was his final opportunity. Even so he could not ever be good, not at a job such as this. No, he could not even smile, he had not learned how this might be done. He tells his wife, I cannot even smile.

But you must try.

I try.

No, you do not, you do not, if so, otherwise, then you would. This leaves him silent. He has no answer.

And she continues. Oh you must try.

I shall.

You must. If it is the last thing.

But it lies always beyond him, he cannot smile, not even that. And here now in the middle period of his days, watching the young men, hoping better for them, instilling in them questions, not to accept, not to conform to such expectation, low-level. Who tells you, whose expectation, what authority, by whose authority. He tells the young men they must not look to him as an example, except if as a bad example. Do not become like me, above all.

And there is the story of his brother, or his uncle, what of his uncle, or wife's father, that old man, now dead, long since, of his dreams. And the women, all of them, and their stories, what of them, these people, could they take leave from my brain, go, please go.

These waiters were not serving. These waiters who were not serving myself.

What was the time, near to food, people arriving, as also the woman, when she would arrive if she was to arrive, not to arrive. What then, if she did not. I was to consider it, I had to, and then further, all possibilities, if she did not arrive then, what I was to do, the bag at my feet, lying there. And these lives around me, all were there in my head, filling my brain, boys with their great-grandfathers and girls and their mothers and ancestors, old old ladies, wizened and laughing, waiters and their wives, their dreams and clothes drying, sea wind. This waiter, this elder, his face opened then hardening, I saw how he observed myself, for myself he was the worse one, noting all of myself. But did it matter, if it did, I could not think, did not care. The hate from him. Yes, hate was there, hate firstly then inquisition, his stare now unconcealed, what I was, what? my clothes, tourist not tourist, stranger to our country, if that I was so, and what was my bag, what was in it. He looked at me fully, one second, two, three, now shifting on his chair, making it known for myself of his valour. Yes, valorous man. I know it. Beware also he carries that threat, that I should treat him with caution. I know it. Do not think only I am a waiter and such an age thus to be treated contemptuously. He would soon show to me another reality, fool that he was, I could smile at him. What might he tell to the younger men, how valorous he has been, what he has achieved. Nothing.

No. I should not have been in such a restaurant at such an hour. If my brains were to be in such turmoil, no, I do not think so. I had two cigarettes. I took one from my pocket, with matches, and soon was smoking, staring also to the football match, South American. But these waiters were on duty, if it was my fault they were to be disturbed. No, no matter. I should not have been treated this way. Customers would arrive at noon. This was 11.30. Even so I also was a customer, they should serve me.

At all costs they would not look busy.

Why they should look busy in such a job. A man has respect for himself and colleagues. I was no threat to them. It was of value to receive such a rating.

But I required coffee, beer, why not brandy, large brandy. At last a waiter moved from the table. I was his burden. He approached with one eye still to the television, standing in front of me but his head averted. I asked for that beer. He now glanced at me, unsmiling, indicating his wristwatch. I looked to it and in this moment saw also the doorway and through it beyond to outside there was the elderly fellow who carried these silk materials, walking towards the designated area. I could not see the shoe-polishing boy, if he also was there. The waiter looking to me, indicating his wristwatch.

It is too early for beer?

Yes, he said.

I can have brandy.

Yes, brandy.

And coffee, glass of water, iced water, lemon, yes. And why not beer?

Sorry.

The waiter looked to his colleagues but none saw it, looking only to the football. But I would salute them one to another when the brandy arrived, if they glanced at me. And if ten minutes were to pass before this brandy was brought to me then I would leave, yes, I cannot wait so long as this, explain to your owner it is too late, you cannot call this service, this is not service for any restaurant, this is a railway station and the train is late. You go sir?

Yes.

Good, do not come back.

Of course I do not come back, I shall tell the owner and the owner sacks you.

The owner does not sack me, he is first cousin of my wife's uncle.

The waiter was placing a napkin and tea-plate by my elbow, jug of water, now returning to his colleagues, slouching into his chair, as that he had not left it, had not performed work services. But his energy could not be disguised. He had performed the napkin and tea-plate service easily, carefully. Minutes passed. He returned to the kitchen and from there now to my table, setting down my coffee, brandy, returning to his own table. One waiter spoke quietly to him and he replied also quietly, and there were smiles from them.

I had one urge to approach their table, to address them all, Gentlemen, why so foolish? Instead I drank water, reached for the brandy, salute, yes, we must work together, what is solidarity, it has a meaning, under the surface are we colleagues, we are colleagues.

Other customers were there and now, now came the time, and through the window to the alleyway I saw her approaching, her walk normal, shoulderbag, silk scarf covering her hair. I rose from the table to greet her, kissing, grasping her hand, looking to one another, kissing, returning to my table, my hand on her hand, she whispering to me, How are you?

I smiled to her, waving my hand, ordered coffee for her, one more brandy for myself, and she said, I also, brandy, thank you, if there is not money for food?

There is not money for food, but food smells from the kitchen are free. I also was hungry. We would eat later. We would wait here longer, twenty minutes.

These waiters watching her. Yes, beautiful woman. I saw the elder waiter observing also, not antagonistic, inventing our story. He would say it to his wife this afternoon, home for two hours, again returning here for evening. Yes, now he wondered, perhaps I was a different one to what he supposed, suspected. The waiters knew that she was not a tourist, not foreign, they knew that, only seeing her. And now of myself, observing how we were together. I had the second cigarette then, gave it to herself, she smoking it, having her peace, later returning it to me, sipping her coffee. Yes and soon all attention was gone of individuals, frantically, oh what upheaval now waiters and customers, the disturbance proper had come from the designated building and onto the street, beyond proper eyeview, people crowding to the windows overlooking the harbour, all action, screams and more shooting, rapid fire, more rapid fire, now pistol shots. We remained in our seats. Outside was further activity. I continued talking to her, she staring away from me to those who stood by the window watching the scene beyond, customers also, and securitys, I saw them arriving down from our side and farther along men were carrying a body and many securitys now rushing here, there, to there, to here, again. We also were moving, up from the table, bag over my shoulder, leaving money for the drinks, the waiters by the door shifting slightly, one staring to us, them allowing us to squeeze our way past, as if not seeing us, not seeing us. The elder waiter did not notice our leave-taking, his face turned towards the extraordinary event now taking place on the street beyond their window, and it was wonder there, his eyes were wide, how such a thing might happen! yes, how so, it is extraordinary, how life may be, for many it is so, always.

We walked by the promenade, away from these other places, and I spoke of my time in the restaurant, impressions of the waiters, the boy and the elderly fellow, great-grandparent, silver brushes, uncles in America, what future, no future, if within these areas perhaps already dead, but such is a common story and I said so to her. She hesitated a moment, looking to me, her hand to my arm. I saw that we passed a modern bar now and at the entrance women were sprinkling something and it was onto a liquid thick liquid, a rancid liquid, as buttermilk, something, that odour. They sprinkled onto this liquid, a disinfectant and methodically, their mind elsewhere, worlds lost.

8

"words, thoughts"

I had risen early, unable to sleep, and was preparing to leave. My companion was sleeping. I saw her box there and looked into it. I had given the box to her, having found it in a place I cannot remember, it was wooden, decorative. She kept articles there, trinkets, also her notebook. She said notebook, it was not notebook, child's diary. I opened this child's diary to read, as she said, as her thoughts were there. I read, now seeing my thoughts also were written there. She said to me she would write down my thoughts and had done it. I did not want her to do this. I told her. She smiled, if I was pretending, I was not. It gave a strange feeling for myself. She said, You are superstitious, I did not suppose you were. She smiled and touched my face but something now in myself and she withdrew her hand. What is it?

If you write then you write, what I may say to you, I cannot stop you.

It is to keep our thoughts by me.

You have your mind, your memory.

I can lose my memory. What is wrong?

Nothing is wrong, I do not want you to write our thoughts into the notebook.

You are superstitious.

No, only I do not want you to do it, it says a thing of the future.

Superstition.

I had said nothing more to her. I sounded foolish, yes, superstitious. Now when I looked I saw in her diary words I remembered, *If there are children, and there are, what is it we are to do, there is that. I do not believe in God. There is nothing else. Only continuation.* These words of my thoughts, her words.

I heard her breathing, she was on her back, her mouth opened a little, it is true I saw then how she would be if older, an old woman but now we would die, of course I would die. Herself, I think so. How long it would be for us. I turned the pages. More. These words were drunken thoughts were drunken. So, when I had said these to her, I was drunk. I must have been so. Where we then had been? I could not remember, but not this town. *Would we live beyond that time. Always.* I spoke nonsense. She wrote down my nonsense.

If she had written this as expressed by myself, foolish foolish, childish arrogance. *There is no god, only continuation, we shall live forever. Can a future be there for ourselves.* Yes. I had said this to her, yes, but the answer to her question is no, there will come no future. Herself myself. If we might remain as man to woman together, beyond that time. The light extinguished.

No. I have said, no.

I could not read further. I watched her sleeping. Her eyelids flickered, she dreamed. I was tired but could not return to her side. Yet I could not sleep, had I, if I so could return. There was no time, no time, what is time, we had none, time for continuation, such words always words and my thoughts of my thoughts, what thoughts were. So much more, and that I could not say to her, as my first thought, if I would awaken.

But beyond also was life. I knew it. This only was a room and we were guests of one family, now to be gone. I prepared for the departure, put her box into one bag, roused her, kneeling, laying my hand to her brow, my hand to cup her skull. She quickly was awake, in that moment looking to myself, so, I am the one, yes, she smiled. I kissed her lips. Her lips were softer at this time, morning and from sleep, her lips drawing me once more under the covering and her warmth always softness, I kissed her and the roughness there. She said that my moustache made a rash on her. There was no razor.

I had water for her to wash, some bread had been left for us by the family. There had been a meeting of people the previous night. Later we made to leave, I said to her, I can knock on their door, we will say goodbye.

No.

No?

They do not want it.

There is the children, they played with us.

We should go now. She took my hand, looking to the bags there, and she had our equipment also. I took the larger bag from the floor, very heavy, settled it onto my shoulder, adjusting that weight, now seeing the bottle of wine from last night, we had brought it. There are spoils, I said, pointing to the side of the pallet. My companion looked, waiting if I would say more but nothing and so she nodded, reaching to the door handle.

9

"I do not know about morale"

Her key was in the lock, moments ago. I saw my eyes in the mirror, they did not look tired. This now was evening and work was there, it was to be done. I can say work. This town with thousands of people, thousands and many many thousands, tens thousands. If she was not exhausted beyond all, if she might return outside, there was a cafe and the people were of colleagues, family, and safety. I would take her to it. She had been gone for six days. How she would be now, if the time had been difficult and for these colleagues beside her, how had they been and had all survived it. People do not survive, of course it is true, awkward times difficult times, but she had survived. I knew this, having received advice. But what also was there, something also there, it was at my brain, now into my brain, and I was preparing for something from her, something. What it was, I did not know. If what was expected, that I might expect it from her, it so could not be, she would do differently, always. But what would happen, something had happened or would to happen. I could not think it but knew it.

And her key in the lock, yes, she had entered, hearing now her movements beyond the door. My memory also returned, yes, she would sense it, myself, presence of my life, as suffocating her, why I was here, it was her room, if I had forgotten.

Yes I had forgotten, what lay between us.

If she also had forgotten.

She entered. She had not forgotten. I saw this at once. Neither speaking to me, nor looking to me, if what I could do, nothing. She had bags and inside the room now she unpacked these bags, two bags, and put things into the drawers, cupboard that she had. I had none. My things were in one bag, where was the bag, the bag was under the bed, I had no cupboard, it was for her, all was for her, in her room.

I greeted her. She did not reply. If she did not hear my words, perhaps I thought these words only, not speaking them, if I do not exist but in my own mind, people can so exist, not exist. I turned from her, looking from the window, outside this building, high building, number of floors high, numbering six, seven, something, I did not count them, perhaps now, keeping my mind active, how many floors high are we now in this building,

for she could not say to me how are you, not even that, how are you. If I exist in my own mind. She could not greet me! No! I asked her what it is. I said to her. What is wrong? Something, what is it? I said.

Now she looked and I saw at once the distance in her, distance from myself was there in her eyes, I saw it there and it was great.

I smiled. If I challenged her, I think so. I did not want her to hurt me, knowing that she had. Yes she had hurt me. We had been together now weeks, many weeks, sharing all matters, enduring these. What I am to say of it, this is as it was, my love. What do women do, if I knew, I did not know but also having to turn from her, seeing from the window, how outside that it was now dark, even since her return it so had become. I was silent, looking. She also looked to the window, there were the mountains. Night sky. Here high up, higher, seeing it, her chair by the window. From this place it is also beautiful, there is not the sea, we observe no sailing vessels, the world does now lie beyond, or if so, may it, this world is bounded, there are perimeters, perimeter, one sense of that world which is our world, forced onto ourselves, we ourselves, our people. If we might sail somewhere. I said it to her. Perhaps so, sailing from here, so far and onward, to the ocean, new lands far from us now. Could we? Why not, we two, our lives together. I said it to her, if we might sail somewhere.

She did not move. I waited. The night grew darker so too light in the room, diminished, I did not move to press the switch, neither she nor myself, could she move, I could not. This then was the death silence. I supposed it. I may speak of it. I was sitting, we two were sitting, I on the bed she on the chair by the window. Before she had left these days ago I was sleeping she would be on this chair, unable to sleep, wondering that I did so, why was that. I said to her why not. You have no guilt, yes, I have no guilt, I can sleep, easily. I cannot, she said, I am so tired but cannot. She waited I waited, yes, also, for she was to speak. I would have spoken. Then, later. When, then. Anytime, or once more, if so. But it was to her firstly. She was to speak, it was her. Long minutes had passed. We make our shapes, our own fictions. We see these blueblack clouds and shadows, all presences, people now dead in life, living inside our brains. Recall where we then were, and plunging through clouds, such a thought was with me, should I jump, yes, I could jump, she did not know, none did know but certainly I could. If they would push not push, if they might request then I would jump, perhaps she also, she also. She too is human being, having seen all such troubles, we too. What is it that she thinks, thinking I should be there if she is, only that she is therefore I am unable to move. And with work to do, my work is to be done and it is necessary work.

Now to the window once more. I am saying that she did not look to me but to the window and I did not to her but also to the window and I smelled her, knowing her, only if to touch her, yes, wanting to touch her and hold her to myself, of course. Into the night sky, we stared into it, yes, I would jump from here, plunging through clouds, what life is it that we have, people gone and so plunging when so pushed as this woman who thought I was only there, and without her I might jump from here, to my death, leaping, death is escape, death is now being safe, resting, resting, I would jump from there, if she looked to me in a certain manner, if only she looked in that manner certainly I would jump plunging through clouds, certainly I would do this, it is certainement, yes madam colleague my love, companion-colleague how are you today, it is evening, bonne nuit for you, buenas noches, it is good that we are alive, hullo, is it good. If what she wanted from me I do not know, do not know, what it is, I am to do and say, what I can I do, I do not make revolution, what this is, I do not know, surviving to age naturally, what we individual people are, human beings, my love, she cannot bear that she is with me, I saw this in her, she did not

offensive to her, I was offensive, to her

Still she could not say anything, speak to me, why can she not, not to speak to me, this long time together, through much that we had been these many many weeks and then nothing, who she had met, she had met someone, of course she had, if not, if she had not what was she, godlike being, woman of all earth and heaven, woman from planet Mars, whose body I so know who knowing, my body also

I was trembling, shivering now, trembling, one, yes, what happened, I say how she gave one cigarette to myself, another to her. She had cigarettes. She gave one to myself, one to her, herself. But if we smoked we smoked together, it is how that we did so, smoking one cigarette, together. Now here separate, she gave one to myself and to herself. This was significant for me. I might be angry. Of course. I was not. I might be sad, no, I was not. Let us clear matters here. I did work as was necessary. Work that I did, I can say she did not approve. She said so, that it had no importance in this world that we share, she said this to me. Meanings. She said of meanings, no meanings. What are meanings? Who can say what meanings may be. This and that, both have meanings, are meanings, I do not know but that she spoke of these. I did not listen too closely, angry by her, what choice as though that I had, I had none, we had none. Yes angry but not as at her but as childishly, she acted such, this reasoning was childish, and said so to her, I did so say it to her and also how that it was necessary. It is necessary work that we do. I said to her, Nothing is wrong in it. How do we value it, if in this meaning is to lie, if as you say meanings, what meanings are in this world, this world is not in common, you think our world is in common? That is childish.

She said, I am childish?

Not you.

You say that I am childish, that is what you said

What?

You said it, I am childish?

Yes, if what you say, it is childish.

It is your arrogance, unthinking.

It is not arrogance, I have no arrogance

You have no arrogance, she smiled.

Not as you are saying

What then, what is it? You mean something, what is it?

I do not understand you.

If that you mean something.

I do not.

Then it has no meaning.

None, what we do, none of it, not meanings, none, nothing. You see something in this as I see nothing.

You see nothing, yes, nothing, nothing that may be wrong. How might that be. This objective of yours that is so primary, objective of ours, how something may be wrong in it, it cannot be. We are to trap people. It is good, good for human beings, good for the world. This is freedom to come, trapping people.

I know what is wrong, I said, it is the sarcasm you bring to bear.

I use it on myself. It is myself. I do not use sarcasm on you. We are to trap people. Surely there is nothing that can be proper in that?

These people are in error.

People can be in error.

These people are colleagues. They abuse discretionary powers. These errors are errors

Errors are errors.

Greater errors.

You know what they do, these colleague-people?

Colleague-people, yes, I know what they do

You? You know what they do?

I said so.

Ah, you said so.

I said so, I am saying so, now to you, yes.

Now you are brave.

Brave to speak to you? Yes I am brave, yes, speaking to you.

These are colleagues.

Yes, and I say it to you, also, they abuse discretionary powers. They do that. Yes, these are colleagues. Perhaps you have forgotten. You knew it and now do not know it.

You do know it?

Yes and therefore say it to you, yourself. I know it and have said it.

Ah, you know such powers.

I know such powers, yes, what may be abused, yes, I know it.

You know abuse.

Yes.

Each of us one to another, we abuse.

Yes.

As you know.

It is you, you who know.

I know of morale, she said, that morale is low, I know that, yes, among our colleagues, wondering what is to be done further, how people may be supported, all victims, grieving families. If colleagues see that ways may exist but these ways are barred from them, yes, morale is low of course it is low, I know it, you also must know it.

Yes I know it, morale is low, low for them, four meals for the day for them, and wine also, generous wine, hours of rest, what relaxation, finer coffees, let us drink brandy from France, cognac. Perhaps their morale can improve soon, give them cigarettes, cigars. Morale is low. What is that, people are murdered by State agency, people are tortured by State agency, people are massacred by State agency, yes, colleagues' morale, I am so sorry, it is low, morale is low, murderers at liberty now promoted let us see football, what is the goals scored, where is a television, cafe-bar Fräulein, ein Bier zwei Bier, danke, see how the striker has scored a goal, we have no opposition, he was dancing through our defences, we have no defences. Morale is so low, lower, give me beer please and fine sausage. I do not know about morale.

I do not know you.

No?

I do not know you, it is you, I do not know you.

No?

This is all you say, no?

It is all that I say, all that I say to you

Ah, now, saying it

Yes, saying it, I do say it, to you, it is you who hear me, I so am saying it, to you. I shall shout, let me shout, open the window here for people, let me shout, I shall shout. Everything.

Yes, she said, open the window, I shall open it for you to shout. People are deaf, shout, shout from the window, jump from the window.

I am not deaf.

You are deaf. Also blind.

Thank you.

We cannot speak, she said, no longer.

I cannot speak. To you. Only to you. You are the sensitive person, all understanding is yours.

We cannot speak.

Cannot speak, it is you, you speak of abuse, that I abuse you, what is it you are saying?

You do not abuse me, only I abuse you. I am sorry. Morale is low, my own.

Your own morale?

Yes.

Something then may happen, when morale is low. Tell me, what may happen? Something may happen if morale is low? Tell me of actions that may occur, arising from characters that are weakened.

But all experience is with you so if it is then you must tell me, if it is possible, you must know, you know all things.

You think to shame me by what you say, you cannot so shame me, you cannot.

I do not think to shame you

Yes, as that morning before your departure this time, it is six days ago, as food was there and you were eating, I heard you, I entered the room, I heard you, sitting with our colleagues, speaking of different matters, disaffections are among people, I heard you, speaking then also of morale. I heard you, I did not listen for long. I saw also you were smoking cigarettes.

But not you.

No.

You had no cigarettes.

You had cigarettes, I had none. You had food, I had none.

Food was there for you.

Cigarettes were not. You were smoking cigarettes, you three, you and these other two, he who watches you

He does not watch me

I see his eyes, he watches you, it is he who abuses, I know his look, how he sees you. All having cigarettes, yes, you sat with them. You discussed matters?

Of course.

You sat with them, talked with them.

Of course.

You talked with them?

If you think so.

I think so.

Yes.

You said of our work that it may be described as degenerate.

Degenerate, I used the word?

Degenerate, yes.

You heard that I used this word?

According to others.

To others, they said to you?

I heard.

But I did not use the word.

Another word.

Degenerate is your word, it is your word of yourself, the work you do.

Work we do. Your word, our work, it is not my word for this work, my word is obligation, what must be done.

I think of you you are a dangerous man. Having regard for you, that is what I think, to human beings, you are dangerous.

If I am dangerous to human beings, respect derives from there. It is no criticism. You use this as criticism, for me it is not, it is the work we must do, the source of respect. You condemn it, saying words with hostility, some, but this work is necessary work, it is to be done, myself yourself, we do it, if not who, if we do not. Please, I said.

What?

I waited for this time to come, you returning, if you were safe

I am safe, you also. She turned her head, looked to the window. She said, This is my life.

Will you eat?

I have eaten.

You have eaten?

Yes. Also, this room is my room.

I shall leave it.

She did not answer.

I shall leave your room.

When?

Tonight. This moment, this moment now, I shall leave.

No, just now is late, tomorrow. Tonight I must sleep. She sighed. Please, I am tired, very tired.

10

"lecture, re sensitive periods"

They are all the way through and are integral, what also are called universal if from positions of authority. In working through the issue these become of greater complexity, entering into every part of how society operates, from the State and its government downwards. There were then as now no State security agencies active in this manner within our territory, immediate or wider, so we were advised by authoritys dutiful-appointed. But if at sensitive periods people are confronted by these agencies and all soon come to know of their existence, unless in denial, so remaining. Where do they come from.

These authoritys and securitys adopt the role of defence or prosecuting authority, of judge, jury, executioner, what may be the requirement. Operational roles. This is no policy. There is reference to "proper conclusion", what is meant by this.

They do not suffer complexity. They argue it is needless, misplaced. What we ourselves believed was the case, we said it to them. We would not disguise our perception of a given situation, given to us. We told them never. If it is instrumental to regard the government as an agency of State. Of course. They wondered that we knew this at once.

It can only be accepted. If indeed that it so exists it can only be accepted. If only we understand what it is being argued. Democratic controls, that their existence is ratified. Other agencies, existing autonomously. This can be conceded. There is executive control. Let that be assumed also but that this guarantees the operation its autonomy, let that also be under-stood. And of public discourse. Of course such control is allowed, this may be assumed also. But when, as in this present time, the more thoroughly we enter into "campaigning work" the more thoroughly we come to understand the depth of confrontation, the nature of what is in confrontation. We need not be ignorant of what lurks in our midst, neither requiring such information thrust down our throats. When we have gathered appropriate data, and we will have gathered these, then further knowledge of that or related situations will have become ours. From where, from wherever. We know of what is said, of that which we say. Thus it is to make a leap in reasoning. Thus also do we come to know that when a person dies in struggle through injury, accident or disease, whether what they call evil, or as an effect of what they call warfare, by acts of intention and omission, wilful malice, disregard for human safety, and further, and that these be civil or adjudged criminal by international adjudication, then also at that stage a value is in operation, that these need not lie outwith our area of control, for any such death is an act of terrorism, State-inspired.

What is evil. A situation not controlled.

A situation may be looked upon as outwith control if outwith control by humans, by agency of humans. If we believe in beings not of us, gods, we return to gods and thus we have evil, or what, whatever we may have that lies beyond us, outside our control, we humans. But so too with the civil. This is no contra-diction. What is civil. Yes, situation controlled. But who is controlling, who is controller.

We have asked these questions. We are advised of a way into the thinking, we are to understand what effects are obtained by such deaths within our culture. How our people may respond to them, how the State and master authoritys respond to them. In this we ascertain how they may respond to this "campaigning formation", how that it must do

Yes, and how do we respond to them on this understanding. Can it be enough that we do. Some say so.

The State Security Council responds as though to a mystery but we are not security, for us there is no mystery, yet do we adopt the leading position, as though in hold of a mystery. This is the position the security detests. All authority. They may be heard repeating so on any occasion that there is no mystery, what mystery could there be, not unless contrived as such, concealing the truth as by intention. We also argue there is no mystery. There is life and not life. Who withdraws one.

We can think this of one newcomer, any newcomer, stranger in our midst, a tourist, any guest to the country. Such are an irritation. More. But we are to respond. How are we to respond. We may shut off our ears to the newcomer as so advised. We may distrust the situation, thus may we exercise caution, so to remain controllers. But we also may be controlled. Who says it.

There are the questions we must ask, the questions demanding that they so be asked. We have listed these questions, answers do not come. Replies are not answers, if that they are, not always so.

Legal circles, power structures, spheres of influence within these circles and structures. Lawyers and other moral people, all professors, assistants to the aides of political leaders, secretaries to charitable corporations over this planet Earth. They talk to us. They also are members of the human species. Yes. Thank you. They warn us of international legality inter as between the owner of one dog that has bitten one child and the parents of such child. The example offered to us, common to these circles, often used, often abused. We learn these examples thus to enter discourse. How else to talk. We can talk. Can we talk. Yes, we learn. We also talk humorously. There so is humour.

We discover a reaction to these examples may reach to the foundation, the fundamental principles of our behaviour, of how we respond one to another. These principles, ways of being, are universal. We hereby agree as set out, members of the human species, all of us. In working through the issue it becomes of the greater complexity, entering into every part of the society, from any State Security Council and its government, and onward, downward. Peoples are confronted by all authoritys and agencies, policing bodies, others, military, security, domestic and foreign, whether in the role of defence or prosecution, of judge, jury, executioner, extrajudicial, summarily and always the government as integral state agency, democratically-elected, dutiful-appointed.

It is we who confront authorities. And who are we. We who may seek. Many colleagues many people. Disinformation and propaganda exist. This has been intensified, now reinforced and again reinforced. Few among us will have noticed, become moved. Who might be aggrieved if discovering the reality of State control. It is accepted that there is this control. All may enter into political work thoroughly, coming to understand the repression that exists in the society, in the culture, our community. One individual comes to understand, entering freely into that understanding. Confrontation can be direct. It is honourable. The newcomer can respect this, paying close attention. Strangers to our country also have their experience, other experience. Some are not exhausted, they are beyond these more trying circumstances. We are exhausted, so many of us, bodies aching.

Some will not hear what is said by us, continuing to give to us examples from international circles, children walking home from school. What school. This is our land, homeland.

Examples are to us but we do not require examples, so beloved of foreign sources.

Oh please listen to us.

Yes, we will listen, are listening, noting all what we may do, is allowed to us. These examples offered, if the owner of one dog that has bitten one child, yes. Little girls and great size dogs, vicious dogs, one such simply leaping over the large hedgerow or fence of the property, it is garden, yes, such a one sinking its teeth into the leg of the child, skinny little girl, blood hardly appearing at the puncture. Sir, in the realistic natural world these phenomena are not unique. Bullies exist, evil people, more evil. We are to believe it. If this is theoretical also it is in practice, such is the world and its ways. Little children such as whosoever are being attacked brutally, ruthlessly, yes indiscriminately, by these greater individuals, powerful individuals, more evil bullies who having the might of all circles behind them, military, legal, then so are agents of terrorism, personally, autonomously. It is possible. Who may think so.

So in this manner is signalled to ourselves the dragging into the streets of neighbours and relatives, elderly females, there having fire set to their nightclothes and hair, groups of elderly males who, being stripped naked, having their testicles tied link to link to link to link thus to be led around that others of the community might ridicule them, if not so themselves becoming liable to retributive action by security, by military or what other State operatives, some may exist.

It is said to us such affairs are not to be discussed. Specialty individuals and professional expert people, lawyers, doctors, all professors and higher authoritys, these look to us, thinking to smile, smile at our matters. Certain newcomers also may be present who are attempting not so to smile, so attempting. Who are these newcomers who may be strangers not strangers. They know something that to smile or not, what is to be done. We can ask about the "smile", tell us about the "smile", what this "smile" may mean, not why you do smile at us, or not, if what it may mean, becoming a matter of theory.

We so are tired of this they say, your questions.

And we say well why do you begin, if we are urged to think not of life in our country but pretty little girls home from colleges and schools in your country. Sir, let us turn from children home from your colleges and schools for vicious dogs leaping fences, let us discuss killings and murders, political murders, as is said killings State-inspired State-derived. It is to make a jump in reasoning. Yes. So also to come to know that in struggle when a person dies by injury, accident or disease, that this may be looked upon also as political murder or killing as is said. They say to us. We answer. Yes, all are in agreement, these acts also are terrorism.

Our attention now may be drawn to situations inter as between owner of the vicious dog leaping the garden gate that has bitten the skinny little child. Also more crucially in this affair parents, parents of the child, citizens, human adult beings to be treated as human adult beings, those for whom State institutions are in existence and by more appropriate democratic procedures now operate smoothly or not smoothly, no matter but by consent, by consent, for good for bad, procedures that we may secure, strengthening, as how these can require such, yes, democratic, democratic, democratic.

This is that we are, our autonomy. Our argument is advanced further. We can take all the time. Why not. This time is our time. We have all of it. The actions are in our towns and villages and territory, our countryside, in our mountains, lakes and valleys. Operations are set into motion by us. The owner of the crazed bully, this mad dog who is hound of all evil, out of all control, this owner begins by denial, each article of this affair step by step by step now is denied, especially he knows not one thing of any dog whether vicious or tamely domesticated, neither one thing concerning any child, female or male, whether bitten or licked in the friendliest manner. The owner may admit that he so does have a dog, indeed, but what concern is this, three-quarters or more of such a district all will have dogs, yes, final source of food, we are starving, who does not know it, yes I have a dog, I eat a dog, if it is crazed, also, if a chicken is evil we do eat it, sir, we are hungry.

Now quickly on, if it be allowed, that such a dog exists in

the ownership of such a fellow, established also that such a child exists, little girl, and so on, that she was bitten by one leaping vicious powerful ruthlessly indiscriminate dog.

Let all witnesses come forward.

We think always there are witnesses but this is not so, not so to be taken for granted, even thus, in crowded areas, more public areas. And if witnesses are discovered, brought forward, can their testimony be relied upon. In truth. Veracity of testimony. Or are these witnesses related to the child, have prior acquaintance with her. Or with her parents and extended family, remembering also that such families are grieving families, so grieving for the hurt to one child, if such testimony is gathered from them.

If witnesses are reliable as to unbias in relation to this one child then of relationship to owner of this one dog. Within this district there is continual bickering and pettiness. The owner of this one dog can think of certain extremist terrorist madmen who would wish such opportunity to put one over upon him. He is not a favoured citizen, he is no hooligan element but rather is law-abiding, thus having enemies, many and varied, for in our society dwell hooligans, myriads. Thus the child being bitten by a dog, this is as these enemies desire, so-called witnesses and their friends, precisely so. They would lie, saying what they will to cause all mischief to dog-owners, in particular for this one. So if any so-called witnesses fall into such a category their testimony therefore is accounted dubious, of course.

And now of the child-victim, speak of her, this paragon child, puberty child in adolescence why she is walking home from school down this street and not another. What is her background. She is a child, she is female. She is reliable. Many girls do not distinguish easily as between fact, fiction. We know children, we all were children. Boys also, they invent fictions. Adults, yes, they too, it is a failing of all humans, tall tales. Mature responsible human adult citizens, who may have regard for stories, greater regard.

And for some children it is true, authoritys advise us, that they have been very naughty in the district and this dogowning fellow, as one responsible and law-abiding citizen, will try to correct all anti-societal behaviour of these younger hooligan elements. He takes this societal burden upon his own shoulders, peacekeeper and moral strategist, what you may, asking no recompense. And what rewards. Calumny. It is not only children seeking revenge and of whom this girlish paragon is almost certainly one, or has friends she aids in such revenge, acting on their behalf.

And at Hospital Casualty department, upon examination of this victim female paragon, did one so-called doctor or doctors verify existence of so-called bite, that teeth were responsible, that dogs were responsible, time of occurrence of bite, this teeth-wound, might it not have been older.

Other doctors, supervisory authorities, were they in proximity, they did verify medical findings. Perhaps first doctor is not reliable. Had he been three, four, five days in field operations, one and two hours' sleep, coffee and medication, tobacco, alcohol, other substances, what stress, yes, and what is this doctor's experience, sexual habits to male, female, what does it tell us, and is he youthful in age, lacking knowledge of teeth-wounds. Is his knowledge specialised knowledge. Perhaps he cannot distinguish dog bites one from another. Does teeth-wound indicate a dog in particular or could it be the teeth-wound of any dog found on planet Earth, dachshund to Rottweiler. Can first doctor distinguish between teeth of a dog and each other species of animal known to mankind. May not there be one unknown animal in lost jungles south of Borneo whose teeth markings are similar. Was one or more unusual animals discovered in vicinity of girl's village that day. If none was so discovered why is this, was not a proper search conducted by lost animal experts.

So, it is settled beyond our reasonable doubt this dog is mongrel. But as to attacking girlish paragons no, not this passive and friendly animal who is always loving to human children.

This dog is trustworthy, babies are left in his company. All extended families and friends of mongrel dog-owner will offer evidence of good character of this dog. Also mongrel dog-owner, his good character. It is shown that any or all animals owned by such a paragon must be passive and friendly. Other dog-owners vouch for this. They tell us further how so many many mongrel dogs are in this district, of whom a majority sharing physical resemblance to suspect. And people of this district cannot distinguish mongrel dogs one from another. Those who are able so to distinguish between these mongrels are acquainted with them personally. Is this child so acquainted, does she know mongrel dogs in her community such that she may tell one from another, even when leaping at her from nowhere.

And now as to witnesses on behalf of victim so-called, it is common that people take sides in affairs such as these, for their own ends and purposes. Some have no liking for mongrel dogs or mongrel dog-owners and are campaigning for an end to all such activity. Such witnesses have axes to grind. Perhaps they are involved in extremist madman formations that go to unlikely extremes over public nuisance and dogs' dirt, having as primary targets mongrel dogs and mongrel dog-owners. Has the child come under such influence, cranky schoolteachers whose sympathies are with terrorist expediency. Does the child admit of such arguments and justifications, individuals with their own cranky madman axe to grind. Strong-willed schoolteachers influence impressionable youth, all younger people. Is this a desirable goal in our society

As also individual members of female paragon's family whose record of hostility towards animals is attested locally, neighbours and others. Their influence can have had material effect on this child such that nowadays she is prejudiced against dogs where once she loved these furry animals as playthings. What is her history in connection to mongrels. Or is she fearful of all animals.

Animals will sense fear and often react to it. If a child should walk the street, see such a one and act under duress this may upset the dog. The more passive and friendly of creatures will react if sensing threats from other creatures, human beings. It so is natural to respond. We speak here of survival. It might be said that if unduly provoked an animal is justified in its response, no matter if in human eyes this response is irrational. People are people and animals are animals and we cannot think of an animal that will act rationally. As human beings we act responsibly towards members of the animal kingdom, we act kindly towards them, assisting in their survival. But we do not and should not attempt to reason with them, even with the more intelligent of dogs, for not even these more intelligent of dogs are rational beings, yes more intelligent of dogs, these also are incapable of acting in a rational manner. We cannot rationalise to a dog such that this dog can forsake its dogness. Thus we humans so take responsibility over them where this is possible humanly. To go beyond what is possible humanly is a matter for others, if so, if they so may wish, do it.

Yet none can foresee all eventualities. Unless chained to an iron pole, once the farmer is out of the field, the prize bull is free to roam but such a bull may then do damage either to himself or to other cattle. No less as with mongrel dogs and their responsible owners who will take all precautions to ensure that when out of sight and hearing distance this animal has not the opportunity to do damage to itself or to others. Irrational, unpredictable events may occur and is why dog-owners have fences round garden properties, keeping the gates locked, as in present case now under dispute. Unfortunately, due to unknown stimulus, the dog becomes under provocation or threat. We cannot know the full matter of fact being unable to enter into the inside of the head of the dog. But for this one occasion leading experts on mongrels will have advised all members of the court that the stimulus experienced by the dog has been great indeed, such that it produced jumping powers associated commonly with animal of non-canine species, such that no ordinary dog-owner might have predicted reasonably, the pedigree of mongrel dogs being open to speculation and if somewhere one ancestor chanced to be member of an ancient species of doglike creature with peculiar jumping skills, perhaps bred in an unknown jungle south of Borneo, for what other explanation is there, then we cannot say.

It is probability, these questions. Actions of loving parents in respect of their injured female child-victim are justified. Parents so have freedom to feel aggrieved when their children are attacked in one ruthless indiscriminate fashion. Yet if children are in the process of development, all learning, acquiring reasoning skills, judgment skills, those that we may expect reasonably of more mature persons as toward democratic responsibility. It is to be hoped that this experience, though nasty, will produce a worth-while lesson both for one child and for other children of the district. The owner of the mongrel cannot be held culpable beyond what might be expected, reasonably, of any dog-owner, that the precautions taken by him were reasonable under these circumstances, which are wholly unique, wholly singular, in this especial and specific instance. The international court makes recommendation, fully unbiased, based wholly on factual data, to the dog-owner that in future he takes pains to discover the genealogy of any mongrel he may own before agreeing to accept responsibility of said ownership. The court here has no doubt that, if so found, this dog-owning fellow would erect a taller fence and/or gate. Yes, and international adjudicators further recommend to all mongrel dog-owners that it is advisable that on the grounds of any property all animals are in the back, better than to the front. Thank you sir.

There are many misunderstandings of these legalities, being designed to bring justice, designed to settle actions between individuals, to advance freedom for some but not nor in spite of others. It so appears equality is in all individuals, but this equality is mysterious, having much to do with essence or essences held in common by all individuals.

It is with difficulty we refer to "all individuals" as humanity, leading as it must to misunderstandings and confusions. Regard humanity as one wide-ranging community of individuals where difference begins from that one fact, community, where one law may be applied. Economic and social difference are individual qualities, sometime properties, and will enter the process of individual cases.

It is indicated that we talk not about one law but another. Societies differ, laws differ. Colleagues irritate international experts through a failure to distinguish one from another. Our history can be an example, exemplification. Yet in earlier times our "campaigning formation" was susceptible to these arguments and examples, colleagues entered into these debates, adopting proposals on conference platforms, lobbies of political chambers, yes, we did accede to these channels.

In cases dealing with political crimes, horrors, atrocities, precedents are of minimal value, also one case succeeds and we may not assume a precedent is created such that future State responses will have altered. Each case is prepared uniquely, as unique, so, a phenomenal occurrence. Yes, of course. Sir. As one case succeeds in however limited a fashion so will the State and wider community, international community, determine future victories, now preempting, from day-to-day operations of democratically-elected governments (dutiful-appointed), work on behalf of its masters, delivering all appropriate legislation, appropriate as so and may so, working through these issues when and as so they may occur, and what then should we designate evidence, what then is proof, how truth can be so determined, whose burden might that become, tell to me a victim, and is this consent. If all the way through and integral then explain to us how this can be. What also are called universal, if from outwith positions of authority.

11
"old examples"

Who would seek a compassion, which must concern a future and I saw no future. Beyond that moment lay nothing for myself. Who is trapped, animals are trapped, humans are animals. This was my country yet not my country. Why I was here. It was to question from the past, having no meaning for the now. The elderly man had arrived with his righthand man, who was a dangerous man. Both had names known to myself and to other colleagues.

All concentration now was on this demonstration, fully placed to the elderly man whose role so was primary. We were in a cleared area in that section, I can say our section. We were seated on a floor, backs to the wall and yet relaxing, stretching out our legs, the dozen of us. Others may have entered. A fire had been built. I had thought to be near to a window but spaces all were taken and I could sit where, where I might.

There was the area beyond and some had returned from there with wood and also water, there was no wine, no brandy, if someone had cigarettes, I do not think so. There was little talking. I could not grasp what was said, having to pay close attention to gesture, to facial expression. People were exhausted, I also, straining if to concentrate, so to listen, also that I might observe. I was not excluded. If I thought so. I know that I was not. There had been strangeness, a strangeness. I can say it, but not what it was, yet something, there was something, yes, sensing it, I did so, it was to happen, what?

Moment by moment I became stronger, gathering this from somewhere, yes, stronger, more. The elderly man was here and to talk, to lecture, of course, all lay within, all aspects, only what form of this, how it so may progress.

An introduction had been given to himself by a colleague. It was courtesy also, these two having travelled far to this section. The elderly man acknowledged it. Our colleague continued, the introduction now a prefatory comment, becoming also a lecture as does happen if there are philosophies or principles of action, of course, what these might be for one, for all, and for us now at this more difficult time if our beliefs are not fixed, not in strength, there are these things we must retain and at what cost, any cost, these are our precious possessions, neither gold nor silver nor the more modern tools and weaponry, all technology, neither trust, betrayal, all questions akin to this, yet more primary.

Near to the exit I saw the righthand man watching, watching, if he might intimidate us. Yes, myself. He could do it, this was a dangerous man, all now knew it, his presence only was intimidation. Those who did not know of this had listened to the introduction by our colleague who now was stepping aside. And the elderly man was there and continued to speak, saying of beliefs or principles, what actions that we are to do and must do. My eyes had been closing earlier, I have said exhaustion but now no longer but alert, hearing the elderly man's voice, now understanding that he moved towards a difficult ending, that was to develop and lay in that ending.

I had thought it a narrative. It was no narrative. I saw some looking to myself. I knew it. Acquaintances, yes, all were so. I knew it. We had come in the first batch together, and from awkward situations, situations of adversity, greater adversity, adversities. Even so.

There was the nervousness. If my colleagues here awaited a sign it was concerning myself, how to look upon myself for all thought that it was myself. If I was not the one.

Now a further thought from myself, that I was not the one.

If I should be in fear. Why. I do not think so. I could have smiled. We were younger but not so much so, that our minds did not exist, also that we were together in these situations, I have said, of adversity. Uneasiness and how to conceal it, not one from another, if we had been together in such affairs. Do not worry for myself. I smiled to them, this reassurance to them. Nothing is unexpected. Is this to be learned, when may it be learned, what of their images, concatenation, where this meaning may be discovered.

If there is selection then it is we ourselves, we are in selection, have been selected. If it is myself then they also may accept responsibility, if imperatives do exist, yes. We can consider our parents, who did not accede but did not comprehend, so turning their heads from us. If our parents turn their heads from us, we do not do so.

I had hoped they would understand this about me. I thought that they did. This now was reminding them. During the recent activity they had watched out for myself as I them, one to another, as always. Tasks always were delegated as this task also was delegated.

It passed beyond remark when they saw that I was not disturbed. They each themself will assume none but them, not he not she, having endured such torment, they and their people, each of them. But also they had the loyalty. They listened if I spoke, and if I spoke of that especially they listened. As one, another, all of us, we would learn and much so was to be learned, we knew this, I knew it, to the depth of my mind, heart, also heart, yes, I say it.

For now I also was learning, in the presence of the elderly man and the other, and younger colleagues could begin from that. He spoke of betrayal. He asked if we knew how long were the human entrails. The righthand man meantime looked to me. I shrugged but as in reply to the elderly man's question, if it had been a question, I was not now certain. When his colleague continued to look towards me I said, Yes, and the sound of my voice, booming. I wondered about the others. Matters of loyalty, betrayal. If they should wonder of myself.

The elderly man had made a sign, directing the same question to the others. A woman made a comment, clumsy comment, attempting humour. He ignored her to continue speaking. In past weeks I had heard him on two such occasions, picked that up about him. He was not courteous but perfunctory, seeming without personal interest. Of course he had seen very many people. They come and they leave, some disappear. Guests also. The elderly man would have known many guests, foreign people. Some had been colleagues. He had spoken of this.

Now again he spoke of this. I was concentrated now, knowing it for certain what he said.

Nothing else is possible. What else could there be? I could not think otherwise.

I now understood that the understanding was to me. I did not take it amiss. Why should I? I was in that position. He told of a very difficult example, during the occasion of a very difficult and awkward incidence, very awkward incidence. He said how these things should be reviewed as examples and did we understand this, it was very important that this should be grasped by the company. He explained it over and over again, asking if the point was grasped. And again, did we understand? I found his colleague, the righthand man, looking to me once more and so again I said, Yes.

It had the effect of making a silence. None moved but the elderly man who stared to me. You understand, he asked.

This time I remained silent. He nodded, moving towards me. He gripped me at the back and side of the neck, at first too firmly, choking me and I had to grasp at his wrist. He was directing me over onto my back and I allowed myself to topple, onto my shoulder yet if there had been one option, I so allowed it.

He patted my head twice, pulled back my shirt and drew one finger down the centre of my belly, rib-cage to navel. When he spoke his voice was harsh and now too rapid for my comprehension. I now had no concentration for it seeing his arm, shoulder, knotted veins on the back of his hand, wrists, how all power was there. He had withdrawn the knife, yes, thick-bladed, a breaking-knife, gouging and ripping. I saw now the righthand man, arms folded, only watching this event.

Also a vigilance, towards something, there was this. I had the part to play in it. I could see that colleague, righthand man and there was that in him too, I was certain, but what was it?

And who would seek it?

I waited to learn. The younger ones would note this, some [as] patience, others I do not know. But I could not grasp all that the elderly man gave, if he might speak more slowly. Also the harshness, there was that. I say that there was a harshness in him.

In his voice, his manner.

I expected indifference but this was harshness, hindering my comprehension. Also I was seeing his colleague who now observed others in the room, yes, as they looked towards the elderly man, towards myself, he so was alerted, was alert, more so attentive. I was having to control myself so not to struggle, could not. I knew it. The elderly man's voice now. Colleagues, he said, it is for you, how you must learn this thoroughly.

His gripping now my neck, choking me, could not see his eyes and grasped his wrist, I did do it, if not I do not think, now blackness, in my eyes, spitting lights, spits of this, blue, something. I would topple. I barely could see his colleague but yes he was squinting across at me, a glimpse of him. I saw him. I saw that man and know it, curious as to my origins, my people, from where I had come. He did not know, neither the elderly man who would not care. They none of them, none of them. I told them nothing. They knew nothing. I told them nothing, not the elderly man. No, not the righthand man, who would seek anything. And find nothing. Yes and find nothing. But I waited to learn. I would wait to learn, and so see nothing beyond that moment, for what may I say I had given myself, if to death, I so had done it.

The concentration of the others centred on the elderly man and his demonstration. I no longer could see his colleague but he would be staring, no feature altered.

Now I was gulping I think to speak, if I may so, having to gulp, if I can speak, but the elderly man's grip forced back my head, settled back onto my windpipe, the heel of his hand to the top of my chest so that I only could gulp, he exerted the pressure again and it was sudden and I saw into his eyes and there was nothing there for me, nothing, I was not here for this man, if my flesh would be ripped. The knife was flat to my stomach, upon it, and its point pressing, I distinguished it, I wondered how long till I heard the voice, when it would come. When it did so it was from a direction too difficult for me. Still the elderly man stared down, his grip arrested on my neck. The pressure there was great. His colleague had moved elsewhere in the room, in meantime, and I could look for him, could smile, but did not see him, could not. The elderly man was listening, only listening. I watched, he saw it. He saw also that I waited. I knew to wait and would wait. The elderly man, his colleague. The response would be from them. Even so it was now that the other spoke. This was the one. I knew it, knew it. Even now, he did speak. There are no friends, he said, there are no others.

His voice had rasped and was followed by silence. None in the room seemed even to move. I waited also, and then could move onto my side the grip of the elderly man so having relaxed. I thought to recognise whose was the voice. I knew that it would come again and I would understand the familiarity. I knew that it would be so.

The fire had dulled and there was not much light now and also a smell, yes sweetish, also was this coal dirt or dampness, something. I looked where I could, seeing their eyes to me. If they had thought I was not of them. They now knew was truth, lying in this demonstration, all younger colleagues. Perhaps this earlier had been denied. If examples might be heeded, not heeded. I saw the elderly man's colleague towards the rear of the room, as though lounging. He was not lounging. I saw also his look to myself, a curiosity. Yet there was the haughtiness. It was a fault in him. I knew it and so could have said it, argue of it, I saw it, yes, an arrogance, what arrogance was this, a righthand man. I thought why the elderly man so had selected him. I would have known. I would have been so capable, I could have succeeded, neither with arrogance.

Now the individual spoke again. I recognised him. He spoke to all. On the other hand, he said, his voice rasping, and this you must know.

But he did not finish this, instead he looked around the room, the resignation strongly there in him. Others had entered. I knew the shift in atmosphere. When the elderly man made his move he did so methodically and I thought then of his grip as an old vice, rust settled on the underside, seeming always a fraction too late. Yet such a vice need not grip at the correct point of impact. But once settled scarcely could it be prised apart. He patted my shoulder now, murmuring something, that my part had ended.

The righthand man was not in the room. Nor the third, this other who had spoken.

I would say this, that none had allowed a proper opportunity. I had not received it. Thus I would say I was not treated fairly. I had closed my eyes. I hoped that the younger ones would see this and know that I could not enter into this world if not by selection which had taken place as one effect of this demonstration. If I am to have an opinion, I so could not be alive. Of course the elderly man would know, would not know, what of that.

12

"I do not go to his country"

I know who watched for us, myself herself. He carried stories, he was a story teller, fabulous fairy tales for news agencies, crossing this world the next world and all other worlds of this and outside universes. Yes. He sought stories, sought that I might advise him. What did he want from myself was not mysterious. He might turn tables on me, what of "campaigning formations", so he thought. What he did think I do not care and did not, also that he thought I was a fool. He called me friend, he followed us, spoke also to my companion in quiet places, a fool, thinking quiet places were secret, calling friends, friends, thinking we are so foolish. You are unlike these others, he said.

Unlike these others, what do you say?

Friend, he said, and there one could kill him, yes, how is your throat today, but I would not kill such a one, nothing. If he is dead then he is, dead, if his throat was sliced, why not pistol, who has energy, it may be said, of course, yes. He has disappeared. All people may disappear, as also my wife, as also my companion, as also other family and friends. Who does not disappear. This one day he came to our section, mister teller of fabulous fairy tales and myself and my companion lay under the covering. I said to him, What is it you seek from us?

What language could he know. There is a language shared, man to man, with woman, why he did not leave, and watched

us, myself, what did he think, why he was there watching us.
He knows, man knows. He was there. Thinking I so am foolish
we are so foolish. Why? I do not go to his country.

13

"if I think nothing"

Always there was danger. I then thought so, how she was returning to her own place, I knew these risks, what routes, if securitys should be there. It was not practical, and if the curfew was there. Safety only is for strangers, colleagues also watch for them. Who does not know it. From our first meeting we became intimate. Other nights following, some she would visit, some not so, or again she visited but did not stay. I did not visit her place, only she to mine. I was not suspicious. If she visited one other man, I do not know. It is said she visited one. I do not think so. If it was possible, yes, she might go to him. If she had done I was not affected. How that might be, men and men, jealousy for what reasons. I had been with her and if it was not to continue then it would not and what was it that I might accomplish, if to change her will. This woman was strong, stronger. I thought that she was. Good fortune was to myself having her and I was grateful, certainly.

I said these were dangerous times then in that town and in shadows such risks, all colleagues took them, so also that night of her disappearance when many authoritys and guests to our country were there, a cultural evening, an event of importance for our "campaigning formation". Social gatherings, all such events, these may be duties. Authoritys and foreign people, media people also, these with us, photographic, that these might meet one another and see things, other sides of our lives, our people. This concert also was for higher colleagues who would seek support, domestic, foreign. All things were needed, tools, material goods and medicines of course, hardware software, all of everything anything, finances.

We were in escort team, my companion driving, I by her side, protector, weaponry. We came by certain routes in one convoy and so would return by certain routes, twelve or fourteen vehicles, up down up down along along along, along, up, down down round, round circles, all due care. We were sixth or seventh vehicle. We two had brought three persons and would return these afterwards to their houses, one a guest to our country. Upon arrival they entered the theatre, colleagues were there, securing for entries-exit, all safety, safely. We two did not enter the building but parked the vehicle then, bringing it to the parking area, returning afterwards by foot. Colleagues also patrolled there. One street beyond and parallel were military and security. We knew it they knew it all knew it, standing off from us, we from them, later would be curfew time.

So, we did not enter the theatre building with the others, but after the beginning. It was excitement. I have said this. It is nothing, I always was so, lusting, what I may say, I can say it, without power, I was her lover. If I was hers, if I was. We returned by foot not to there but behind so to the alley, and into shadows, a doorway, we were together. Here was the smell of burnt burning things, food, chicken, lamb, onion, we had not eaten, these smells were good, I remember, was hungry. If she was excited by these adventures, I do not think so, not so much, yet these were risks and greater risks. Yes I pulled her to myself, she pulled me to herself. We were lovers. We were. What I am to say, I did not abuse her, what to say I can say it, herself myself, I opened her clothing. What to say I touched her, yes, yes touching her, gripping her. Yes, gently, open, her breaths, catch in breaths, her breathing, her clothing. If power was with ourselves, I do not think so. Later we were into the seats for us in the theatre. Other colleagues then saw us so, entering later.

All lights on stage and dancers were there. Or if it was music, perhaps, in the traditional style, I think so, musicians were there, also dancers. Dancers with musicians. Yes. People enjoyed it, I think that they did, authoritys, foreign guests. If it was boring. Older people may enjoy these evenings. My companion now with me, my lover, I can say it, and if one artiste was on stage, musician, poet, dancer, anyone, what I heard only her, saw only her, smelled only her, whispering into her ear, her skin, hair, her slender fingers, seeing how smaller was her hand from mine, yet this woman who was so much strong, stronger, yet if her body seemed to mine lacking in physical powers what strength, where did it come from, how women may have it, such marvels yet allowing her hand to rest within mine, trusting in that. We two then had been for weeks together, three, four. If we would remain together, who could be foolish, so thinking, for how long. Always. What always may be. Her own partner thought so, he now was dead. She did not know for certain, but supposed it. She took my hand again into her own, settling mine onto her lap and warmth there, we might sit, her hand now onto my lap, if we were bolder, it was darkness, and the change also came in her and her breathing, and that sound was beautiful to myself and then that I saw the one watching us. It was then. I saw him. Farther there to one side. Staring, yes, seeing my companion. My arm now I put round her shoulders. I thought if he was known to myself, was a familiarity there about him. I thought so there might be, I whispering to her, if she saw him, did she know him. I saw that she had seen this man. He was there to herself, she knew so. One moment then and she looked and he turned from us. I wondered was it absently done. If he was a security. She did not think so in this place where all were trustworthy, were so to be, but also I knew and so said it to her that there is no place where all are trustworthy, such a place, one other planet from here, where, no place. We sat then in silence, I did not look again to this man. It was in my belly then it was anger. If also it was fear, why not, if there was, I think so, what might it have been.

Now was an interval and we were walking at the entrance hallway and lobby where tea or coffee, drinks, food also, there was bread, cheese, cold meats, salad. We were hungry, all colleagues. If we might eat, if others had finished. We were standing back from the authoritys and guests. Her hand was into mine. Now colleagues could move to there and she whispered to me she did not want to, want not to eat. Why not, could I eat her portions! She would not eat with these people. She said it to me, had said it one earlier time also, authoritys and foreign guests, saying to me, Do not let them see us eat, they shall not see me eat.

What is wrong, we are hungry, we can eat?

No, I shall not show them.

I did as she, so, a hole into my belly. There were notices on the wall, events were forthcoming, news information, we read these. Now it happened that I saw that fellow again, yes, watching us. I could not believe this, he would be daring as this, challenging. He was on the other side where food was, having a cup in one hand, sipping tea or coffee. My companion did not see him. I took her arm, as natural. I whispered to her. I do not know, saying to her, but personal words, personal. There was a feeling in myself, strongly emotional. I wanted to hold her. Sensing something. I was. I do not know. But strongly in myself. Stronger. If a knowledge of loss. Loss to come. I do not know. We have losses always, always, but some can live, why not we two, that we might live, we two, why not, why others and not so for ourselves, if we loved one another. I whispered to her perhaps these words, other words. Personal words. I cannot remember. I cannot remember but I did so. But in my belly, something, twisting. She grasped my hand, tightening onto my wrist, now touched my face and left me. Left me, yes. I saw where, walking to the room for women, bathroom. And the one who was watching also had gone. What I am to say. He had. I looked but did not see him. If he had followed my companion, yes, I thought so. What else, what one may think. Other colleagues were there, one came to me, gave a cigarette and matches, saying two foreign guests were in his vehicle and would be to their house later, also other colleagues, there would be wine, brandy, perhaps, he hoped so, if we were to come to there afterwards, my companion and myself, they would welcome us. We spoke further, one minute. My companion returned. Our colleague was smiling to her, touching her arm. Elbow, yes, he touched her elbow. I thought why he had done so, if there had been a need. Why he had touched her. If such behaviour was normal. I looked to his face, only smiling to her. And the bell ringing, the interval ended. My companion wished to return to our seats. I did not, wishing only to return. To my section. I could have gone then from this cultural evening. Yes, what is to say. It was not anger, I was not angry. If so, yes, I would say it. But troubling to me, by these events, troubled, yes, I was so, nor comfortable, these people being there. I wanted to be away, we two. I said it to her, we might walk outside. No, she would not. But for one moment, I had a cigarette, we could smoke it there. No. She said there was one performance to come she must see, more dancers, musicians, but young people, many related to friends. So we returned to our seats.

I could not enjoy anything, not of this performance, barely could I watch it. Yes it is good to see children, we see their faces and there is brightness and future hopes but these older ones and adults also, no, I could not enjoy them, how it may be possible so to do, if it is amateurish, amateurish, and boring, more dull. It was. I thought it. What is to say further, trivial banality, if it is traditional, and only, why, what century is this, do we look forward, backward, to our grandparents, grand-parents of grandparents, do we have monkey dances. Foreign guests also have music, dance, laughter, as we do, yes, they also as we have ours, but there are many towns, many communities, traditional yes, also modern, younger people with music, excitement of this, loud poetry also, shouting and with all passion, yes for our people, we too, having many many things as these foreign people in our many towns these are there and here were in one town only town, say township, where local colleagues may not know other things, do not see other things, so cannot be judges. A band now entered and a troupe to follow, dancing on stage, grandfathers. I could not sit there. This was not entertainment, I whispered to her, thinking if we should go soon we might wait outside, smoke one cigarette, if not I should scream out, I am in agony, whispering this to her.

She did not answer me. I saw her eyes, beautiful, how the beauty of women's eyes, beautiful and not as men, women's eyes are not, men's eyes differing. Now what she said to me that he was there, this man was there again watching her, always, she saw his face. Yet when I looked I did not see him, neither elsewhere. I said, He is not there.

Yes.

Where? I cannot see him.

He is watching.

I cannot see him.

He is there.

Do you know him?

He is watching.

Who is he, this man, who is he?

Her teeth biting onto her lip. Her head, straightened, shoulders, body stiffly held, her attention as to the performance of the children. This was to myself, rigidly holding herself, as against me, it was, and I put my hand to her arm but could not touch her, would say something to her but did not, waiting only until the performance might end, the applause of people, but she soon turned to me, whispering, What is wrong with you? If you are jealous, stupidity. It is do you know him, you are my protector, you are, why you are with myself. It is to myself this man looks, it is my safety. Do you know him, have you seen him, where he is from, what he is, colleague, I do not think so, what suspect, what is he, security, he is military, where he is from, does he know my husband, what is he wanting from me, what is it, why you do not protect me, instead so foolishly asking questions of myself, do not ask them but him, go to him, where is he, find him. We are protectors, watching one to another. Now I may protect myself. If I can, and I can, if it is only myself. Who is he. I cannot speak to you, you are an attacker, not protector.

My companion was onto her feet and walking to the exit. I did not follow then. Children were on the stage, now from it, making their exit, the band behind them, and the applause from people.

I walked to the front hallway and lobby, could not see her, so to the tables, bench seats, rooms for men, for women, no, I could not see her. I waited, she did not come, so continued to wait.

People were there, and to the exit. Perhaps if she had gone outside of the theatre, would she do this alone, if she so was so foolish, she would do it, I knew her, if only weeks yet I knew her, anything she might do, she was capable, taking all risks if so necessary, she would do it, in all situations, I knew her, difficult situations, more dangerous. I went outside, walking to there, here, that way, now if already she had gone, so by the side of the building, very dark shadows, as is known, also one street from here where were all military personnel, not in view for us but were there, quietly, waiting, waiting, when was curfew, if colleagues forgot this, and if so important, these guests to our country, were they, if they may stray also down dark alleyways, if they too may disappear, what then would happen, if colleagues did not protect these VIP guests to our country, what of foreign sources. I walked by the alleyway, along there, taking the cigarette from my pocket. I had my matches, to strike one onto the wall, draw the tobacco smoke into my lungs, I had not smoked since afternoon, and closer by one rear entranceway, lighted by one lamp, little, and again the smell of food, but then also came the hand onto my arm. It was her. I breathed, only. Passed the cigarette to her, I think so, that I did. What of her, lifting my arm, she did so, lifted my arm, placing it round her shoulder, settling her head there, her hair against my face, smell of her skin beautiful skin I closed my eyes, drawing all into myself, breathing her into myself, filling my lungs with it of her the smell of her hair and the smell of her flesh. Moments in life in history. What seconds may be. If in history, one of us dead. This is not dishonesty. These are the thoughts and were the thoughts, which one, the one of us to live, for one would live yes beyond the other, are we not children, let us admit and not deny, one lives beyond the other. Thus what of we two, if one what one, if it would be one. I tightened my grip on her, my fingers touching her upper arm, bare, to my fingertips, flesh of her upper arm, muscle of her upper arm.

I thought always that I knew her, in these few weeks, yes, always.

What I am to say. Is integrity, what integrity may be. We two. I cannot say more. It is known.

Now I could not stop it, how my mind thinking, my physical always, I could not stop it, never thinking and held her now more tightly, more. What I can say more, I cannot be ashamed. I would do it, always in lust, I could not stop it to her. But she stopping me, touching my wrist. This would not happen it was dangerous for us, military all were closeby, yes, also but my lusting for her, always to touch her, feel for her body, pressing her to myself, farther, within shadows now moving to rest against the wall of building and she allowed it, her arms around my neck, lifting her her body was upwards sighing to me feeling for my penis and I could move quickly to inside her, being inside her, entering, so beautiful but stopping she stopped now, and her tension, Oh, he is there, he is there. And when I looked she was from me, moving apart from me, now walking. She pointed. It was into the shadows, farther, in that direction from myself, past myself, away from herself, and I stepped then, slower, along that alleyway. Nothing. Nothing was there, he was not there, none. No person. I looked there for one minute two minutes, longer. Nothing, nothing. I returned to the street but she was not there. Inside the theatre. Neither there, not by the doors. Colleagues were by the hallway entrance, securing entries-exit, none had seen her. Perhaps she could be safe and somewhere. They said so. What of the parking area, she might have gone to there. No. Perhaps I should wait for her, she would come soon. In ten minutes vehicles would be returned from the parking area, she knew it, and later curfew would come, she knew it, schedule for the convoy, of course.

If I am to deny everything, we are human beings and have thoughts. She was not there, where was she.

What I may say, work is to be done I so do it. These are duties, we have acceded to them. The convoy was there, authoritys returning to their houses, foreign guests. Vehicles always must be in line. One key is for each escort, if trouble arises. Vehicles always must be in line, ordered, these are basic matters. I now was driver of the vehicle. One colleague came for my companion, escort-protector. Our passengers were to the houses, four miles from the theatre, we drove slowly, properly, arriving. An invitation was to all colleagues for one house for relaxation, food, refreshment drinks. Colleagues were my friends and we spoke together. To return in search of my companion was not possible so to do, but next morning only, this was the first time. I knew it. Only return to my section. She would return to hers, if so if not so, but what I might do, nothing. No, nothing, it could not be done, nothing. This then was possible. Nothing. Nothing. I could walk. Where to walk. I may say. When tomorrow

I might drive, driving southeast, I would so to streets of her childhood, narrow streets that were her familiar streets, and in that zone I would stop the vehicle, leaving it. Morning. It was not cold, smelling also the sea, and walking far down hill, steeply and not some open areas but if where women may hang clothes, and far down to where she had brought me days earlier, showing to me walks from childhood. I said to her, If the sea was there, might we walk to there, the sea is freedom, all gateways, yes, she brought me, saying Of course we may go, securitys will not be there, if the sea is there, where can they go, they are not sailors, if they might flee the country. The estuary was there, closer, and one river also, that bridge also, smaller bridge for walkers, that we might cross this bridge from centuries past, we were keeping to the side and within shadows. I would search to there, all places and thoroughfares, I would search them, those to lead us to us, the morning is tomorrow.

What might be expected. Neither from myself. We are human beings.

We became intimate from the first evening when we met. I knew her from previously. I had known him also.

Her partner. I said it, she had her partner, he was her husband, a man held in regard yet with his own habits, known for humour if telling colleagues of matters, we would smile, jokes, stories. She also smiled in speaking of him. Yes, colleague, good fellow. But two years now had passed. If he was dead. All thought that he was. I did not say this to her.

I thought nothing, what so, what I am to think. I would not look to her if he was there, he was not there, having been gone now two years, some thought dead, I thought dead. He was dead, I knew it. I would not say this to her.

I remember that she dropped my hand, having held my hand then dropping it. I reached to her arm but if she tensed, her body rigid if against me and I brought my hand away now seeing her face, yes, such anger there. I knew it in her.

But let me say firstly when we met together, weeks only had passed, I speak of one meeting for colleagues, she came to that, she and one other, also female. This was late night, discussion matters, issues then raised for future practices, some critical, some defensive. Older colleagues respond to criticism, it is normal. I had had instruction. Others had made that decision. What people may think. They can think it. Thoughts are in freedom. Younger colleagues have opinions. I thought of the future, what of our "campaigning formation". I would raise matters for discussion. There was a past also some colleagues did not consider, I considered it. But firstly tomorrow I would return in search of her, next morning.

"a pumpkin story"

The ticket was in my pocket, the goods also with me, these in the bag strapped on my shoulder. Not strapped down meaning by this I could lift the bag from myself easily. Soon I would be gone from this place, good feeling. I saw from the office of the bus-terminal. Near to here were lines of vendors, some having barrows, boxes, selling vegetables and fruits, other produce, meats, other articles, other people, yes, seeking, desiring, what, requesting, and of these, customers, travellers are customers. Military and security were among them, also inside the terminal building. I came outside, looking for somewhere I might sit to wait, two hours more. I walked to the other side where were military installations, all personnel. And from there and round farther was the bus and two mechanics working, the hood lifted to the engine. Inside a woman was cleaning on the low level and I might go upstairs. I looked for a destination but none yet was posted. I asked this woman and she told me yes it was this one for myself. I stepped on board. She looked but said nothing. Thus I was the first, first traveller to board, this was why, the two men at the engine having shown no interest, if not noticing myself, perhaps. I went onto the upper level, sitting halfway along with the window, all windows were open, it was not hot. I took the bag from my shoulder, put it to my feet, knotted the lace of my shoe to the handle. The long wait to come but with my book this was a pleasure, long waiting was time to myself, I might read, sleep a little, if it was possible, yes, I closed my eyes. If it might be peaceful, that was my wish, but what a wish, smaller town, border town.

Soon others were thinking such thoughts as myself, the bus becoming busier, new people searching for places. One hour more to leave. I saw now a second bus was behind this one. No sight of the drivers. Beside me was sitting one man and his suitcase on his lap, resting his head there. His eyes were closed, not sleeping sleeping, I think not, resting his mind. Men worked far from home, travelling to or from one place and another. In front of myself to the window was a woman, thirty-five years, I would say it, so supposing, she wore darker clothes, if religious clothes. I did not see her features other than one moment as she seated herself. It was next to her the one had come, the younger fellow that I am to speak, placing down his belongings to safe security on that seat. He spoke quietly to her and her answer only was by head movement, assent. He would say how none should sit down on that seat. And if his belongings should be stolen, she should see this did not happen, none should steal his belongings. He thanked her then returned below, not looking to other travellers, if this was carelessly done. He appeared from the bus exit, stepping outside.

Vendors had come to our two buses from the other side of the terminal building, selling to travellers. It was very busy. On this bus also it was very busy, full seats, families split one and another. Many people gathered on the street below, families, all relatives, leavetakings, farewells. Near to the barrows with fruit and vegetable produce two vendors of water, people queued for them, water for the journey. The younger fellow also was there, not with the water queue but standing with elderly people, older man and woman. They were not drinking that water. The vendor was near to them. I do not know that these people had bought the water at an earlier time. All people are thirsty. Yes. Not all people queue for that water. People are bitter. If this water here sold was not liked. Where that water had come from, of these vendors. I do not know which water was sold to people, it is I am supposing. People perhaps are too much bitter, some might say, not say. These mountains beyond, they also have water. Only days since I had come from there. Water is in the mountains. The elderly couple and younger fellow might have come from there. I do not know.

Water is in the mountains, obtained in the mountains, obtained not obtained, perhaps it so may not be obtained, perhaps sealed off from people.

It is factual information. Pipes are from continent to continent, vendor to vendor, water is sealed off from people, going to vendors.

Vendors may be local people, also foreign. Water and oil, these are international. Rivers may be pipes. I have heard them so called. It is not sarcastic. Rivers can be pipes. Sealed not sealed, some may be. Oil also is sealed. People do not say oil-river, rivers are of water, water gives life but of a water-river people may say of it it is a pipe. I have heard it said. If water is sealed off from people what is it, it is a pipe. The river is one issue of water, more, issuing not from the sea but from the mountains into the sea. Rivers are in the mountains but where is the water. Foreign lands have rivers, all have pipes, pipes are crossing borders, international.

People say this, I have heard them. They are bitter. Their home is there and their water is not. There is no river, not of water, not of life.

What I am to say. Water is controlled, life is controlled, people have the water, governments have the water, people possess the water, governments possess the water, possessing the lives, the lives of people, day-to-day life.

What experience, experiencing

I am asked to say this fact or this fact, this other fact. What is expected. I do not know. It is known why I was there. I speak of these people as I was inside on the bus. I was reading one book. I had some, I had six, seven. I had with me seven books.

These were the books to be stolen, later, my bag taken. The books were different books. Books may be different, those of mine were different. Also two new ones I came upon. What books, I cannot remember.

It was in that same town, near to the border and beyond there. Yes, others. Of course dangerous.

I had different books. Theoretical works. Also old books. It is not sarcasm, old books.

New books old books, theoretical works, computing. Languages of computing. Other languages. Languages that may be possible. We can say models, adopting innovatory techniques, amalgam of logic, linguistical, in algorithms, not so modern.

Not so modern. If old ways are not discarded. If medieval times are considered, if we move beyond then, we can move beyond then, medieval times, if it is allowed, progress, yes, progress not progress.

It is not sarcasm. Old ways often are discarded, progress is backwards. It is not sarcasm. If religion is medieval, I do not say it. I am not a religious man. Who has the authority. Who are authoritys. I have my questions. These questions may be put forward if it so is allowed, who will do so, who may question, who is to speak, so is allowed, then do so, tell it to me, say who is arbiter if our lives so are determined, who is to determine them, if these questions are, or are not, who is arbiter, what religious man, what is that authority.

All theoretics. These questions are from books, old books new books. A book such as that does engross me. Or computing. These books also, any books. What I am to say if this is not true, it is true. Some are new books speaking of old history. If these treaties were between countries, between states, inter one to another, of 80 years and 800 hundred, 8000, that duration, if it be so, what may be denied, if one is to deny, what, if this is our land? can such a thing be denied. We are not gods seeking verification, what is our proof, show it to me, if birds do not

103

sing and babies do not cry, call to witness, please show it, otherwise we are beings on planet Earth, some humans, what may we do if evidence is demanded of us, we ourselves, that we exist?

I would not deny these books, speaking of old history. What can be denied. Books are not to be denied. Who has books, have books, who. Who has history. Some have no history.

It is factual information.

Old struggles, old campaigns, old propaganda. From other countries. I cannot remember more of them. Revolutionaries, famous figures, personality people I do not know, intelligentsia. Of other countries. I do not remember, anyone, peoples.

I do not remember which countries did they come, I do not know. It is not sarcasm. Historical books, technological books. These were taken from me during the period of the disturbance. The bag was at my feet. One book was not taken. I held this in my hand. I was reading it.

I was reading it. The others were stolen from me. I say so.

Who has my books. They may read them, gain pleasure. Perhaps the woman wearing religious clothes. She might steal them? Religious people do not steal. This is said. I am not sarcastic. Religious people are good people. They will not rob from others, unto others, so, as they themselves, into temples, mosques. Perhaps they can read them, stealing my books they now can read them, seeing from medieval times, the collars and veils are by our eyes, progress not progress, give your authority to me, I also am a father, father of your father, all fathers, I am father.

The revolution is the technology, this is said. People say it. I do not say it. Geometrical solutions, what is digital problems. I read for interest, instruction but also interest, only myself. A book such as that will engross me. I came upon it in that town. I bought it. From a vendor. I do not know the vendor.

How can this not be possible to say. I do not know the vendor. There, I have said it.

Which one.

Yes, which one.

Magicians may fly. Also animals, yes, all pigs, planet Mars for martians, colleagues of mars.

I would not describe these border towns as treasure-trove towns, treasure-trove villages. Not book treasures. Other treasures perhaps but for book readers, for teachers, for students, an embarrassment. The authoritys may be embarrassed. Here is a culture, it has no books. We shall die for this culture.

I cannot say the vendor who had these books. Other treasures are there. Drugs for sexual assistances and medications, weapons or livestock, fruit produce, vegetable produce, wines, alcohol, brandy, jewellery, trinkets, yes local brandy, it is dangerous yes to health, and livestock, all may be purchased. I do not know about people. People can be purchased always, yes. An economy may build. There is trade in people. Who is to be sentimental, I can be so, if it is possible, I think so, that it may be so, if it is children, our little sisters and brothers, if we may sell them.

I am a guest to these districts but knowledge is available. None may not know. In recent years also are stories of upsurges in the interchange of articles, yes, all services and goods, so it is said, luxury goods, hi-fi machinery, computer machinery, computing goods and telecoms, all phoneware, hardware software. We hear of it. We do not see it. I do not see it. Yet was one vendor having one typewriter, no electrics, no paper, I do not think so. Among the people also, if it is near to the border books can appear. Who is to say, it is random. I have books and had them. If there is laxity people make use of it, as they may wish, what is possible, they buy they sell, we buy we sell, we are human beings as are they. Who is surprised. I do not know why.

There was much vegetable produce, fruit, flesh meats, some decaying, giving off odours, ripened, other foods, pastries. People eat. Always. And for leavetakings, always. I did not buy. I had eaten before coming inside this place. Good food. It was a restaurant, I ate in it soup, and fish also was there. I was alone. Colleagues did not buy this food. No colleagues were there. Where these fish came from. I asked the waiter. He did not know. Waiters do not hold such information, I am sorry sir. Good fish, oil fish, I still could taste it, smell it, and here by the bus-terminal I was not hungry. Perhaps for the journey I could purchase some fruit, I thought perhaps, yes but did not, I did not go to buy, thinking someone might sit on my seat. If I might be allowed to return, if I had stepped onto the road below, military were there, who can say what they may do, risking to my health. Militarys are such hazards, securitys also more.

It is not sarcasm.

Now, thus, I was on the upper deck of this bus. One man next to me, man and his suitcase. His eyes were closed, resting, coming from home, working to someplace. In front of me one woman, religious woman, she did not move, perhaps she too was sleeping. Next to her was the younger fellow, his bag there on his seat.

I was tired then, now also I am tired. Exhaustion. Every thing. It is energy. For life, living, for energy, oxygen and water, we breathe, how do we breathe, breaths for living, where do they come from, we get our breaths, steal our breaths. I do not talk of the mountains, there is no water in the mountains, no water for people.

Pipes, enclosure. Who does not talk of the mountains.

The people were on the street below. What I am to say.

Yes, I was reading that book then and from the side of my eye saw down to the street, near these barrows with fruit and vegetable produce. The one was there by the old man and woman, elderly. Certainly it was a farewell, there was that finality. Many farewells, embraces. He was their grandson, if grandson, I think that he was. Each passed something to him, money, trinkets or jewellery, silver and gold objects, I do not know knives, cutlery, family treasures, I do not know. These would be there and found on his body, money of course, savings of money of course, elderly relatives to the young fellow, dreams and hopes, what they will do, and so they give all to him, it is an exchange, offerings to god and all other spiritual beings, safe-passage for our children, protection of our young and future.

These old people do it. The young offers hope for the future. All family hopes can be based on him if he is a young man, more than young woman, yes, I am saying, it is older people and what they do think, of that future, it is not myself, it is themselves who think it, yes, what does the future not hold, but pumpkins.

It is not sarcastic. Pumpkins are everywhere. In our culture, our country, whose country, who says "our", yes, pumpkins are everywhere.

They are everywhere. On sale, yes, everywhere.

Pumpkins may be soft and ripened, vegetating, rotted. Thus then was one military who fired the bullets to kill him. If he had insignia, perhaps so, shot by pumpkins, perhaps he will have been honoured, State authoritys to say it of him, death with full honour attached. No rotted pumpkins to be there then, slashing onto that insignia, if he had insignia, this security.

It is not sarcastic, sarcasm.

Returning now to myself, on the upper bus section, flight deck for our people, yes, to all galaxies where is found planet Mars, all good martian colleagues, it is not sarcastic.

I continued to read the book. What anger may be. If anger will move matters, events progessing through anger, if that they do, some think it, yes, I am not one who thinks it, books do not live, they are passive, coming to life as visceral, read by people, human beings, it is ourselves, we so.

But what.

reading books. Computing languages, algorithmic tasks, let us resolve, possible not possible, what we may achieve, all of we human beings, that we are, our moments, pavlov moments, it is not sarcastic.

All were aboard and the driver also

All were aboard. I thought it, hearing the engine turning and so the driver also was there but no sooner than the disturbance. Relatives remained on the street below and their relatives on the bus. Loud voices, I looked, yes, brave military, shouting military, all voices people voices shouting shouting. Now men were pushing out from the bus, pushed out from the bus. Military had boarded, pushing pulling, what tasks are performed by militarys, these are major operations, major operatives engage, all military and their insignia, large insignia brave insignia, finer military and their finer decorations all decorations, all personnel for gallant death with honours. These were honourable men courageous men men at the bus inside outside upper level lower level and on the street, brave men major men major operations, pumpkin operations, I am not angry.

Angry is sarcastic?

What is sarcastic.

Soft and ripened, vegetating, rotted. If what is under our skin, what might it be, if not blood, bone and gristle, sinew and muscle, what might it not be, arteries, beating hearts and souls, spirits of peoples.

Yes.

Families bid farewell. Under the nose of the military they bid farewell. A family bids farewell, it is a sacred operation. Sacred things. Give religion to me, not vegetating, already rotted, what it now is, what persuasions are we, if we have persuasions, what might they be

Now all were aboard low and upper levels of the bus we travellers and from outside faces raised, staring upward to us. I saw them, open faces, happy not happy, they bid farewell, when shall they see their loved ones. Never. Never shall they see them.

I tell the truth.

I so was witnessing.

I had the book but was not reading it now to exclude all else which was not possible. I so witnessed. Two travellers were ejected.

Only two. I so witnessed. I did not see from the other window. I could not, two eyes only in this head, remaining in one seat, myself.

Yes the younger fellow was of that two, he it was as second fellow pushed from the bus. The first fellow was the other. Each of these two pushed individually by militarys, five. Five military men major operatives all insignia for brave gallantry, these for the younger fellow, taking him from the bus, pushing, knocking, I do not know but for this one, grandson of the old people. Pushed out by five. Yes, what strength was there, youth is strength, yes. Five such military men. Why not six, seven men, eight men, warriors from Japan, wrestlers. It is not sarcastic. Youth is strength. Eight Sumo wrestler-warriors will push this younger fellow. A regiment is necessary. Bring these to our territory, peacekeepers so may do, bring them and bring them, all must arrive.

Other personnel, also securitys, many, they were there. I am saying it. Many were shouting as seeking information. They looked also to us, upward shouted also to us. I did not hear them. My ears were not suited to loudness, all shouting.

Vendors had moved

moving backward, from these lines of vision as also relatives and others of the travellers, not to be in sight of these personnel.

And now these two fellows were in view fully, isolated by these vendor barrows, it was these two, the younger one and the other who was pushed firstly from the bus. He was thirty years, our colleague. He it was sought by security, now taken by the militarys. I saw it I knew it. I looked, I saw, yes. This was a colleague. I did not recognise him but I knew it, knew it, who may tell this to myself, please, please do so do not do so

Yes, they shouted at him, pushed him felling him and up he rose, up to his feet, yes, onto his feet, standing, they shouted at him again shouted, knocked him down again, he rose up knocked down rose up, felled, rising upwards, yes, rising, yes, still he did, rising, felled, yes, having made the decision, thank you.

What decision what is decision.

All know what decision. He had made goodbye to his people. His people were not below, as that when they knocked him down and he rose up, he stood, waited, simply he waited, and all knew. He did not seek death, his head was bowed, it was to come. All we

How not to use bayonets bay on-ets for goodbye babeee. Bay on-ets may be used on younger fellows as on babies, sacks of grain as it may be done for children when all are surrounded and by heavy numbers face bravely our infants, why not if these are the foreign fabulists who may write it, academic experts who are into our country as servants and clowns to our master author-itys, all monies and riches from our colleges to these foreign professors, specialty experts who may say we do exist, or not so, who is to buy my words, all newspaper media, other servants all servants, such politicians and other personnel, allied at foreign office. Why not use such. Sacks of grain also are human beings. Yes. Come to our country, all pumpkin vendors and elderly people if surrounded by military personnel, younger people.

It is not sarcastic. Time is not ours.

People may oppose humiliation. If time is not ours. They will oppose humiliation but we have no time for that oppos-ition, all such forms of it, if there are others.

We have none.

Kill and not kill.

Our bus will depart the terminal, when our bus is departing the terminal, do not ask questions, military judgments summary judgments, what is it, exercise that judgment, power is summary, execution also is summary

that now, from

As the first fellow pushed out from the bus, our colleague. What is your human rights for human life if you are not human, you are human, are you human, what life do you have if you have none you are not human, let me kill you, it is slaughter I am butcher. Where are your identification papers is this your country if it is so show us where are they. It is supposing, I am supposing. I thought it. They were shouting, angry voices, very loud, I could not read my book and was looking down to the street below. Yes of course. I did not see the elderly male and female. It was the first fellow that one military shouted at, first man pushed out from the bus. It was this first man knocked down rising up knocked down rising up and shouting at him, shouting, these military and insignia, insignia men military men shouting at him, parading for us the colleague, yes, I now saw they knew it.

These personnel parading for us. I then thought so, yes, they parade for us, it is a theatre for travellers, relatives, vendors, all customers, suspected colleagues.

But soon this parade was not so by this first man, who he was and decisions that had been made, who had made them

And some will oppose humiliation. Also militarys, having regard one for another, respecting themselves, we are great men, greater, and with all weaponry, see our weaponry.

We have experience. It is predicted. We can say, Opposition will come.

I do not know if he was grandson. I say that. Perhaps son, nephew, neighbour I do not know. What could he be. He was led to one side, he did not look to anywhere, could be looking to anywhere, be to anywhere but did not look to anywhere. This is a way, method, who will survive, we shall survive. Who understands this, all understand this. We have the experience. What humiliation is. People do not look to anywhere. He looked to what only took place and in front of him, as happening there, then, his eyes seeing only that.

If a moment, who says, I do not think so.

Honourable militarys, honourable securitys, all honourable

operatives and personnel, yes, all were foolish. I say it, am saying it and am saying it. With such experience, oh such experience, held by such personnel, one may never witness such experience. What was happening, death was happening, this human race, inexperience that information was not possible, better bay-o-net better shoot, simply execute, this power is here, now kill him, better than such for no purpose wasted, energy for nothing, buses will depart the terminal, shoot this first man, it is better for us also, bus-travellers, better for all, we are a practical people.

I thought it might happen. I saw the curving line of men's faces, from men's faces, military and security faces, to a dead man on this street. I could say it, my experience, all of ours, this first man knocked down rising up knocked down rising up

predicted by all, our colleague, and I watched it, so witnessing.

On the upper deck people stared down to that street, none speaking. The first man was looking now this way and that. Crazed emotions were onto his face. I saw it. We waited. If the bullet would be fired into his head, when, we waited, yes, when, we knew this and waited, simply this, we waited. But not the younger man who did not wait who now was become maddened and his act signalled this. Wrath, rage, humiliation. Where his elderly relatives might be, I could not see them. Their grandson, who that he was, now his act, stepping to a vendor of vege-tation, pumpkins, this box upon which these pumpkins rotted, lifting the pumpkin and throwing this at personnel, and one military, if insignia was there on his heart, oh such dignity, higher military comrade-colleague, how are you this afternoon a pumpkin is now breaking onto your uniform, splashing, proud uniform

what I am

None can say. The pumpkin was lifted, the pumpkin was thrown, it hit onto his insignia breast, splashing, and how he started, military official, now staring, wild in his eyes, widened eyes, big and roundly, now seeing us on this upper flight deck, we travellers. All people were stunned by the action of the younger fellow. I can say this first man, our colleague, who now should be dead, he too stared, only staring, as with everyone, and military and all operatives, shocked by one action, splashing pumpkin.

I say this was a pumpkin, so witnessing. Others have said watermelon, this is a watermelon story. Now the military official was stepping to the younger fellow, firing bullets into his head immediately. These military were not maddened. These are experienced fellows.

No disturbance followed. What was to happen. I did not see the elderly couple.

I did not see the first man. If he was removed from there. I did not know him, nothing of him but that he was our colleague, I have no doubt.

We can ask, we may ask.

I also may laugh, and at these questions, who is to forgive, if of myself. I ask it.

Other details.

No disturbance followed, buses depart. I said. This is the pumpkin story, or watermelons, I now have narrated it. What is memory, if I who was there and so bearing witness to it, if times may arise for opposition, when do these times arise, what was the time of the younger man and we travellers who could do nothing, what time is it for myself, if questions are to follow, if they should, not for myself, who am a practical man.

"wine from one religious"

You have told me you are a religious man and you have told me of the religion itself, as held by you.

I have stated this.

You also are prepared for attacks, and all hostility.

Yes.

If I may say, a man from your culture is less likely to hold such beliefs, also anyone, if he has such beliefs, man or woman, often they remain secret.

I was surprised you have asked me.

I would ask you, where is honesty.

Where.

Such beliefs are considered foolish.

Yes.

So you are foolish?

You charge me with foolishness, it is a serious charge.

Then why smile. Or not, yes.

Charge me.

I charge you with foolishness.

If so then so. I do not care what people may think of me, you also are a person. And you asked of the religion, which is my religion, which is amusing to myself.

If I may apologise.

No, it is myself, I apologise to you.

There is no need, only advise me, I am asking these questions, having faith in your answers.

Thank you.

You have said it is your own religion. You have invented it from your own head.

Yes.

There is no god but your god.

Yes.

I have told you that for other religions this is blasphemy. You have replied that you do not care.

Cannot care.

Cannot, yes.

I cannot.

You cannot care.

That I cannot care, yes, I have told you, for it is my central belief, I stand or fall by it, all it, of it, remembering that my god so may resemble an ordinary god.

And of other gods, complicated gods, having complications, gods whose nature is not ordinary, whose nature is extra-ordinary.

Yes.

These are the preferable ones.

Yes.

What of these?

I know little of them.

All religions down through these many centuries, ten or twenty, fifty, how many years on this planet for human beings, one million. If other planets, how many religions are there.

I do not know.

So also religions on this one planet, thousands, how many?

I do not know.

What of them?

I do not know about them, but if a distinction will exist radically and that it is a matter fundamental, if so, I do not know

But from all such religions radical not radical there can be one to suit all, all peoples may find one truth for oneself, yet you have one for yourself, invented by yourself for yourself.

I cannot care.

Explain further arguments to me.

You are deaf to religious matters.

Only my ears. My mind will listen.

You said you have repugnance for religions.

I had such an upbringing, it was my mother and father, all families, people there of our community, all believing in gods yes and all prophets and evil persons, yes and also if all gods had all relations, mother father, what sons or daughters, we children would say, we had heard, some had watched a television if they may be christian or muslim and for the "god", all-powerful beings, and in his son mithra also devils, ghosts, these animals also having spirit beings and too almighty trees and bushes and all-powerful waters or darker shadows, deities, entities if we say entities as that spiritual coming to you in the dark, piercing blue light emanating from these skulls and who is to be in such light, who, we children hold the covering over our heads that we shall hide from all spirit beings, yes, but they also were amusing, for we children, only ourself. Yes, such an upbringing. Who can speak of it.

None.

What might be said, if one so does it, what can he say?

Nothing.

I thought to ask of yourself why only the christian or muslim god that it is not, that yours is not, as you have said, and why that it is not one another, from the jewish, the sikh or buddhist?

I do not understand.

You have said.

I apologise

Yet you have said it.

I apologise

No sense is there

Yes

If it is religion, I am speaking of religion. I, I am speaking of religion.

You are the religious man.

I am the atheist.

You are the religious man.

You are the religious man.

Though I know very little.

I also.

I know very little.

Yes, as myself.

I cannot dispute it.

I understand that we are to be together for several days. I may watch you closely. I may learn from you.

I may learn from you

Yes.

If I so choose.

Yes.

Perhaps I do not choose.

Yes.

If we are to be together for several days, between us there seems no ground in common.

What of the enemy forces, surely these are in common?

You take this for granted?

Until in error.

I cannot so take this for granted, if it is possible for yourself, not for myself.

You do not trust colleagues?

I shall not live forever.

You regard the enemy not as enemy?

Yes

But not as I understand "enemy".

Yes, I shall kill them.

Of course you shall kill them, if they come to kill yourself.

But I do not believe you if during these acts you also shall love them. Why do you laugh? You must answer, I cannot understand you.

I shall now pour further wine into your container, further wine also to my container. And, I say to you, say to you now, as I am pouring this wine, your hand is not shaking, it is enough for you, now my own. Yes, I also drink, all health to ourselves, and telling now something different to you, if this that I have invented no longer is religion, religious.

"they see you"

You are not from their place. These people do not see a place where you can have come, they do not understand there are so many places, that they are throughout the world (places), they have not that understanding

but the world is small

but not as they think it

I do not believe that they think it.

You have had (no) reason to give the opinion. Are there not occasions when their faces haunt your waking hours unwaking hours, when you sleep, am awake, these faces,

yes they crowd in on my brains mind, mind of my brains, what I can say may say if to

mind of my brain

what I can say about it. They see you and think you are of alien species.

Yes.

You ask them to do things.

They would do them, achieve them, at cost to themself. I could see these faces, music of these faces, in these faces, yes, yes, as a camera is there and the children crowding into frame of the shot, large eyes as all children

And what.

What.

Finish what you are saying. Finish. Finish what you are saying.

I am not saying, I say nothing

17

"split in my brain"

The pain in the back of my head did not begin from so great a point and if a fall then such that it withstood the greater impact though I was stunned for some period of time as I may state.

I had not set these things down. They would have laid that charge against myself. Their decision had been made and if that what could I do but nothing.

Not to antagonise. Beyond that.

I could not rationalise.

I was the suspect, they said that, to me also, yes, I listened to them, heard them.

No, I said nothing, what could I say to them, those who suspected me.

They harboured these suspicions. This position was theirs. I scratched my neck and one said to me, Do not scratch your neck when we are speaking.

I continued. The one looked to myself. I did not apologise.

His voice was at such a distance.

Soon I had entered into my own self and things that I knew, knew from myself, if he had assaulted me, it was as nothing, he and they cannot know, they think of death that might be of them, ours is unimaginable to them. I stared way way beyond. I saw how the wind feels that it moves by its own force. A split had formed in my brain caused by the shadow of an act that I committed unknowingly

It was unknowingly.

A matter of power, the matter of power

mattering

The freedom not being a true freedom which I knew even then. If based on a degree of exploitation. These are self-evident things. A knowledge that lay beyond the edge of my brain

listening to my breathing, not daring to move

I saw him there, the one, again looking to me, at me. He had been speaking. I knew it. Did I wonder?

what he had said.

method of inclosing myself in nothing but myself so to rid myself,

rid myself of them, all

Them, of them. And the place itself was round me and inside attempting to overthrow, take control

from such an instrument a pattern, and from the pattern

I was staring at the ceiling, and it was as a mirror, I saw myself, staring out at the mountains beyond. Of course screams. I myself had the pain, in the back, of my head

I was out beyond them, the one and those others, what they did, they could do, perpetrators, to talk of hope is to luxuriate in their bosom. There is no hope, there can be no hope, I would not wish hope, that hope

coloured by failure, my visions, all is marked by it

chipping at the concrete, my beliefs' foundation, they think to, as though to weaken the stanchions.

no not pain, not so much, not the awareness of it. But I could not locate where/what it was

The back of the head was broken, my head. It was said to me. I could have smiled

they might admit of terrible things. What are terrible things? What they do to me there in these places tethered and tied a goat from childhood I remember

And of wealthy, wealthy. I would ask.

Of our bodies, they fail to cope, cannot evolve, such that they manufacture

What is manufacture

There are requirements, I said, essential

A tawdry thing

vigilant but submissive, apprehensive

casting barely a glance to where my feet might fall

not able to squeeze, squeeze it

mad as not mad (but they suspect me)

that I would have not gone thus, to have remained only indifferent, loitering, yawning together

My fingers trembled yet I could smile easily, all body.

the dead are inside them, inside me, my feet in the undergrowth, slimy.

they were sturdy enough though ancient

stanchions, ancient

as beliefs

18

"respect is for actions"

Some people are sarcastic, older people also younger people. As I was young older people were sarcastic, even silence, unto silence, asking questions of them and they are silent. We ask them questions they do not reply, do not think to reply, yet also it is respect they are demanding of us, as of rights, entitlements. But I said then as now that no, not from myself, not respect not regard, nothing, unless you show to me that it is an entitlement. Then I shall allow it. So I said to them. You are elderly, we are to show regard for you, our behaviour must be deferential. If it is to be so, by myself, no, I do not think so. I have had a father, a mother. Have I regard for them, inter, one to another, as between? but if between, what, and if I am not an equal, I always am so?

If the day will come when equality is there, it is possible, one thinks it must be but perhaps is not so.

But for yourself. Of course it is asked of myself. I am younger. All ask it of myself ourself, for you also, seeing their faces, for we younger ones, it is true that I see them and knowing it is so expected, deferential behaviour, why? from myself, yes, I am to have such a thing, oh please may I serve you I am younger I may serve you.

Of course it is foolish. If I am thought foolish. It is yourself, thinking I am foolish. I said it to them. Older people. Whose expectations? They are too much. Who holds them. Foolish people. All are to be treated similarly. Respect is not for long and older ages but is for the actions of people. If these are elderly persons and they have acted better then respect is to them, and rightly it is so but if respect is not there, neither shown anywhere, how we are to respect such people. It is not possible, only foolish. I cannot lie.

19

"I speak of these men"

These men stood around, committing sexual acts together, he it was seated. He sat on some thing, not a chair. None else but the other man if he too was there he took his place. I do not know. It was dark, features were not visible. I think he was not younger but perhaps, if he was younger

I do not know the reason. What reason. What reason might there be. I do not know. Not either about women, I do not know about women, it was not the place for women, who did not go there. This was by the perimeter where lay the outer encampment. Far from my section.

I do not know.

Yes I was there. I said. Why should I deny it it was nothing. It was far from my section. I would go walking to there.

What of the man who was older, naked man, he had a top covering. Both were older. I said that, if one was younger, older than myself. He was seated on that occasion. They were around him, they held each their penis, sometimes he. Yes, also, he held it, my penis, I said it. Other men departed. I do not know. What reason. Some lost interest. I said it that they lost interest. They departed. To somewhere. I do not know. Men lose interest, go away. I said what happened. I do not know about these two men. I saw the younger man. I said that I did. Having regard for me, yes, I said it, having regard for me, he had it. He also would look. Of course. I know that he would. It was not rape. I am saying it. Yes, I have heard.

These terms, definitions. Perhaps if it was rape, no, I am saying it, it was not.

These were men. Not women, girls, none would be there, they would not be taken to there, it was men, some older. Not boys, these would not be taken. Men. Men masturbated. Yes men masturbated of course men masturbated. They masturbated. What should I say. Each other. I do not know. Of course each other. I do not know.

They lose interest, depart, go away, they go away.

Who would recognise individuals, not recognise individuals.

It was very dark, I walked to there, I knew men were together, between these huts, in darkness, shadows, they came to there.

He had regard for myself. I do not know what women know. It was for myself and to myself. I know it. Some held each other, he held me, I have said. I do not know. If he did look for me. What is there I can deny, what I am to deny, if other matters, I have heard of these other matters.

Each one of us, we hear them, of them. Some in whispers. Of course I too heard these whispers. I have nothing to be forgiven. I said of his regard, I also had regard, yes for him.

I did see his face. I said that I did not, I did not see individuals. I did see it. Perhaps others, more. Yes. Men did not look to one another, their faces. Not to their faces. I did say that. It is what I said and I say it now that they did not look, not one to another. I do not know what women know. The men crowded round. Some younger, older, I have said it all. They came to there from elsewhere, they would gather individually, I think, one to one, I think, yes, individually, perhaps together. Then depart, some return, I think. None spoke except as in sexual activity.

Sexual activity. They would say things, whisper them, fiercely, yes, some if not all. No I do not say unusual, if fiercely. Not what women say, I do not know. I did not go often. Some went often. I know that. I said that I did not.

I did, I said that I did.

One heard voices, saw shapes. It was there in the shadows by the perimeter, shapes, I was walking. I had gone from my section and was walking. At the perimeter I could see out and to the mountains beyond the outer encampment, I wished to see the mountains and think of my place, home. There were the shapes and the shadows. I did not recognise at first. When first I went. I had not known. This is what I speak, drawing me on. Closer and I heard breathing and saw there the huts, between them, dark, shadows.

I did not know. Perhaps I did think might be. We could not go near to women and we could not

although

I speak of the men, being tempted, how I was, yes, one of them, drawing onwards, the breathing, rasping, is rasping, these muffled sounds, quiet and what is to say, tempting to onwards, to me my heart, I was pounding and tension all, me, nerves of course yes in my stomach

men, this is not surprising. I was not then a psychologist I am not now a psychologist, sexual only, arousal. I went to between the huts. Slow or fast, if I know, why I do know, and if I know. Fast, well then

I do not think of this. How can it be. It is not serious. The men saw me or did not see me. They did not look. I saw the shapes, heard the breathing. Some held each their penis, penises, some out, some did. Who would take them, these two, both men. Yes to me, if that was what one would want, I would want, yes, held them to me if for me, but I did not so want. These grouped together. One with his hand at me, yes, onto me, yes, I allowed it. Of course. I said of course.

I saw then someone seated and men were round him. All were male, he too, if all were then he also, I knew this. I said that I did. Women were not there, we could not go to women I could not go to women, women, who would not be there.

I approached, I had approached, entered. The space had opened. They made the passage. For me, allowed me that I enter. I do not know. A way to enter. I did not think it then. He who was seated had looked to me. None else would to have seen me. They did not look to each other but to their bodies, penis. I have said, yes. And the man seated naked, they lined round him, his back was to the wall, wall of the hut. He pulled me to him. I saw to the other man. We did not look to faces. I may have seen him, older man, not from my section. He had not regard for myself, was not from my section, not close to there. I do not think so. For myself yes arousal, sexuality. I can say it, of course, why not, it was nothing, arousal, I had arousal. Yes he pulled me to him. Other men grouped there round him round me, and the other man there I saw that he also was naked, top covering. Hands were at my shoulders. Someone, had put hands to my shoulders, onto. I did not strike at them punch at them, of course not it was not attack, I was not attacked. He was to my rear, I did not see him, his breathing. The other held me. It was not rape. Held me. My penis. I have said, it is not serious. But it is not serious. Men will masturbate.

There at that place in darkness, in shadows, no sounds, not as noiseless, noiseless, the slightest of wind, breeze only a whisper, the breaths. I did not recognise other men. None did so, so searching for that, recognition.

Only the one man and if two men it would be two men, one followed by one and would have seen, could not avoid thus seeing that one. I did not wish to. I saw the one seated, younger man, I saw him there and knew him, he it was and these others round him. I had not known this of him. Yes his regard for me, I said it. Myself, I would not have such feeling, nothing. He it was humiliated, I was not. He was naked, I was not. These men lined round him, he wanted of me, me to him, pulled me to him. He had others, yes, what else. I had pity for him. I said of his regard.

I could not see. He was naked. Of course men ejaculated. Masturbated ejaculated. Of course. He did not think himself humiliated. It was not myself humiliated. No I do not think so that he thought I thought that he was humiliated, perhaps. Certainly he was. Before these men. I said that.

What I did say, pitied him. I pitied him. I had a regard. I said it.

Hands were at my shoulders. What other man. I did not see other man, other men. Yes the other man who was the older man, yes I saw him. He was from elsewhere. He knelt beside the other. I did not see the features of him, colour of his hair, he had hair, I could not see these things, darkness and shadows and the men there crowded, always shadows and shapes, it was not possible. I did not see the uniform, not a uniform if a uniform. If he had a uniform what uniform I did not see, he was naked, only the top covering. Hands were at my shoulders.

These are details.

I went from there.

I went from there, departed. Men depart. I was not naked he was naked, these two. I was not naked he it was seated, pulled me to him. Of course not rape. I do not know. Perhaps he was older younger. The space had opened, they made the passage, men crowding. He was naked. What man. The other man, having regard for him. I did not know of sexual natures. Yes, I have said. He pulled me to him. Men ejaculate, commit mastur- bation. I also did, yes. None, no men, none others. These two only. Hands were at my shoulders. One only. I think. I said. I had regard for him. He for myself, so having, yes, regard for myself. Yes, I said it. Of course not he. I was not he. I was not naked. I was not seated, not kneeling, it was the other man older man I have said, yes, kneeling there, hands at my shoulders.

Men masturbate, commit suicide. Also, yes, I have heard, it is a common thought, a problem of life, one would waste no time in resolve. I wasted none, then was not such a time. These are musings, lying alone. To say that I was not seated, of course I was not seated. I might have sipped at the water, later, thoughts of life, thoughts of myself.

They had given me water. Who.

Why I had survived this period. As we all, we talk. We have habits, they come to our assistance. If there may be questions, I do not think so. People were violated. I do not hide it from myself, certainly. I ask what might others have done. I myself was not humiliated, not violated. I am certain, of course.

It is for others to believe and not believe. I do not care, psychology, who has psychology, theoretics.

Men from other sections, from my section also. I did not know them. But him, yes, I have said, if he was older I do not know. I said that he was. Both men, seated. If I was younger I cannot say that, not for others who did not look to faces, one did not look to faces, neither one to another.

I had not known any thing. I had been walking and then at the perimeter where I could see out to the mountains beyond the outer encampment, wishing to see the mountains, thinking of my place. One walked to there.

I said there were the shapes, there were the shadows. I did not know, what was this, I did not know but then hearing the breathing, rasping of breath. I might not suppose. Women could not be there in that place it was men. I have said it, now saying it and again, again, yes, it was not violation.

I stepped out. Lying in the hut and alone and these thoughts in one's head, racing racing and if dawn is to break

I have been clear

One wondered about it, there is the taste of nausea, one wishes for water another gives it. Not cleansing, the wish for water, drinking water, it is nausea, what is the taste, dirt and metal, if it is.

People are still. Men not moving, I said men, only men, and

these two one older one younger, I said it. Older than I. I was then younger, of course. But younger than them, yes, than these two. They did not pull me to them. Yes he pulled me to him, I said that. I was not violated. I said that I was not. Hands were at my shoulders yes hands were at my shoulders, what is that

What is there I am to say, what can there be. It is not serious. It would have been said. I would have said. I do not know on these other matters.

This cannot be said to me

We heard of matters, I have heard, in whispers, said not to me, I was hearing, only hearing of the other place but not then knowing, knowing nothing. If there were bodies we know nothing I know nothing

What of bodies, if these are dreams, people who may be friends, not so friends, if we are to save them, enemies, acquaintances, who are they, if these are people, yes, also.

I can begin again. Problems of life. Talk to me of death. Yes it was walking it was walking. I. I was walking. Hours of the morning always hours of the morning. And the silence, only breaths. And shall we be alive shall we be alive we are to be alive, it is said survival. I said that men grouped round and silence, their breaths only. Some sounds. Slight. Noises. Rustling. Masturbating of course masturbating men will masturbate of course of course we are to be alive, I say it. Yes I say it, we are to be alive, women could not go there, girls could not be taken, it is nothing, not serious.

Of course at night time too. There could not be light. Yes we are also alive. Life has different forms. It is my thought that our heart slows, our requirement is lesser oxygen for these several tasks. Any task. What is to be done. In the dark I would walk to where. The outer encampment. No, what other matters. We would see the mountains. Not mounds, if mounds were there, if in the other place, I do not know of bodies.

I have heard. I could not proceed beyond that outer area.

There were breaths.

Where.

Between the huts breaths, yes, breaths of men, not of talking, whispered as breaths, breaths yes as whispers, for it is true I know I think might be, that I did hear of the other place, these matters but I did not go to there, lying beyond the perimeter.

I do not know. What mounds are, if these are there, I do not know.

There was the other man. He did not speak. I did not hear him speak. Whispers, breaths. I do not know. I did not know men there, of course from other sections.

It was the outer perimeter

clearest in the vicinity of the mountains I could see out and see such a vision. I could come to a place of danger, of course. Yes one could be killed to come there, I too.

Talk to me of death.

I have said.

I can speak.

No not when dark. Daylight. Dawn would break. Men stayed, returned. None said to me of the other place. None said to me come to there. If men were taken to there I was not. I do not know of that other matter, if of the younger man I do not know, do not know of it.

My father is old, old man. How should that be said. I should say it. Why I should, I should not.

If men were taken to there I was not taken.

I did not know other men. None others, that I knew. No sweetish smells were there. Yes if the other man was older, it is possible, I think so. Yes dark, very dark, always very dark, and shadows, between these buildings. Men arrived, departed.

It was not possible. It was not violation. I did not see others. I do not know what others have reported.

Men lose interest, they ejaculate, depart. I also. Some

returned, yes, I have said. Nothing is to deny, I have nothing
to deny. It is not serious.

I do not know about that other matter. Nothing of the other
man, older man, he had the top covering, I did not see uniforms.
We did not look to one another, to faces.

Nothing more than that.

I said.

Not me. I do not know.

It was dark, dark and the shadows. Yes then why not. I said
not I said yes then why not, it is nothing, I was there he was
there I have said. I reported, they were there, many such, I said.
Men see only in sex, bodies. I do not know, he had regard for
me. Over and over. Nothing. I know not of that other matter.
None said to me. If others were invited I was not, knowing
nothing. I know nothing, nothing, I know nothing. I know
nothing more. I have said. I did not see him he did not see me.

If he wore the uniform I did not see it. If others were by
force I do not know. If he was at that other place I do not know.
I do not know. I was not one. I heard in whispers these were
whispers, not spoken to me. I heard these others. Whispers. I
do not know. I do not know, do not know them. None spoke
but in sex, and fiercely, as arousal. Not violation. I do not know.
Myself not myself. Not violation. I do not know.

Violence. Yes death, talk to me of death. Mutilation, yes, talk
to me now, now to talk now talk to me. I do not know these
other matters, that other place.

He was not my friend. I did not know him, if he was an
enemy. When I went to there. I saw it to be him, then that I
did know him and saw then that he had a regard for myself.
I did not know. He it was, he pulled me to him. If he was by
invitation to that other place I do not know, did not know, had
no communication, not with him. In that section we did not
speak, were not colleagues, not acquaintances. I did not know
him. I saw him yes saw him, what is that saw him, he was not

in my area. Afterwards he did not return. I did not see him and know nothing.

My mind wishes to turn from this. It is my belief that our bodies are whole things and that mind and body are one, so that the mind, wishing to turn from an object, gives its message to the body and so there is nausea and concentration departs.

My concentration.

I shall speak. I have said it. I can say it again, I shall say it again. What am I to say?

20

"these people"

It was the foreign authority. He pointed his finger to me, saying, Ah but you are known, I am not, I am a shadow in the world. They do know you. This is why you are here. Come now, we do not fabricate. Sit down. A chair nearby him, he was pointing. I sat down, and he said to me, These people move as though wearing dark overcoats or cloaks. They abuse themselves and each other, they believe they are performing heroic feats but they are not.

I only listened. All forms of control lay in my grasp. I was in control, so I considered it, as to how I should conduct myself, more, as in control of the movements governing myself, intently, yes, that I might stare to all such individuals, listening to those who would speak to myself.

Their luck was bad that day.

Vigilant, without cowardice.

People often are innocent.

They continue to serve while others continue to rule. (Who speaks of children?)

A form of madness prevailed. When they spoke none listened, instead making much of the manner that it was said, and if one smiled so much the worse.

Myself

These people were thankful to receive their lives. They humbled themselves as to deities. Among these deities were authoritys. To the authoritys these people offered prayers that they might serve beyond themselves unto death, willingly, all that they asked if to remain as they are and have been, if only to retain that which they had, or have, and if this be nothing, and if it is so, yes, then so it is and is, and to carry out iniquities that they so may survive, clinging onto what they so have, nothing, yes, why of course, what do you ask, let me insert the needle.

It is a great and wonderful thing that nothing is known of this, of any of it.

They do not fight that their families may discover a method of escape. This is not fight.

None propagates this.

If they wished not to confront

A strength can negate blood. This is what they believe. This is the strength.

They do overestimate the position.

They did not see it of myself. I can laugh.

The hatred beyond speech is a commonplace

Who are taught to revere

No distinction, not between adults and children, none

when they looked to me these looks were not such as should occur, and cannot occur, not between equals, as inter human beings

They were patient but watchful and curious in regard to myself, that I survive as I appeared to them. But how did I appear to them. They would invite me to sit, yes rest, rest there. He also, one I had marked, foreign authority, as he said, do I believe so, if I do believe so. All supposed that they knew but what was known by them, if something indeed was known, it was not any thing, not for myself, myself myself, they knew nothing, he knew nothing, thinking I am easily trapped, so, colleague from mars. They did not have even the conception. Was I there to advise them I was not to advise them. If someone else could do it, I do not think so. Was it possible, I do not think so. What my life has been. Do I come from a place, terrortory, is this a place where people are. Am I one person of this people, singular fellow unique man as a being, human being, what I am

what they do to myself, thinking of myself. What is courage. I know it of people

Conversations took place rarely in public, people would not put themselves at risk. To listen, a pause, that was enough.

I am to speak, what I say, to whom is to be said, foreign authority of national security council who is, he to myself, he points to myself. Each other is smiling, patient

no thing beyond the act that they performed in order to survive. Surviving the moment, I have said it.

This is how I think of them, how I then thought of them, that they existed until they might walk no longer, then lie on their backs or sides, they would die.

It is my courage

While they were waiting.

But none waited, there was no one, no children, no women. Men women boys girls all were equal, babies also, hear babies, how they breathe, listen to these lungs, hear these lungs, they are of a baby, the baby is seventy years of age, the baby cannot breathe, baby's lungs. What should I do. I can be honest or not. Who returns to our home

Let me go over it I can go over it. So I said to him, to all of them, such authoritys, who might there be. There is nothing to conceal. What can there be to conceal. I have no home so cannot come to it. Have you a parent, grandparent. There is nothing to conceal. What can there be to conceal. You want it of myself, if you require it

That was said. Yes, I said it to them and have heard it of others

These voices continue. Let them. What can we do. I could have done nothing other. There was not any judgment. But I also must answer, yes.

It is not courage. If they will kill me

They torment

And people also observe. Of course. These emotions are no recourse, are meaningless.

People themselves will gain, from observation. We approve, or not, approve disprove, disapprove. They would begin with myself, observing without objective. I said it to them. Some replied that matters might go untouched, not particularised, seen as future strength, even individually, used by the securitys in bargaining, even as to myself

so what is that that I am to say

my movements, to talk of them

yes there are fools, all know, the foreign authority also, so thinking

21

"if under false pretences"

But those for whom we were perceived they watched us, they watched me. Their eyes might flicker. The feature that was consistent was sardonicism. They were not angry, not irritated. It was beyond a personal emotion but holding true only should the circumstances not alter. If I/we had given rise to inconsistency emotional alterations might have taken place and in the past I had given rise to anger. The most common effect if not immediate impatience was frustration, the frustration of the individual, not unkindly. But soon it yields impatience then irritation, yet within the impatience is the seed of the sardonicism. If the sardonicism was always to follow, if I knew this to hold true always, then on behalf of others I might relax, have relaxed, I think I did. For myself, I had to contain my inner life. Ever-watchful. If I was stopped the mistake could never be theirs, never of their manufacture. My circumstances were awkward and difficult and this was assumed. They were obliged to assume this until they might intuit something other. Once that was made into its place, put into there, then I was altered, become a hostile presence, so that for then, until then, I was present under false pretences.

I know this as a juncture. It can arise on the road to a freedom, what is mistaken for freedom. This idea is necessary to take the step, to progress beyond that juncture, before setting oneself the task, of getting to it.

If I continue under false pretences.

Yes, what then?

It need not be a point towards something further.

Others were offered inducements, I was not. I was not forced, nor physical pressures put to me, onto me. It did not happen. I can say it did not. I shall not deny the thing. Is it reality. Then it is reality, if it is reality it is so.

What then, these other voices.

These other voices never cease. Varied elements, words sometimes distinct. The people there did not notice the voices. They had their own thoughts, deeper thoughts, deeply, more, some having strategies, existing within these strategies. Perhaps they have reached midway, now, perhaps further, soon they will awaken and will re-enter the world. I am part of this world. For now, until then, they do not (cannot) perceive me.

Should I be allowed this?

Yes, not as licence, I should be allowed this not as licence, having come to there. I have arrived to there. Yes a journey

"intercession/selection?"

None thinks the value of what we do diminished. Selection is resolved earlier, it is prior to what we do. What we do is no less integral. It should not be downgraded, this at all costs. To downgrade what we do is a knife-thrust into the core of that culture which is to say their culture, I do not say ours.

Myself and former colleague were among those invited so to enter at the early age, why selected I cannot say but from then, my thoughts of that time, images remain.

If I tell of what we do, I can, I can say of it a concatenation of images and conjectures, this is what it is. But this is to be human. We humans are this. The substance of what we do is it, the essence of any one human.

I do not believe that what we do is not of interest. If only as a confirmation it is validated. Its worth cannot have been overestimated. But what we do only is adequate, neither less nor more. Only is a descriptive term.

For those selected a mystery remains, the power of selection not being with them. They have little power and that power cannot be. If it remains a mystery then how so, this because those not of power are chosen by those having the power but no intercession has occurred, no intercession can occur.

Authoritys and other powers show ignorance of a crucial tautology that may be formulated if roughly, having sense as follows, we have been selected by virtue of our merits, these merits are worthy selection criteria. Further, that these merits, being specific, are of universal application. Upon selection power is/was taken from them [democratically-elected governments, dutiful-appointed].

Prior to my selection they did not know *the* word. I speak of our parents, firstly my own. The reality was far removed from them, such that the name, I speak of *the* word, that it alone left them floundering. There was the conversation where a pause was left by them, when the word should have been uttered they left the pause. I have a strong memory. I was to appear in front of a committee. What committee, district committee, committee of our people. I spoke of this to my parents. They looked one to the other. If I am selected, I said. My father was worried and so I said to him, I am selected. But did not finish speaking this, looking to my mother if she would comment, hoping she might, I think but also as though a thought did exist, shared one to another. He knew of this thought but could not utter it, could not think it. He knew of the thought but could not think it. We may extend this, say clearly that this is an extension of it

fate befalling, events that might take place, a future for myself, what might it be, and in this lifetime would they see me ever again. These were the questions, questions I then thought. And my father, future for himself.

The committee consisted of four men and a woman, each having a copy of the document. When I had entered [my father waited below] and was standing inside that room I saw that they had been discussing a subject, of course myself. One male reminded me of someone, stared to me then began as the speaker. He spoke and it was peculiar to my ears. They were learning of my community, culture of this community, learning from such as myself, the value of their positions increasing thereby.

A woman then continued, her voice the same, then stopped and I was informed by another of the males of the rarity of this occurrence, the selection of myself, such as myself, but that this selection certainly had occurred and certainly had been ratified. Others of the committee confirmed this. A silence followed. I interpreted this as a question and moved quickly to speak but the male stopped me, smiled at his colleagues. He said to me, This no longer is part of your world. You require patience. You will have been under strain. Let me say that you should pay heed to the document with the word and its adequacy. You have put forth the document with the word, its contents are yours. You have understood that this must also be a practice.

Of course these people were members of the group of that now I belonged, I was now within. I believed they might think well of me. It was fancy. I was foolish. Arrogance was a central feature of my imagery and conjectures, causing amusement and also I think wonder. Individuals as myself bringing order to the group by remaining with it, also as affirmation, I think so.

My own understanding had been a hatred, colouring my view of the world, and now within the group I could progress, hate was not proper, not adequate.

Of course my thoughts and imagery were precise, especially then. I would have taken their value for granted. I then believed values were shared. It only was notional. I tried to be as prepared as much as was possible, that I thought possible. I prepared myself. There was no counsel. Not that I would term, not any. I could look, listen, sensing what I might. I had an understanding. It is said of my parents that they had such understanding but I say if so never was it obvious, if my selection did derive from their part, no, not that I could say.

Community leaders regarded me as impertinent, they blamed my selection on me, they said that I was responsible for it, giving me to understand, not using the words

the thing to separate us from my fellows

who we were

I may speak of security, perhaps of securitys, the security, that security, security

23

"she offered"

Yes she offered herself to me. I never heard her laughter. She was a girl. Her laughter. She would have laughed, who does not laugh. I would have walked with her and our lips could not meet.

No I had not heard her laughter, never, but who does not.

Yes I would have walked with her, of course.

These people moving in the shadows, our bodies also in shadows, while our sounds, together our sounds. She cried out, slight but a cry, she too. And she uttered no word, she would not have uttered one. The sharp inhalation of breath only from her at my entry, not having conceived of the size. And when I continued to push a gasp from her, eyes tightly shut that she could not see but then in the darkness I did see her eyes open, looking to myself, staring into me, into my eyes, and her lips moving, her tongue, wetting her lips, looking, looking to me, while around us were the shadows of these people. They moved, these were bodies, I know. We were lying together. It was her coverings. I came to her and she remained. These others lay. She was uncomfortable. What more. A girl there in that place and all of these, shadows moving but people. It was the next night, also in darkness, night, mid night. I would have walked with her, of course. In the light, morning, daytime, of course. At that time all was burning, odours always, burning, all things. These places may disturb. Yes.

rustling, quick breathing.

the children jeered, little children. I would punish them. They did not anger me.

I walked there and also not alone, others walked there. The women also could jeer. Not in voices, nor did they laugh.

Men were there. The women lifting their skirts while treading the steps. They go up, go down.

I could not see.

I do not know, some can have. But she made the offer to me, it is clear. The girl had indicated, I went amid the shadows knowing that she would find me. I know of traps. Of course

None other knew of it. I was alone. This girl knew only myself, offering herself, to myself, I have said.

I lay with her. I know her fragrance. Yes beautiful of course beautiful.

Women do it, they are magicians.

She came to me. This is why I say it.

I never heard her laughter.

I am tired.

These places disturb. I would go and it would be darkness.

People always are moving. There, everywhere. Where do they not move. All people. Children, old people, infirm, should be dead people, no limbs, all were there, all were moving, more, it was no comfort, I have said, for the girl for myself, all people, everyone so found it.

I do not know. She lay and I was to her and no word between us, I entered her but she was not prepared. She cried out. I pressed, entered. Not prepared, I say, if she had been prepared, she was not. A cry came from her. Yes involuntary of course involuntary a cry is involuntary, I am not speaking this to say nothing, if it did not happen. I say what happened. She did not know. She brought me to her but did not know what was, man to woman, she knew but did not, of course, I said she was a girl, I said she was beautiful, girl, woman. Yes. In darkness in lightness, I would have walked with her. Publicly, what is to say. There were children also there. I saw them, heard them, if they might jeer. I would punish them, older people are teachers. Her family was there. Her mother and father. I know nothing of them. Her father hated me. Younger man, his daughter. Many fathers so hate, yet his daughter came to me only. What her mother did see, her daughter alive. Who knows these things, I also am alive, also weary. These people moved on, the girl with them.

24

"most evil incidents"

I said about this area bodies lay, people sleeping, resting, also were three children nearby, these were with one woman, and one other woman was helping her with them and also nursing I saw that she helped with one baby, whose lungs we heard.

I had not been here a long period and such was its history, each section having its own, as its own people. We listened to the ravings of those destined to die. I listened to those ravings. And if death rattles. So of the security who was marked amongst us and was to be dead and would become so I heard that noise, a whispering of it inside his body, spirits of all dead people, murdered people. He spoke to me in our section and it was late night, people asleep,

so,

resting,

if night-time he was to be dead, who was to do this if myself yes myself. I had seen this security outside of our section. I recognised him, that when my companion had been here he had spoken to her. What did he say. If what he said, I do not know but that he came to her and did so. This was two weeks before her disappearance. Now I was alone, now he sat by me, saying of himself how he was content, contented man. His voice was low, yes, and three other securitys were by the door. It was to myself he spoke. The thought then was to the front of my brain that this one man, security, it was myself would kill him. If it was a decision, I so had made it, even before he came to my place. I had thought how to do it, having no weapon, if I might so acquire something, using it, what means so to acquire. But why had he come to my place, was kneeling at my side, speaking to myself.

It was said of my companion who then was how she had been removed. Her disappearance was a removal. Such was said. So, resting, this night, coming to kneel by my side near to where I lay, I said it was late night, I was not sleeping, but as so. There was a covering, I had pulled it around me, yes resting, lying in my own thoughts, times from before her disappearance.

I cannot say of my mind in those days bad days evil days, but becoming accustomed to that absence. I would not see her again. I would see her again. When it might be, if I would. It was possible not possible, what may be possible, life itself, is it possible, as we can conceive, human beings. Yes for some and not for others, what authority, what power, if we have power, the control that we may so make use of it, what do we have, and if so how we make use of it, what are we, who is selected who invited, how are we we who are we who choose, making such decisions, gripped by others, we are enticed by others, so taken, and people have no faces, I see that they do not have, that none may resolve this, for nothing so may be resolved, or if we all must disappear, let all of our people so disappear, we are not in the world, effaced from it.

Such questions, while continuation continuation. How we do it, this is how. So, resting.

And I was cold now the covering pulled around me but as to have gone beyond sleep, if ever again. By it, speaking of my mind and our mind, what is in our mind, we may sleep forever.

What was to happen. She had suffered. What do I dream, thinking of dreams, and of childhood no more enough and enough enough, this security, one who had been marked by some, myself ourself, having marked this one. He knew it yet sat near to me, saying of himself how he was content, I did not know, what that arrogance may be. He held only contempt for us, I say it, and now speaking, and what of myself, contempt to myself, if I also am a man. It was muttering. And this muttering from him, beginning in whispers as of praying, if he was stating a prayer, what is prayer, so low in his voice none but myself could hear. In solitary tone, monotone, monologue. There were these monologues, people speaking in that fashion, it was common but not by securitys. But if he wished to talk with me, I knew it, and he would not begin but after these mutterings. I was having to listen to them and so listened. Religion. If it was religion. I do not know, perhaps, some might say, ramblings, musings, prehistoric idiocy. I cannot make sense of these things, nothing, neither from himself. The muttering altered but all was prefatory, I knew so, if he would tell of my companion's disappearance and of one other now dead, an older woman, he would speak of that time.

These were two issues.

The light came from his skull. Skulls may give light, if the colour of this light is blue, colour from his skull. It is not a colour of life. Death skulls, these are blue. And if I battered this skull, if I were to have one rock and to smash it down and the skull was to crack, shattering, eggshell pieces, electrical sparking. He said how the people he had made dead were people as myself [himself]. I could make sense of it, not moving, my eyes open. He saw that they were. He said how the people he had made dead were people as himself. It was not viciously done. Neither brutally, not as in barbarism, nor the animal as some said bestiality. It was not the mark of the barbarian. Some would say this. I might say this. It would be said of others and be so that all might see it. Yes if he did bully, that he might be a bully for people but he has had charge of children, baby children, elderly women, crippled men, those being without feet without hands. When a young man he nursed such individuals, all things. Therefore we may excuse him, if all executions are duties, carried out as dutiful, all executioners so appointed. Powers are discretionary, they may be. We exercise these powers, executed as dutiful. These people, always they were as himself, it was/is imperative to him, himself himself, these other people, he has never bullied, is no bully, cannot be such, he does not terrorise, is no terrorist, cannot be so. It is not cowardice. If I may think it cowardice, it is not cowardice, what obligations may be, who is a colleague who now a security, if from such as myself he may not conceal matters, yes, from such as myself, securitys do not conceal matters, if their voices are loud, yes, they do not lower them, and if we so hear them, they do not see us, if a duty only, yes, they then may see us.

But this one who had been marked and did see us, perhaps wishing for other worlds. Securitys also are human beings. Some seek that we allow such distinction, one from another, each from his colleagues. This one wished that I might recognise him who is himself, I should understand how that he differed to all other securitys, yes, a human being, I so was to cry out, You are a human being. I recognise this, now am acknowledging this, you are not like these others.

Perhaps it was to have been celebrated. We are to celebrate he is himself and not another.

Human beings may wish for celebration. Securitys wish that we also might celebrate them, as they so celebrate themselves. I might say it to him. You are a human being. Now leave us.

Some metres off I saw the woman who helped with children, also now nursing, lifting the baby to her breast. This baby had difficult breathing, its lungs hurting and would die. How might it not, rescued by angel people flying with wings of medicine. Of course I gave thought to mine, child, as we would have, all that were there in that section, we fathers, mothers. What I am to say. If this is sensible, it may not be so. Ravings, influence of one older woman, elderly woman, whose spirit now was with me.

There was also an old man, he died, I saw his spirit flee from his brain, blue light was there then extinguished, I saw his mouth open yet there was darkness, a moment, that moment, moment of his death.

Across there by the exit wall the other securitys talked in low voices. What of this one of theirs, did they wonder of him.

People come to know of the actions of cowards. Who are cowards.

What actions are the sign of the barbarian, bullying in the use of power.

Cowards.

It was a stench coming from him, excrement, dead blood, there is blood, dead blood.

He was talking. If he had stopped, it is possible, now continuing to speak.

He could see nothing, and for him there was nothing. I lay in that same position, it was stillness, beneath the covering, if the turmoil only in my intestines, and he said of himself how he was content in this that he did, had done, if indeed these people he killed were like others but that they were not, they never are, these people who are like himself and never are others, and so if they are not then why should he feel so, that he does not have health, so health is there in him, health at himself but not for all time, when this has finished and it is he who is the old man, for it is true that he should so become. People will not speak to me, he said, we are punished, why is that, those who will not speak to me.

No. Why is that that they will not? Nothing may signify I only can be such and not other, securitys are human beings. If it is so said then what of fathers, fathers may be bullies, I had a father as you have had a father as all have had fathers, having fathers, who are bullies, of course, fathers are bullies, if not are they fathers, I do not think so, but what we might be who will know it, if there is cowardice.

And he put his hand to my shoulder, continuing to speak.

If I am it is asking, asking of me, what it is, about women asking, children, infant girls, boys, I say no, do not ask about these things and if you do it returns, will return to me. Things do return to me. It is my brains, filling my brains thus must I say it I must say it, yes about the female sex, women, girls, I have a friend, there is friendship between us. This friendship that is between us, male female, one to one, I say it is sentimental, that is that relationship, only that, and what do you say of the woman? You with your lover, she was your lover, companion, your partner? This woman who was removed. She was with you, and beneath your covering, she lay with you, I saw it. You, you will not speak to me but I who spoke to your colleague-companion, woman with you, yes, I who spoke with her, I am speaking to you. As she with me, you know that, how she was speaking with me? You know that I did walk with her, yes, by the perimeter, we walked, she saw the mountains, she saw them. I was a human being so too as she was. So she said to me. She said how the very air had altered.

Why do you not speak? You do lie here. Your eyes are open and you do see. You are not deaf, not dumb, your mind is strong. You may bestow unto me, it is verbal, blessings not blessings, I am religious, a good man, I pray also and for the good. You also, I see it, I feel it, so feeling it in you.

There was the old woman, elderly woman, you did know her, visited her, yes, I think that you did. Your companion also might speak to her and not to yourself, woman to woman, yet also she spoke to me, you do not think so, yet she did, she to myself.

If the elderly woman had wisdom, no, I do not think so, neither your companion. Yet I see wisdom in yourself. I know it. You can speak, yourself myself, speak in answer to myself, what with the woman? what part I had? I had no part. She was removed from here, she is not dead, why do you think that?

you think we are animals from one foreign planet, we are not human beings? We are human beings. You do not speak, why do you not speak, so lying as stone, no living thing. Do not think cowardice for cowardice is yours and not mine, not of mine. You are beneath this covering now alone and no one, yourself now, only, as you are, as are we.

Where she now is, there may be a knowledge. If there is a knowledge, who has it, if it is known, by whom, someone. These people are not killed. You think so, they are not. Children and babies, family, friends, old women old men, our grandparents, no, these only may disappear. What are disturbances and upheavals, so when people may disappear, who is surprised by it, who only does not know, who only can be surprised.

But our parents also, you have not said of them. If you were removed I also, as boys we were taken.

This is upsetting for yourself. Yes, I also. You do not know this? Who are securitys? My father your father? Who are so? In these villages brother to brother? Yes. You are listening, now listening. Brother to brother, you know this I know this. It is upsetting, yes, but it is so. If you are lying to yourself, I think so, revealing to me a sentimentality. It is not truth you have. You say to me cowardice. No, not cowardice. These are brothers we are brothers, brothers now as we then were. My voice is not loud yet is upsetting for you. Do you walk by the perimeter? You may walk by the perimeter. Some walk by there, they have women, have wives. You also can walk there. I am not mad. You think it but I am not. You listen to me. I am speaking, and you listen. What can you say to me? What can you say to me? Will you speak? There are these most evil incidents. You know of them. Others will know of them. Your companion also, now she does know. Thus you think it of myself.

Most evil incidents, certainly they have occurred. We all know of them. You have marked myself, I know it. You think I do not? You think I am a fool.

Yes there are fools in this section, if you are one such, you must know it, if I am the one you think and if I am only the one, if you think that, yes, you are a fool. The possibility is not serious, those who think such a thing possible are not serious.

Continue, listen to the ravings of those destined to die. What happened to her, the courage of her, shame in her courage, shaming her courage, of her courage. Let us hear stories. What stories we may hear. What places are these, if we are to speak, say to me later, later.

"history must exist for colleagues"

It is of how we may stand in this "campaigning formation" of which we all are committed as members, as volunteer workers we may say, for what else are colleagues. If there is criticism of individuals and colleagues of our group it is not from myself as will be ourself. Personal criticism of individuals is irrelevant, is misguided, indicating only ignorance of reality, the situation as material to ourselves.

Colleagues have discussed ways forward. One proposal does not die. It is said that this proposal is new, it is not new. Our "campaigning formation" always has recognised overt methods, actions, political formalities are not meaningless and we so may recognise such again, for times are to come. Yet we have understood from past practice that if so doing we risked destruction before battles were won. We then endured much, we were foolish, enduring foolishness, ridicule, entering dialogue with those known as cheats, liars and cowards, bullies yes, killers and murderers, rapists, rapists of children, murderers of children.

It is what we found ourselves doing. It is a horror, it was so, and if absurd also, of course. If colleagues do not think it seek evidence, advise us, perhaps explanations so may be entered. But if we do not have a choice. If we are forced into it. Tell us, explain to us.

We saw then political formalities, politics that were not politics. This was politics acceptable so to master authoritys, we called it "official politics". We talked of people or groupings as radical who were not radical as now also we do so, talking of democrat people of foreign countries, religious people, parliamentary people who are in these countries as politician-employees, servants of these foreign governments, as European, African, Scandinavian, Asian, and onwards, all geographic formations, all politician-employees having financial rewards, in existence as for corporate international financier bodies and larger business bodies, insurers all of terrorism. Within "official politics" these people were there, we were to communicate with them. Yes, so must be done now if these new proposals from younger colleagues are unchallenged.

If alliances are to be formed worthily, what worthily may be.

But the history of our "campaigning formation", if this is not known by colleagues. Older colleagues can say it. In earlier times meetings also were with authoritys of working-class groupings, socialist groupings, trades unions, religious organisations for charitable bodies, other charitables, all rights bodies, civil, democratic, human, also medical aid supporters, industrial/environmental peoples against horror diseases, horror deaths, pollutive poisonings from all such business industries, mining or energy industries, forced into our territories onto our people.

Yes we could meet with other formations and individuals, experiences heard from older segmentations of the socialist movement, foreign peoples, international workers movements, philosophies from older "democracies". Colleagues sought that alliances might be formed. Expertise lay within such groupings. We knew this. And these were within "official politics".

Colleagues listened to much discussion, arguments or matters then arising, if individuals allied or members of social democrat religious, liberal and nationalist, religio-fundimentio, all such formations, if these may be "more radical" than another, if one individual is "left-wing" may be "right-wing". At larger meetings in foreign countries our colleagues listened to conversations and leading statements from such foolishness, if this one or that one who is of fascist calling is also moral or has scruples derived from religious or ethical code, if a security is a "kind security", or state official is just and fine a person in his own house, saying fine anecdotes to people, if torturers make jokes, these are witty people sensitive people, we must understand them.

Colleagues entered into such discussion if one fascist was "caring fascist", one racist was "caring racist", what one torturer may be, one rapist, murderer of children, yes, murderer of children is "caring murderer of children". And if our colleagues said to them, But we know what securitys are, what are military operatives, what politicians of national government, lawyers, doctors, judiciary. Yes, we know them. We said it to them, We know it. If we are to speak, yes, what we are to say if we cannot say it? They said to us, No, you must listen. "Official politics" is "you must listen politics", constitutional activity operating by rules and regulating principles embedded into stone by all gods and infallible creatures.

Younger colleagues should know history. In that earlier time we also were orderly, knowing how to behave, we are a civilised people, speaking properly to such foreign politicians, introducing petitions and all matter material to our substance as people, also doing it, if under threats of excommunication, please do not excommunicate us, we shall suffer all punishments, oh it is so painful for us, horrible fate for us.

Reports were supplied to these formations, individuals, official bodies, reports on the existence of our people, that we also are human beings as so determined who is to say different let them supply evidence, how then we are treated as animals.

Within "official politics" such information and knowledge firstly is given to these politician-employees, also specialist experts, government servants, operatives from foreign office departments, agencies as overt covert. We supplied to them all latest evidence on behalf of all such arguments, research figures,

157

all, if germane data, all. Colleagues procured fuller reports on the cases of individual victims of State-inspired terror, mutilation, atrocity, arbitrary death, murders, disappearance. What were these individual struggles of people, of punishments to people that must follow, all retributive practices.

Colleagues knew how to exhibit general problems of particulars, but beginning from there. Younger colleagues then trained in these methods and were proficient. Some trained in foreign institutes, returning to our country younger older. Others remained in foreign institutes becoming meelionerrs, younger older, students of martian economics and martian sociologies, now living on other planets in advance of these studies, having palaces made of gold bullion and swimming pools of milk and all champagne from French countryside, what is caviar, yes, also.

Colleagues were in close communication with higher authoritys for influence of "the course of natural justice", if one material substance in these foreign countries as it is so, so if it is said. Higher authoritys, politician-employees, multibeelionerr sensitive creatures, rock and roll music and media figures of famous programs at HQ or branch district levels from other terrortories of the world, these were petitioned by ourselves. Also managers, strategists, directors, leaders, what was possible of corporate worldwide banking and finance operations, mining companies and beef steak industry, also oil and water for our piping systems, quicker routings from one sea to one sea passing over the more difficult terrain, over mountain peaks oh colleagues, we so did it in that earlier time and may do so again, only assist us brothers and younger sisters, younger brothers. I am not sarcastic.

Meetings as with appropriate departments of state, societies of Law, of all religion, associations of medical doctors, mind doctors, aviation doctors and agricultural doctors, all such prosecutors, pathologists and coroners that we might resurrect all older generations of colleagues, colleague-grandparents, all dead people, families and friends, if so mister preseedente.

Who may award support to us. If on single issues we can show you these. If we are committed to the struggle on behalf of victims of terrorist abuse, all State-inspired? We spoke to them. Who else. Colleagues so had to do.

What discussions, questions. We may say meester presidente, of one fight for the testing of terror of all victims. Show to us such terror. Bring to us the more advanced technology, finer and finer scans for heads and scans for brains and for our spirit beings also bring scans, head doctor mind doctor religious doctor, from all so meeting places, temple, church, mosque, synagogue, bring to us everything.

And for all peoples now at risk from state operatives and terror doctors, now at risk from the establishment of all gods' finance houses here on Earth as it is on Planet Mars my colleagues. Bring to us a Hospice for terminally-ill victims of State-inspired terror, Resting Houses for grieving families and all relatives of disappeared persons. Please institute an institute for the funding and coordination of proper research on this subject, wholly independent, freedom from all propaganda bodies. Bring proper needles for biopsies on suspect victims of State-inspired terror [so-called], attempting to isolate these strata, our colleagues shall assist you, if to affix appropriate diagnostic criteria on prescribed horrors, extending the set of terror-related atrocities prescribed by the State Security Council in accordance with external guidelines and rules of behaviour, thus to include all trauma syndromes now established by caring humanities of all European, African, Scandinavian, Asian and onwards, all geographic formations, Amereecas also, who are granted financial reward by these overt covert agencies oper-ating for on behalf of greater business, corporate international, financier bodies of the world, all insurers of terror, those that do exist, not as so told to us as for official purposes, please, what is our prognosis, if I so am monitored, I so am being monitored.

I can know this presently, what historically, if it so may be known.

Younger colleagues will know history. If it is said some may have said it. I too am a younger colleague.

Yes, precedent. What precedent is. If to effect change through precedent, what precedent may be. Colleagues tried so to do, speaking to media, all various, communicating directly and establishing contacts for radio, television, journals, all news-papers, globally from internet, yes also, website magazines, email factsheets, fax all press releases, scholarly articles and features, imparting knowledge, acquiring publicity for our lives and deaths, holding press conferences, academic conferences, all conferences. We consolidated and extended our contacts, peoples in the world, all humanitarian bodies, human, civil, democratic rights' campaigners, all religious charitables, organisations for world health, safety in every environment and workplace also.

If groupings had the interest in our struggle but not only it then also there were links in to these as "struggles-in-general", what "struggles-in-general" may be, if these are something, what thing might they be. Such questions.

What of learning also, in these new proposals, looking at former colleagues older colleagues, how these did peruse and study closely theoretical works, all computing and languages of computing. Other languages, what inventions, if they might have been, if new languages were there, are such languages possible, we could propose such models, adopting innovatory techniques, amalgam of logic, linguistical, in algorithms, all modern technologies but to remember also that these have derived from somewhere.

It was reinforcement that our "campaigning formation" so might strengthen.

So colleagues did spread and make stronger that network, maintaining our communications system with associate individuals, groupings, yes abroad, abroad farther and all elsewhere if the universe may broaden or towards infinitum, onwards if so these Star Wars, are we into exile, where is Planet Mars. If within our own terrortories colleagues sought to advise and support all associates, other formations if these so were desirous, actions so for all people, healthier people, in safety people, all human beings. Colleagues held meetings formal informal to establish personal contacts, also within dubious agencies, if we might so do we must so do.

Might so is must so.

State, yes, securitys and all personnel, military, educational, industrial banking groups, external officers for international welfare, for the diaspora, for rights of all victims who are human beings, all military, medical, legal and religious professions, leaders and disciples, all prophets, executives in foreclosures, we established personal contact with such individuals, overt covert, please not to foreclose us oh master authority.

From our monitoring work on all violence towards people, all abuses, terrors, State-inspired, all atrocities and horrors. We gave of ourselves to others. They would look to ourselves. They must protect themselves.

What are sympathetic bodies, and to a "campaigning formation" such as ours? We discovered. Where were management meetings, and seminars for business economics from foreign terrortories.

People would be there for us. Colleagues, it is we ourselves who were there for such meetings, elsewhere that could have been. Colleagues distributed leaflets, colleagues giving talks, assisted also by more famous sympathisers, foreign sympathisers.

From ourselves also the organisation of educational workshops, displaying reality of struggle, what struggle may be in general, information also of our own, these foreign capitals and greater cities where if people might come to know and understand something, if truth may be for our people, what it might be, truth for our people, for other peoples. We would have supporters and sympathisers, intellectuals, others, gestures to us, solidarity for us, rock people, art people.

Our "campaigning formation" supported and advised all people who enquired, seeking from us informative writings, all humanitarian, rights bodies, from all other countries and terrortories, all colleague-representatives from these foreign "campaigning formations", speaking to field workers engaged in newer struggles or if in preparation for such a beginning.

What of education groups, yes, we had these, here is the history of our struggle, the history of our movement, here is where all stripping and removal operations began in our lands.

What are people's own assets, land and water, crops or oil, mountains and valleys or forests if we have these, what, what we have, are these yet in existence or picked clean by master vultures. Here also is where our people's involvement developed in these townships and communities of them, here from help and advice groups from community homes and safety of these homes, making them so, local issues, who has no home and bedding, who has no food, how are babies fed, if inoculation is desired, medicals, all pharmacy, necessity, girls must survive, what is tortures. We have all tortures, history of torture, it is history of our people, yes, History of Torture is History of Our People. We said it, sloganising.

All questions, such questions, women spoke with women, village and community. What women were there our colleagues discovered, women always in struggle, seeking out women, advising and supporting, imparting skills and technique, offering to them organisational experience, receiving also if it may be. Volunteers also came for us. Women knew more of disappeared people, they came to us, offered advice, sharing with us. Now colleagues monitored disappearances. How so to do. Offering advice and assistance to younger, newer colleagues, inexperienced volunteer workers.

Ask us.

Colleagues established contact with people of outer communities, leaders there, tinier pressure groups, tinier campaigns in tinier townships, little little villages. These were distrustful, that the involvement of our "campaigning formation" would bring to them trouble from securitys or military. It so was for them, and so would be. All retributive practices. Colleagues convinced them not convinced them, not convinced them. But also learned, inter, one another.

What of day-to-day management, of our secretariat who held monies, domestic and foreign. These are important matters. Who operate technologies, who perform diplomacies, who have these skills, we discovered them. Can one speak, let him speak. Can one discuss foreign affairs with foreign guests, at what level. We discovered them. Who can take telephone calls, improving our data-bank and filing systems. There is information gathering and dissemination of knowledge and currently-available research. What is world history of State-terror, State-torture, slavemakers, displacements, all enclosures, law-making and withdrawal of all human resources. Yes, if people have all medicines if we have none, what information. Treaties of kings and master authoritys, all mafia families of royaltys that now are binding for all time to infinitum. What of these. Colleagues obtained such information from the world beyond, all worlds beyond, and not then wwwdotcom. Or if not if someone might assist practically in these things, who it is, we found these capable individuals, and all stories may be told of that time, earlier time, if younger colleagues seek learning, know only the history of our "campaigning formation". I too am a younger colleague.

If it is a clearing of our head only, the nonsenses, sand

grittings are into our brain, if it is clearing it is possible and if so it is good. Time is short, always is short. Colleagues can find the many points we have missed, greater variety of them, many. If it is a necessary freedom of expression of conscience, yes, they must have it, know of its presence. What they are to say, yes, say it, have no fear. What is constitutional, not constitutional. If we are to lay down our lives. Colleagues should create agendas, their lists, listings, all items. Beyond here and now must come open discussion in all meetings, as to get such open discussion organised it all may be raised. Of course. This has not happened as to be better. Many have thought themselves under suspicion, that they so would become, thus have been fearful to speak. Problems then arise through natural ignorance. Colleagues must speak, speak publicly.

26

"perhaps some men"

She lay beside me, looking to the fire. My hand then lay at her breast and she allowed it, until putting hers onto it. If something was wrong, I did not ask her. Over several weeks I knew her, and what not to say, if something was wrong, I knew it. If it was the woman's time. Her being close to my body, she said it was the need in her, not for myself but all men, any man. I said, Men are not different, women think so but not here, men also have such a need.

Perhaps some men.

No, all men.

Some men, if any. She raised herself, reached for the water. We also need warmth, other bodies.

I do not think so, she said, passing the water to me

Then comfort.

I said she was naked, she was not self-conscious. I lifted the covering, she returned beside me. I put my arm round her and she lay on me for a long period. I do not know how long, my shoulder and upper arm aching but this was a moment that should extend and the ache meant nothing to me. I said so to her. And that you are not self-conscious, it is complimentary to me.

What?

You trust me. The male has a need and a need also is to be trusted by women.

She did not reply but there was movement from her and

I saw something in her face and I said nothing further. It was more than one hour since our last sexual intercourse. She got to her feet, went from the room. The fire still burned, barely, I did not replenish it. She returned with drinking water and also wine, placing it nearby. I watched her. I said, You are a genius.

She was uncorking the wine bottle, herself drank from it, not offering it to me, nor returning beside me and I had raised the covering that she might return, instead she knelt by the fire. Silence for minutes. She did not offer me the wine and I did not ask. Until when I saw that her mood had turned once more I said, Why do you think that of men? Not to be trusted, surely that is what they want, trust in them? Even those who wish to abuse.

I waited but she made no answer. I again had raised the covering that she might return beneath, she ignored it, sitting near in to the fire, her side to me. I put my hand to her back, rubbing at her spine. I saw that her shoulders lowered. Now she straightened. There was the need to relax but no, if it was so, she did not allow it. I said to her, You cannot relax. Why is that? You do not trust me? What shall I do? What is it that you think? I smiled. You will not give me the wine?

If you want the wine take it

Yes, I said, taking it to drink.

I cannot relax, she said, it is foolish to ask, why do you, always asking it. She moved further from me. Men's want is to be like women but you are not and cannot.

No, I do not think that.

Life is this moment for you but not for us, we are women, we think differently, live differently

Fight differently, yes. I smiled.

Arrogance. Fight differently. What is it you mean?

I do not mean anything, I am sorry.

But tell me.

I do not mean anything, I am sorry.

But you think it

No

I cannot understand you, except I think the worst and know this is the way of them. What is the worst, then that is men.

I returned the wine bottle to her and she corked it, reached to place the bottle beneath her coat, at her belongings. Her legs were nearby the fire, she rubbed the side of her thigh. If we had a cigarette, she said.

Your feet may burn.

She did not answer.

I raised the covering. You are tired, myself also, exhausted, come under, we may sleep. I put my hand to her wrist, lightly there. She did not notice. Then she did and looked to me. I said, What it is, tell me, something is wrong.

No.

Yes, I know it.

She put her hand to my face, her finger onto my chin, the groove there. What is this? she said.

Tell me?

Nothing, nothing is wrong. She studied my face, her finger still onto my chin, now she looked to my eyes.

I said, Tell me.

We shall live forever. She nodded. It is not sarcasm. She turned her face from me and there was the stick and she poked into the embers, the fire dying there. It was more than one hour, if she thought of it.

"nonsense song"

I found that I was singing. She heard me. It was not singing as she thought. It is a nonsense song, she said.

Yet if it is, I am singing it for you.

If people were to hear such nonsense it would give embarrassment.

Not to the creator of it, it is my composition.

All others.

No.

All others would scorn it.

Some would offer encouragement, praise, not all are lacking generosity.

You think I am so?

You are dependent on others, you should have confidence in yourself, I am your man, if you should praise me, why you do not, familiarity.

She laughed.

Strangers would praise me, our enemies. My song is so beautiful, it could not be denied.

You hum this one song, it has no melody. It is a mournful mournful sound, it is mournful. Yes.

Mournful! It is yours, I composed it for you.

I do not want it, she said. Her hand now was onto my chest and we lay for some period of time, her finger twisting hairs on my chest. I was tired, sleep would come. Moments are good. Yesterday into this day, if tomorrow is there. Moments with her, seeing her eyes now, but alert, a light glinting, continual movement, her hand on my arm, her mind roving afar, breasts flatting onto me, heavy beautiful. I do not know, if she thought something of myself. I thought of my daughter, infant, who that I had not seen for more, longer than one year, who never could be at peace, if I put her onto my knee, staying there, restraining her, weighting her down. I would have to do that, and if she was kicking and struggling with me, not able to be still, tethered to myself and if I laid her onto the floor would come her breathing in gasps, lungs of oxygen, I was her guard, now she was free, my daughter. This was after that my wife had not returned home, I had gone to her, it was by the sea near to the home of her grandparents. These two now had my daughter.

Nonsense song. You are singing it. She slapped my chest.

Again?

Yes again, you do not know it?

Some have said that my singing is very good.

Your mother.

My mother?

None other could lie in such a manner. But I have a question.

Yes.

If I may ask it. I can ask it?

What?

If she was speaking to you, then why?

What?

If you can answer this question.

Ask.

I asked, why the woman was speaking to you.

Many people speak to me.

Why was that woman speaking to you?

What woman?

There are many women? Yes, they look to you they speak to you. You know the one. One woman who did so, she spoke

169

to you, I saw her face, smiling to you, I saw her. Why? If this was indicative of contempt. Contempt for myself.

She pulled at the hairs of my chest. I shall torture you. These women speak with you, why is that? This one woman who was very pretty. No, if I ask you, why is it?

What?

They speak with you, these women, younger, older, anything, if you are any place, I see them, and they talk to you. At our last meeting when the stranger to our country was there and talking with many of us, his discourse to us, yes, this other fellow, I saw the woman there, she watched only you, yourself only. I saw it. What was it, she heard nothing of that discourse. Such manners also. Here is a stranger who speaks to us and yet this one would not listen to him. Why? You did not see this woman watching you? Yet she did so, why?

Because I am so handsome

Yes because you are so handsome.

You are foolish.

You make yourself handsome for these women?

Yes.

Yes, so, you are handsome to see for these women, so why should they not so address you, she was speaking to you, it is what you wished.

If that one addressed me I can say nothing. Males address females, beautiful females, so females address males, handsome males.

So they will address you handsome male.

If so

Yes, my own life is altered by your presence, why not that of others. You are a dangerous man. Perhaps we should worship you.

Why are we fighting?

What do you mean? I do not understand. We are fighting, I do not think so.

You are fighting.

Who is fighting? Who is fighting? What are you saying now to me, I am not fighting with you. I am not fighting with you. I am not talking to you. Neither can I say more, I cannot, cannot.

What.

I cannot speak to you.

What, what is it?

Our life is passing.

What can we do?

Nothing. Nothing.

I do not ask

I am sorry, nothing.

But what I am to do, if I may do something, what, I am sorry.

Oh.

I am to do nothing. Except the work that is there for us, what else, for myself, myself, I cannot say more.

Where is your child? Where is your child? Where?

With her grandmother.

All males are enemies. She breathed deeply, I felt the breath on my body, now her hand from my body and was a discomfort beneath my shoulder and also her breasts there if they would give discomfort for her, so shifting the position I lay and she also. Later she said, Hearing you say that, I do not like it.

It is not serious.

I do not like it.

I said, We should have a pallet.

Even as she wore clothes, clothes for both sexes, she transformed them. As that women do, yes, but her way was different, I saw other women, they did not look as she did, she was one only, beautiful and as the female shape, in the trousers was obvious, her waist and hips, breasts and eyes when she smiled, beautiful, as now my eyelids remaining closed and if hearing

171

her laughter, her laughter. I then suffered depressions, I do not say greater depressions, clouds only, darkening. Yet these would not vanish, overhanging me.

28

"father/family"

Some men would not have taken part, as I understand, travelling continually these areas of waste, always burning, fires, stench of smouldering rubber, thick black smoke. These men had sticks or poles and dug among it. Poles might be long and thin, having iron hooks fashioned at an end. Men carried these poles balanced on their shoulders. Our colleagues were not with them. I saw the father of the one requested, he wore dark clothes also, black or dark blue colour, and the vest as termed amereecana where across it above his belly reached the chain of that watch fine watch, I remember it, pocketwatch. Where he got it. If the son would know, it is possible. If I asked him, I cannot remember. Heritable goods, family goods, elderly relatives. His father was a man who performed obligations so, with dignity, as he thought, to the ruling class, and this watch may have been their reward to him, perhaps stolen but I do not think so. I say it only as possible. He knew the town, all perimeters. It belonged to him, as how he walked as how his son also walks, I see the walk, I see his father, I see the arrogance. When his son was selected his superior he said that the boy was no longer his son.

So with my own father who believed I also had power. I did have power, but not as he thought. It was necessary he held this opinion, proper that he so believed. As the general situation such opinions held as by parents would not interest myself, nor colleague, colleagues, yet in the form of specimen, yes, it is possible. If we considered the lives of our parents, these were a form of nightmare. But for younger men what the lives of adults are, who can say. When I had entered the teens I could not have used certain words and terms in their presence. I had to leave and I did leave, was taken, it may be said. I could not have remained with them, conscious of that inferiority, to have coped with the knowledge.

Yes superiority. If it is to be so transformed, I make no objection, and can say it, now say it, as with my former colleague I held that superiority, over my father and mother. Who will slap his face in her presence, in his presence slap her face. Who will slap one's face in my presence, slap my mother's face, father's face, presence of myself, who will do it to my father, father of my former colleague, and to we two, who will do it.

What is there.

I can speak of one night lying in my bed she came to me, my mother, and spoke and I also to her, beginning with the words *When I return from*. I cannot recollect more of that, *coming to home*. Her reaction was strongly affected, how it was that she shrivelled, in front of my eyes losing weight losing height, becoming this ancient woman, manifestation of power-lessness in front of my eyes, and she knew it well. She could say nothing to me. I had advanced to a level beyond, beyond which she would not understand, neither to have withdrawn.

Yet we ourselves had made that decision, myself herself, one to one, I know it now, perhaps then also I had the under-standing, as my former colleague, yes, at that time we spoke together.

We acceded to obligations.

And our parents, taking pains to hide worldly things for the sake of each other. I can have sympathy. What is not possible, not permissible. These things had entered our lives and through this the lives of our parents and elders, forced to concede their inferiority. If choice did exist, did it so for we two, no, I do not think so, we had none, it was to be accepted and we accepted it, as must they. We had no choice, acceding to obligations, I have said.

Then of my former colleague I would say he had that imagination, necessary imagination. Decisions were taken early, from when, when is it, when for myself, the age of twelve.

If in those days my father had friends it did not continue. I remember how he would stand, hands in pockets, head cocked to the good ear, his head nodding while he looked off that he might listen the more intently (the sight of a speaker's face disturbs our attention). His gaze would settle on myself. He had a mannerism, how he would shake his head, meantime in the act he would have established not only his inferiority but that he was not discontented, not a discontented man, often dangerous. I recall how he looked to me, frowning, yes distracted, not with comprehension, neither occurring to him that I might pay heed to this. No reference was made to these encounters.

The company of my father was acceptable to the community, company of my former colleague's father also. But the community was of them, not we two ourselves.

My father could not speak to me on matters beyond the immediate, continuing to lead me on forays upwards of the river, and we would find there different things, lumps of rubber, metal or wood. He led, moving quickly not quickly, slowing as he thought, searching for all things, bodies could be there, deaths that need not have occurred. This was how he said it to me, need not have occurred, people who need not have died. There came the occasion of the white clothing. It was among the undergrowth, ferns, sunflower plants. It had a sleeve torn and was of no value, also stained, of course blood, I did not touch it, my father did so. We found that body, of a man, each leg snapped above the ankle as so, laid on the track for the train wheels. My father did not say this to me but it was known, I knew it as did he. I told it to my former colleague, then boys as we were, he listened closely, asked of the dead man who had been of our community, from our district but had not been here for some long period. Who had killed him, we then thought securitys, we made inquiry, securitys not securitys, if military were in the district.

Impertinence is a worldly quality. For our parents it would have been beyond them always. An exhibition of impertinence had a peculiar effect on them. I knew it as a child. They thought of me as "godlike". Yes, I believe that to have been true. But they would stand together. After the selection had been made known I saw my father look at me as though become aware, and only now, that a secret had been kept from him. My father believed I had kept a secret from him. I do not know of my mother if it was the same, if it is possible, I do not think so. The possibility of my selection was not kept from him, nor from my mother. For the lives of parents it would have been not so difficult could they have considered themselves accomplices.

What I am to say.

If I so could do, I could not, if such a choice existed, it did not. I say it with certainty. I cannot say this for other than myself. I am saying nothing of my former colleague. I know nothing of himself and father, his mother or other family, I know nothing. We only were boys together. Beyond selection we moved separately. I did not see him for years after it, ten.

For myself, imagination might lead further as it was to do and from then, the break having been made by myself, no I did not see him for some long period, I have said years, ten.

29

"I bore him no ill will"

I bore him no ill will, did not see him either as cause of evil. What terms, what can be said. He of course had the authority, anything. It was more than nominal. If only that I still would have allowed it. He was not a fool but responsible. The hunger in his eyes was for something that for me would not exist but yet had its meaning. He had asked that I accompany him and it was complimentary. But his authority, he used this with me. He could only use it. I do say he enjoyed it. Authority is not irrelevant. I say he did enjoy his. It had moved beyond good humour. At first I thought so, the joke lying between us. Later, no, he had authority, he used it.

Yes, I felt emptiness. Also emptiness in him. Knowing of life I never would have. I would not live. He hoped that in knowing this I would act in accordance. What this did mean, in accordance with the death to come, my death to come, was it close was it afar, what was it, I am young, younger. You will not live beyond this time. I looked at him. He supposed that I had this knowledge. If I also knew it. Something, this is what I am saying. He could have seen this, his eyes searched into me. I said, I shall live. But he did not say more.

He was not godly. If he was a spiritual man I do not know. Some said evil. I do not know evil, these terms. Hunger in him, yes, but what was that hunger. Not for life, he also would be dead, he also knew it. He had no children.

I would not feel much.

Unlike others who would use such knowledge against myself and others, harbouring suspicions always, all times

He was regarded highly, by colleagues, by superiors.

Yes.

I do not know evil.

What is choice if there is choice if what is meant by it what people will know, our people do not know. If there is a people what one, can I know them, if our people may know these others.

The proof is our burden. These peoples luxuriate, thinking that we so choose. They luxuriate, as our children.

But what of them. Agencies, may to be international

our children.

Beside this what else to call it but fire, passion, for me to witness and who else but not his own people, he could not have allowed that. Why? Why can we not allow those near to us, those with us, to understand that this passion is present, ever present. But for me, yes. I was to hear his story, I would to hear his story, of course, know his life, yes. Man of action. Yes. We all, men and women all.

I have said it how when he knelt onto me, pinning me down, the stench of him, sweat, urine, if he had committed abuses, but he did not commit abuses, only the stench, if it was so

but could not now look to myself and said, On the floor by your head there are insects wriggling there. I have crushed them, three four five, family of them. There are wooden boards by your head. If these insects crawled from there, it is possible. This family of insects have walked from your head, from your ears. Are your ears clean? People do not examine ears, why not? There is a wish to kill you. May we? I am representative. If you present the problem, where lies the burden of it? What do you say?

I would not look to him.

It is only to yourself I am speaking only to you. Listen

Who would care about such things. Himself myself. He did not care I did not care, if death is to come, of course. I had no regard for it, for himself. I was aware of it, of one I must discover. My mind was wandering, I forced myself, again concentrating concentrating. There were these recent events, difficult events, men crowding into the section where those activities occurred as that intending to compete with each other, of course taking all that they could, if exists respect sharing one from another, manhood one from another. I cannot believe it. And is it a small matter, grave matter, I cannot believe that respect was so shared. If it was possible, I do not think so.

They made full use of the laxity. None was surprised. If I could say why. Men gain strength, perhaps women also.

He whispered, They will return, it is clear, certain, we cannot act other. You were in earshot. Yes. It can make no difference, if these are your own people, whose own people. I am not familiar to them. There is no individual basis, personal basis, none. No, nothing is known to themself, so they pretend, smiling, the smile allied to fear. It is not only of foolish people. Listen

The sounds now were there, not thumping. If they were, mildly, not loud, for the sound of it had come to me as through a fog, thickly. It is this therefore that I think the thumping was controlled, perhaps a knock, coded. But then

I could not, if the cold is there.

What

But what I was to do. Older questions return, and tiredness

not young however I would say he would have been thirty-five years, great shock of hair. It was to this man they referred. The other had escaped? I think so. I thought that the man killed was one of these but perhaps not, discussions were there, several did discuss this and other occasions. If they spoke to impress only listeners, myself and others, yes, I do not know why, only later he was killed.

30

"leg wounds"

It was tiredness, being so tired, we two. If exhaustion is healthy tiredness, I do not think so, tiredness of our work, operations, what operations, some speak of our operations, some of duty. I speak of this land, it is difficult and hills there and he was leaning to myself, onto my shoulder, could not walk. I am strong enough and if he also is strong, strong man, stronger, I too, and he is not so heavy, I could take his weight. But that night, what of it, we had found a space but there was little shelter if a sanctuary, there was no covering only clothes, what warmth, none but we two and I recall the shivering, shivering, and could not get warm, a time when I never never could get warm, and the wind through us my colleague the same, and shivering shivering I could not give warmth to you my colleague.

Later was the sweating. I was lying tightly to him, and that was pain and I did not understand, nor then knowing, but later and all was thickness stickiness, stickiness of that, and by moonlight I saw it now the blood, blood all, and when we ripped the material of the trouser seeing how that the right limb also was damaged at the knee, swollen there and colours of the flesh ugly, yes, I knew they would sever this leg, so I thought, it would be cut from him, yes, I thought so and he also, looking to these wounds, if some other thing might happen or, if this, until later to myself I thought I saw it in his face this further a puzzlement, I saw it there, it was a puzzlement and he did not look to me, not to myself, if so he was thinking not leg wounds may be fatal wounds, no, how can that be it cannot, if so he was thinking, how can it be? if leg wounds may be fatal wounds, we neither of us conceiving of that but how that tomorrow must come of course day will break and how he might then walk, how to do it as so we must, moving from that territory, if escape, what escape may be, he to rely on myself, of course, and for walking a stick of wood and tomorrow I would find one and it was tomorrow he was dead, next morning. What I say now, speaking of him. I shall get a stick for you, it is a stick for you tomorrow, crutch for you. He was gripping my hand, yes, greater pressure, applying to it. His brow was fiery now cold, sweating cold. He looked to me. Tomorrow there is a stick, I said it to him I said I shall find it, there is a stick, I shall find it, we may escape out from this territory, you may walk, this leg will heal.

What sentiment. Tomorrow I made the escape out from that place, yes, leg wounds may be fatal wounds. He knew it, if there was a truth. I do not know his look. That we then were alive, yes, as one, no, did I feel that then about us, no, himself myself, warmth of my body yet that night, what of it. What we do say. I can discover what we say, in that process. It happens and we act, look, it is happening, we act, act is the knowing, saying, speech act. What is your language? If it is my language. He slept by my side, was dead, yes, I think then, holding onto him, if he was dead, yes. Sentiment. I do know sentiment and international agreements, heads of states, yes our colleagues I do know. Sentiment. But I could not get warm. Not that night, shivering I to give him warmth my colleague his body, he lay and his pain was there and in his voice, he lastly was talking, and now the blood, blood, so much of it and on the clothes and I to his leg it would not be staunched, using garments, my garment. And later I was sleeping, stopping sleeping, could not waken, he only by my side and there was warmth but later again was cold and I was awake, so cold, colder. This was how he died. We then were together.

31

"if I may speak"

A relative or neighbour was recounting stories from his own childhood, how life then was in the district, if songs and dancing were punishable offences. Beyond was dark, wintry, the nights then closed in before evening mealtimes and this was it people might enjoy, all children thinking such a time exciting, older people talking together, stories taking much from family history, community history, also invention, and all knew it but that such inventions would derive from these sources.

We were in this house for one evening only. A few years had passed since the killing of the family's two elder sons by State agency. There was one other son, younger son, also two daughters, married, whose children were here in the house. The younger son was a colleague alongside us on this duty, escorting a guest to our country. He was gone presently to assist in other preparations. His mother and father were seated near to a window, his mother looking to the door, thinking if her son might return quickly, his father was apart, staring to the window, away.

Our guest was not foreign but one who now lived abroad and had returned home for a period, busy period, many meetings, many people, a lawyer. We had two vehicles. We were six colleagues, three now outside this house, stationed. Myself and two others inside, the son as said, and one older colleague who had known the lawyer from these earlier times. One month ago military personnel had fired into men and boys from a football match, killing some, newspapers said was rioting, so also radio, television, all media, servants to the State. This was the lawyer's return home, why he was here. Before his visit the family had thought him to be dead. They were not people who followed news events for overseas to come upon his name in campaign writings, political writings.

But I should say when it was known he was returning on this visit few among us knew his identity. We were not advised of it. Not myself. If to be taken into trust, if it was not necessary, it was not and I did not think such a thing, decisions were made. His name was familiar but I did not know of him. It was the younger son spoke to me, saying the background to it. The lawyer had come to their home when he was a boy and would stay overnight, people would come, there would be meetings. This was a difficult time following the death of his brothers and all harassments and retributions then endured by the family. Our "campaigning formation" had assisted the family in their struggle for justice, labouring against the State Security Council, offering advice and all personal support for advocacy matters. My older colleague could speak of these days when such work was undertaken. Our "campaigning formation" then expended much energy on this, work of value to individuals, so is argued, but if such energy might have been expended elsewhere greater successes could have resulted. No longer do colleagues attempt such work. These points so continue to be in dispute among colleagues, some arguing for a return to it.

The relative or neighbour had finished his stories now and our older colleague spoke of the lawyer, explaining how he had come forward in support of our "campaigning formation", how in those earlier times for such professional people so to come forward was not known. None offered specialty assistance to victims and grieving families and if only sympathy, not in public. Only colleagues attempted to bring such cases to justice, if things may be shameful to a people, scandalous behaviours, horrors and all atrocities and cannot be listed, cannot be discussed, if people cannot know of them. Only colleagues were tackling such work, work for opposition people against all master authoritys, military, securitys, these agencies, servants of the State. Professional specialty people were despised, lawyers, doctors, all professors. Few offered support. This one now our lawyer, this man was unusual, his name so becoming known. He received all provocation and harassment from State agencies but continued helping colleagues come to learn such advocacy matters. Charges of terrorism then had been laid against him, the State prosecutors seeking to bring him to trial that he might be sentenced to many years' imprisonment, many years. Now he dwelled in foreign countries, had done so for past years. People all were pleased by the lawyer's visit. Yes, he was alive and did not bow and did not scrape, he was no servant lick-spittle but one of our people, fighting for our people all peoples. He remained hard-working in these foreign arenas, knowing many authoritys, higher authoritys, knowing the views of our "campaigning formation" and speaking of these if he might where he might. It was true of the situation and none was more respected.

I saw how my older colleague attempted to lead the family into these historical accounts, pointing to certain factors concerning the case of their two sons, also the struggle for everyone as it yet continued. When the father did not engage my older colleague looked to the mother but she also, not answering, not taking part in this, looking only to the children, grandchildren, yes, but children also may learn. If people understand this. Children will learn. Allow it. Many colleagues are young, younger, they have learned. Adults spoke to them, did not hide things. If the younger son of this family, how he became our colleague. Has he learned of the world. What of the death of his two brothers. Are things so to be kept secret from children. I also have a child whose mother is somewhere nowhere, she is disappeared. What we may say. What I am to say to her, my daughter, nothing.

If we must lie to our children I do not think so. I now spoke of this to the family and neighbours.

I spoke further, of how these older ways of working brought greater failures to our "campaigning formation", bringing little satisfaction, only notice from foreign sources, helpful sources, yes, but what change this did have in our own country, nothing, there was no change, nothing, authoritys did nothing, only laughed at us, employing more securitys into our towns and cities, now more, all military personnel. All here knew it. Were we to stand back and allow this. The lawyer listened closely, he was not smoking, I saw it, he always was smoking, not now.

The son of the family returned, was by the doorway listening, hearing all that was said.

I told how on this visit home colleagues were with the lawyer six days, many meetings had been arranged, talking to many people, informal formal. This morning had been one meeting in a township and many of the community attended. Military had known of it, stationing themselves outside the building, provocatively, intimidatory, calling to men and women from here, wishing to trap some for fighting, the excuse for them. These in that township were known, would shoot to kill. It was where only one month before they had shot dead men and boys from a football match. This meeting was very difficult and we still were waiting for information. We did not wait for food but left thereafter, driving this one hundred miles, but easily, safely. The military knew our movements in travelling but did not harass, only monitoring. It was sensitive for them, they would not touch this guest, foreign journalists and individuals also monitored this situation. Tonight was one informal meeting, community leaders and local colleagues coming to one house, later we would leave to go to there. Tomorrow very early we would drive many more miles, to one large meeting at a town, larger, very many people, more. Military would be there, of course securitys. We knew it, received warnings, as this night also.

I explained a little how there were many tensions among colleagues on this discussions-journey. All things were happening to us, person contacts did not arrive, failings, failures, what as scheduled nothing as scheduled and all other major factors minor factors all petty detail, I cannot list. People do not think of time. We may travel one hundred miles and people think of it we have come from one street around that corner. Come in ten minutes to us.

But we are one hundred miles from you.

Okay if fifteen minutes may be necessary, we shall wait.

Yes!

I saw the lawyer watching me, smiling. Our older colleague now continued speaking. I was glad.

Much of arrangements and organisation was specialty involvement for myself, but if an arrangement was not organised easily, easily for everyone, the lawyer would apologise as for everyone. He and the older colleague travelled in the same vehicle, also with them was one other colleague who was a vehicle genius, more, if for his greater abilities, if he had not been present, yes, all would have been lost, I can say it.

To all such matters, greater tensions, the lawyer said to us, What can be done, not everything can be controlled, do not worry. He sighed often but said not much, if sometimes also his eyes would be upon us, seeing how we did respond, and to us also how did the military respond, if colleagues were there, if they looked to us, if we so were intimidated, if the military were so from colleagues. Other times he did not look, his eyes open, but inside his own head, Often he yawned, if he might apologise, not always. I think he did not notice. I may say that I watched the lawyer. I wondered if he listened to people.

And if events might be awkward, more, for turning

dangerous. How would he then act? I had no doubts we had no doubts, his actions would be accordingly, appropriately. Yes, I knew it. All colleagues respected him, I also. He had disks with him for a computer and sought access always to a computer but for this week so far he had not received the access. He had brought one with him but something had happened to it and he did not have it now but having secured these disks to work in preparation for such troubles and copies were with other colleagues. But computers were not available in this territory. When he asked of the younger son if a computer was in his family the younger son said there was not and thought there was not one in the town but did not know, and left us to assist in other preparations. Later a typewriter was brought for the lawyer but only he looked at it. He was a man with a bigger stomach and was heavy, wearing clothes such as white shirt and a tie with designs on it. Some might look to his clothes. The family had given him a better chair and it was near to the fireside. I saw that he was not comfortable, too warm and also with food, biscuits on a plate on his lap, of which he had not eaten, nothing. Younger children watched him, hoping for biscuits. Family members and neighbours present also watched him. Our older colleague yet was talking. If he would stop soon. He could speak for periods of time, longer periods. Many were now in the house. One might be anxious. Who knew all who crowded here, we so were relying on the younger son to the family, he would know identities.

One hour more until we must leave to the next meeting.

Now the older colleague was not talking. He looked to myself. I would not speak again. And so was silence, it was not comfortable. Some looked to the lawyer thinking to hear him with his own tales, hoping so. Since his return home newspapers told stories as to discredit him. Yet people enjoyed these stories and wondered of him, were such things true, rumours of famous people, beautiful actresses, did the lawyer see them, stars from movies, sex movies, also rock people. But the lawyer did not speak. I say colleagues also were disappointed, wishing to hear him speak, and he did not speak, having further questions of him, what struggles, how foreign people thought of us, if we were worthy. In one week he had spoken only a little bit, good morning, hullo how are you, good night, and was tired often, yawning often, did we bore him, of course.

Now was a longer silence. More looked to the lawyer but only he reached for his bag, took from it a new pack of cigarettes and gestured so if he might smoke, giving the pack to the younger son, waving his finger, so that the younger son offered cigarettes to family members, his father also, who took one. Colleagues might escort authoritys and foreign guests who had materials yet did not think to distribute them but the lawyer so had done for those days with us, all cigarettes, if he had brandy, yes. The younger son held the pack to others, not many took one. But a woman, older woman, she took one, looking to the lawyer, I noticed, it was staring, staring at him. She was older and her face was thin, what, ravaged, wrinkled wrinkled skin, all folding and inwards, her shoulders rounded, thin, and her back, seeming twisted. The younger son took matches from the lawyer and gave lights to smokers. He did not offer so to the older woman, instead looking to his mother who sat near to her. Now he gave cigarettes to myself and older colleague, one also to himself. I saw his father watching him and watching also myself. Now came the cigarette smoke in clouds. A daughter of the family went to a window, opened it.

Let me say of the older woman that she held the cigarette awkwardly and all over she so was awkward, did not know what, sitting upwards, then crossing her legs, now raising them onto her chair, sitting forwards onto them, holding her feet, ankles, head bowed, rocking, backwards, forwards, her upper body. I saw her eyes close, spittle from her mouth as of a trance as people may do, I have seen it in tragedies where are traumas, people remaining so, in tranced. Her eyes opened. A child was nearby, little girl, the woman looked to her.

I have said how people were in silence. They remained so, but for this cigarette interlude. Now it was over and again was embarrassment and again my older colleague was speaking, looking to myself. He said, I am thinking of a fellow we escorted many weeks ago, more, two months three months. He is now gone safely from our country. Some here will know his name.

My colleague now mentioned this person's name. The lawyer was interested, knowing the person very well. Other family members and neighbours had heard of him also and were interested. He was known widely and liked also by colleagues for whom he had become a great entertainer and imitator of people, this was a greater strength that he had. None had known of this until escorting him, coming to know him as now we were knowing the lawyer, and so my older colleague continued for some brief seconds, when the older woman began to speak, yes, suddenly, interrupting, looking only to the mother of the family. The older colleague stopped talking. The woman said, Who fights for us now there is none fights for us. She pointed to the lawyer. He is good man, what is good man, is he? He would fight for the sons of this family but not for my own. He did so, for punishments, those who killed two boys, they were punished. Your beautiful boys! she said to the mother of the family. They were punished who did so, evil men.

There was no punishment, said my older colleague.

Yes, said the woman.

No.

All knew their names, these evil men so were punished, their families, punishments. Who fights for us now, there is none fights for us.

The lawyer was smoking his cigarette.

People were uncomfortable. The younger son looked to his father.

None fights for my family, said the woman.

Our older colleague said, It is disrespectful what you say.

I may speak.

You may speak, yes, of course, but why should you disrespect people, I do not know why.

My family is missing, they are dead, I know it. Nothing is to be done, I am alone. It is not my family, I was of it, all are family, say it to me, you may say it to me.

My older colleague did not understand her.

Say it to me.

What, what I am to say, it is not only your family, it is all families.

The older woman looked to the lawyer. Say it to me, please. You are the famous man, good man, lawyer for all people, families as we are grieving, you are supporting us in our grief and fight for just behaviour and we may not know, if we cannot. What will you do for us, what is it? Do you tell our stories?

He only is one man, I said.

The woman did not hear me. What will you do for us?

I said to her, He will tell our stories, he will tell them to all people.

No, she said, stories for our people and stories for foreign people will differ. The stories will be of a different kind. There are the stories, yes, they can be the stories one will recount but some will not. Some cannot recount stories, these stories any stories.

I do not understand what you are saying.

The older woman turned to the lawyer. But think of yourself, she said, only who is famous and know so many people, important people famous people, famous famous VIP people.

What is famous? I said.

Famous, replied the woman.

Yes, I said, I can say it, it is when the securitys think to execute someone but then think no, then again, should we, they cannot make up their mind.

We are not famous, said the woman, they kill us.

Yes, said the lawyer, but our colleague is correct, it is good to be famous, I do not deny it, people often are confused, thus at the airport my arrival caused greater consternation, authoritys so were shocked, what they did do? Nothing, only stamped my passport entry. I did not say greetings, I wished that I might, I did not, I am not so brave, merely I passed through the terminal building, so to my colleagues who waited for me, hoping for better luck.

The older woman listened closely, and others also, the mother of the family, father of the family. Some shivered. Colder air was into the room now from windows open. The lawyer continued speaking. What do we ask of our colleagues? We all are in struggle. Suffering, yes, everyone, what is wrong? I shall speak. If I may speak what I am to say, I shall say it, I shall say it here and I shall say it overseas. For now at this time it is plain to all that in this room are brave men and brave women, who endeavour only for honesty, for this only, who so have been fighting for that and so shall continue, will so to do.

I saw the younger son's face, excitement was in his eyes. I saw his mother watching him, the father not so, only staring to the window, away.

We waited, if the lawyer might continue, or the older woman to speak. Other people also. Each held a story, stories. Moments passed. The lawyer had one new cigarette from his pack, lighting it from his former one, still burning. People watched this. Now the younger son again took matches, moving to the older woman, striking the match and saying to her, Auntie, here for your cigarette.

The older woman put the cigarette into her mouth and he gave the light to it. Thank you, she said, and saying his name, touching his hand.

More silence.

The lawyer said to our older colleague, What of the fellow you people escorted, who is now gone safely from our country, some here will know his name.

Yes, said our older colleague, gesturing with his hands, speaking to all in this room. This is the imitator of people whom he speaks. One greater strength that this fellow had. We had not known of it until we were his escorts. Let me say to you how he spoke in the voice of all people, women, yes, foreign people, whosoever, everyone. At night we could lie in darkness listening to him speak in voices that were funny to us, voices of higher authoritys, master authoritys, all personality people that we might know, yes, cartoons from television, what is it, Bugs Bunny, who else, Donald Duck, these voices also.

Our older colleague laughed, pointing to the children who were listening.

Yes, these voices familiar to yourselves, he would narrate stories to us in these voices also quack quack quack, I am Donald Duck quack quack quack. Then speaking as two people, man to woman, husband to wife, having conversations together, this also was quack quack quack and we thought it the more humorous of all interludes. If anything such had happened in the past, we never heard it, not anything like this. And let us remember also of this person that he was a very important person, personality person, VIP person of all rank and stature, of the more high international authority, higher authority, from Washington and London, Paris, Berlin and Moscow, Beijing, Stockholm also, here now arrived and with ourselves, living, sharing, sipping alcohol also for he took this, brandy from France, so he said was the better for all drinkers, brandy from France, one may take it with breakfast cereal.

Yes, the lawyer smiled, drawing smoke into his lungs, wiping water from the sides of his eyes. Yes, this is the fellow, he gets him.

My older colleague continued, of this personality international person coming from our people, offering lectures to all other peoples while in his other voices speaking many parts, people of our people, asking questions of international authoritys, historical questions, moral questions, intellectual questions, questions premised from all offerings, reconciliations, and of a more foolish nature these reconciliations, murdered and murderer, all things.

And when my older colleague paused in this, requiring more breath, I also could speak of the fellow, imitator of voices, and I said, Yes, as these, victim and perpetrator, violated and violator, inter as between yes, yes, you have murdered me, I forgive you quack quack quack, do not think badly of yourself only murderer, and to orphans of violated women, mutilated men, yes, I forgive you quack quack quack our rape and murder are nothing, cutting at my breasts and genitals, come to me that I may kiss your cheek quack quack quack, where is your religious house, let me enter that I may know your most high of most high, that authority, he above all others that I might know to love him as he loves our mothers and fathers, your god, come.

Yes, said my older colleague, but remember also how it was said, if we were helpless in laughter, we all were so.

Yes.

And something further, perhaps you may say it as you have said to others concerning this same fellow.

What?

You have told it to us.

I do not know what it is.

Yes, said my older colleague to the lawyer, this is an important thing, we were talking after one discussion meeting.

Yes, said the younger son.

My older colleague looked again to myself. And all others now looked to me. If I might have answered, or if to have said something. I looked only to the floor, only could do so.

The younger son said to me, I may say it? I remember how you told it to us.

And so he told it. His father had turned from the window, watching him. I listened but did not hear, it was my own story of when the great man, the imitator, was with us. One night we had journeyed a long distance and had found a location and were resting. It was in one camp. Military so were closeby, we could not accept hospitality from local people, if bringing further recriminations against themselves. We had not much food, very little, and it was night and it was quiet among us, trying to sleep but it was not good, but for the great man who had begun to speak, telling all stories, and colleagues listened and found it good, but I could not hear these stories, could not concentrate on any such thing that might happen and why this was, only, that my companion had returned earlier that day and was there by my side, if I may speak of her, I lay closer to her and how we were not touching, that that could not happen between us in this situation, and yet people were not fools, it was now known we were together we two, if colleagues saw one they saw two and when the great man was telling all such stories in all such voices in support of colleagues through this difficult time I could hear nothing, nothing, breathing only in her presence, my companion, and I whispered so to her, and she whispered in reply how when the great man had been making all colleagues laugh there only was a loudness inside her head, filling her ears and brains, crashing of many voices, many many voices, voices of our people, providing a discordant thing, lacking all humour and she felt then she might soon be dead.

What more. More. This was that time, difficult time. How it was told by the younger son, I did not hear. All others listened closely to him. Afterwards the father and mother were looking to myself. It had gone well for their son. I nodded to them but not to their son. I would speak with him, also our older colleague who now gestured with his hand to me, saying, Our people have a love for stories.

All people, said the lawyer, putting the cigarette to his mouth, now looking to his watch.

32

"I cannot remember"

She argued how it arrived as a thought, to set down my time on this planet Earth as of a life yet to come, her own life, having the faint recollection, from infancy, sensation of death, between the anticipation and reality, recognising its similarity to leavetakings such as this one, one of hers, of myself.

Voices were everywhere, peering into our heads, singing in our own rhythms. They are real enough, those reminders. Elderly people know it. She would say it. Some say memories. I do not say memories for these may not be as they were, and they belonged to her.

Outside of itself knowledge of the source derives from a mixture of fancy and hearsay

She no longer desired knowledge. She said so, looking to myself. She made use of the eyes in my head. Illusions are from inside. She said it to me. It is that my vision is coloured, and always has been coloured, beginning from separation, from my parents and family. She spoke to me as though understanding was hers, belonging only to herself.

This formed the leavetaking.

I had not set these things down and wonder of these rare occasions when it did fill my head. Not now. Illusions are from inside. Yes. I knew I could. It did not stop me.

What then. I do know these questions, she did not know

these questions, not at that more complex time. Such as necessary, as might give

I thought that I may have been

if that I was

Thus that it was false. But it became only false. were-couldby w I wasI thought that i. It was a fantasy while waking and no dream. could could, can feel it nowwe tightly yetwaslingd.

This necessity was the stronger on myself our time was so limited nowas in relating past, if past to the present, why, must I, but if so then as that I might be ruthless.

Much that is said is said needlessly yet the formality may seem necessary.

She thought we might become a history, we so might be one, saying this, whispering this

insufficient, engendering false modes of living

By attempting such a manoeuvre I gave access, was giving access, by virtue of the attempt, giving access

Already false, in the act of consideration. By mapping "the considering" I thought to be offering a demonstration. The distinction between the two lay in the store set unto them

She wanted to tell of her time, herself myself, we two, becoming a history. I would be approaching that method

The arrogance was all that I had but not so herself for whom always lay more than that and from outside of herself, having marked her life since childhood,

since childhood she had marked her life, its moments. The time passed. I now relate some of this, of that life, having had, lives continuing

My heart is a normal heart, signalling my death when the beating stops. Her death as the beating stops

I have no language now. My means of communication are holy, created by myself for myself. Her disappearance now.

I can tell of her time, it may be all that I can do, setting myself here, one thing already known, its existence, by virtue of that, while beyond, considered by ourselves as the possibility, a possibility. My wife was here and she was mother to a child, my daughter, I was with her and them and we do not know.

"there was no other possibility"

At these rare instances an energy was channelled into my body as from the living, I could feel it, I knew. What do you say. Below the window were clouds. I was on a staircase. There were staircases. Down below it could rain, but if where I was no, it could not. And if falling I would drop through clouds, causing them to burst. These are patterns of thought and imagery derives from there. I watched four birds, these were doves, one followed one, one followed one.

My eyelids had closed, resting. Always dreams. These are from life, forming life. We were trudging through mud, a valley, by the side of an old track, railway line, as so, I do not think it, do not know. From the long grass might come an animal. On this occasion any occasion. The area was dangerous and people did not go there. It was that section, of course, there were bodies. We discovered them, yes in the grass but not only there. It might be as though individuals had lain themselves down toward that purpose, await their own death. People now see it in this way. Now they do. They have said it to me if these were strange characteristics of people, how people so act, and were these older people only, or younger, men, women, did they so act.

I had climbed from there that evening. At the side of the main entrance was a parapet, the stone surrounding fractured, short flight of steps, I remember. There were ferns, we walked through them, picking into rubble, see for anything, no not trinkets, not jewellery, sifting gravel, is teeth, and the blades of grass. Weapons. Not food. Weapons, the means by which it might be obtained. Later by the outer perimeter I walked a route I had come to know, it led me via areas known for danger. I feared others, of course, but this danger also as advantage, it could be adapted. I saw people, they had manufactured a fire, making tea or coffee, brewing it, the odours, also burning waste, and wood. A girl then was with me. She had lived at the sea, a harbour. She said all there dreamt of travel. Now she dreamt of home it was returning to there. I told her I also dreamt of the past as future but let it remain so, what it is we are to do.

These people also prepared food. We stood there, not able to leave. I saw some fellow arrive and gesture at us. None responded that I saw. And he came then to us, asking who were we, why we were there, to where we would travel. I had a bag, I hoisted it onto my shoulders. It was the more simple move, making it and so I did make it. The rain also. It was the time to leave, if this was possible. If it was not possible. The fellow looked to the girl, yes staring. There was the yellow shawl or scarf, she was wearing it, lace material. He reached with his hand towards it and I saw worry on her face and she said, No, but he gripped the shawl or scarf, pulling it off, from her shoulders yes others now were staring to her and he now touched her arm where it was bare and I saw on her face

I could say nothing to him or to them all and wished for something, and if I had something, I had nothing

She had her fingers on the end of the yellow scarf, she gestured at him, it was threatening. How could she threaten it was ludicrous absurdity she should do so and antagonistic to this man hostile to him, what else it might be. He frowned at this, what else he would do, looking to me quickly. A distance from us I saw one other man raising a hand as to wave but turning his head, signal also to one other man. The girl also saw and her face. Now my memory entering, seeing her father, arm round her mother and she turned from them that she might not see them for a last time, spending this last moment not seeing them but these were not here, simply myself, herself myself. What was the girl thinking. She was with me but I do not know. Why she was with me also I do not know I do not know. I remember it seemed I was sleeping sleeping and salt spray was into my face if from the harbour, lifted beyond that wall, splashing. If I was to vomit I thought I might be, I was vomiting and the clouds spun and the sudden squawking of the birds, seabirds, noise of the sea, but where was the sea, there was no sea where I then was. If a river was there, yes, I think so, if from the mountains where rivers may come. These flow downwards, of course it is possible. I remember, it was not in that town, it was beyond, and was rising, land, into mountains, these are from borders.

During the weeks prior to then we were together, conversations leading to smiles, smiling, soon to silence, discomfort, finally. I said her parents were there. Yes, and other family members. Her father watched her, thinking I did not notice this, he watched us, thinking how she was with me but I did notice. What could he do, nothing, nor the mother. I was with their daughter, yes, while they were present. Others too were present. We lay together, as children not as children, whispering not whispering, sharing air to breathe, musty air, and touching, touching, we had a covering, lay under the covering, we touched yes, yes each other, who, of course. And the securitys might be there, yes. But in the dusk, half light, no light, shadows and dark, darkness, no one to see. We would remain together as so, if it was possible. I stroked her arm by the scar, there was a scar on her shoulder. Light had faded. She had the scar, I knew it, could feel it also, touch its lines, and if the security returned. One security did not care. He saw us, he did not care. Other securitys were there, we parted. Not to break the peace between us. Then also the movement of the clouds, blues, greys. The change had come.

But these others, family, mother, father.

what past, thinking of the past

She studied me, studied her parents, what would become of us. I thought she would choose them. She did not. I touched her with my fingers and she trembled, and inside her, I thought her sickened, that I witnessed her hatred of myself but this was wrong, she grasped my hand and held it there to be at her my fingers if I was inside her. I was from another place, I did not know, I had thought an obligation existed and was settling it. I surprised her in an argument with her mother. It was later, it was myself, she argued for myself, for myself. I walked on.

Now by the outer perimeter, burning waste, and wood and she

I saw no other possibility, none other existed.

She could not look at me but with embarrassment. But then as now from her mother, hatred, what else.

I did not know it then. It was to have made a difference and did not. And at that age, no, I do not think so.

I remember her story of leavetaking, her family, that the moment of departure was magical. On a pier listening to the calls of the birds, smells of the sea, vegetation, clarity of air, a fresh wind nipping her ears, as she said, of her ears being nipped, girl's ears. At the pier the water lapping against the wooden stanchions, tiny fish among the weeds, also debris, she recalled debris. What debris? Signs of what? She did not know, but was shaking in excitement, heart resounding, having to grasp her ears. She said how she would place herself by the shutters of windows and listen for a long period. I listened to her for long periods. I could not tell the time but by the light and the sky, now she might sleep, yet in her mind as she said how her father yet was watching

white ash, charred wood in lumps, blackened, disfigured; encircled by the bodies. And voices, mutterings. I heard them, saw no other possibility, none other existed. This by the outer perimeter, burning waste, and wood and dangerous for some, us, I knew it and by the fire was a smell

They were there at the fire, rain drizzled, the breeze only slight. I had become aware of a whining and moaning, it was all about me. What was it. I stopped walking. The girl was not now with me. Where these men might be. Who was with me. I listened, uncertain of the direction. These sounds were not human, not the girl, not those who were at the fire, and so walking, walking, and I reached the end of there and thought of the river, there was a river, and a footbridge, and I crossed this footbridge, and to the other side, being anywhere now, away, no other possibility, none other existed.

"if she screamed"

The security was pointing at his penis. This is the enemy, he said, why do you blame me? It is it. I blame it too. Look, I do not even call it him! He smiled and watched us, holding it out so. It was not erect. He gripped the girl by the back of the head and inserted it into her mouth, it too soft to push. He now could have held her but did not. The girl's father retched, he retched again and drops of vomit were on his chin and upper lip. We saw also that he urinated. Another security shook his head, wagged his finger at the girl's father and said to us, He is able to bear this, he is not a man, a man would have killed himself. Instead he messes on the ground, messes in his trousers. What kind of people are you, are you people.

A woman nearby whispered, and with surprise in her voice grappling with an answer, They do not think we are human beings. They do not think we are human beings. This is why, they do not think what we are.

Another of the securitys heard her and knocked at her between the shoulders. She fell to the ground. None went to her. She lay, she was stunned, she stared back, seeing us but also the staring, staring of ourselves, now taking the weight of her body on the elbow, daring not to move. Not even move, the position of her head, she could not accomplish that, that it might antagonise men further. And so the violence of the act perpetrated on the girl was not witnessed by her.

each of us

space
each of us, the girl too.

Afterwards the security cleaned his penis on her hair, looking to us. He was thinking of something, what he might say, if he might say something to us. I did not see him looking to his colleagues until another had stepped forwards. Now he smiled and called something which I did not hear. Behind me securitys were laughing, quietly done. The second now opening his trousers, erection was there, moving to the girl, stepping as to pass the woman on the ground. From behind another security shouted at her, You are not good enough. You see that.

Here the woman began banging her head on the stonework. I heard the noise of this, the thumping, and if she screamed, I do not know. I would think of what she had said, if she was mistaken, perhaps, if this could be something she believed, perhaps not, I would think about it, considering it only if later
passage from my mouth, my stomach
but how long since I had eaten, later
it is also a numbness, below the jaw, upper neck
our eyes are open

35

"I have brains"

And in that section to the top of the stairs, the smell having altered. It was a germicide. I was alert, my upper body now settled from the tensing and from behind the sound, the tread of a security whom I was acquainted. Surprising to me, thinking he was gone, perhaps dead. If someone had told me he had been so taken, perhaps so, such rumours, perhaps one had been whispered. Now here in this section four securitys, and seeing this one. He did not recognise me. He walked, hands clasped together, a bold walk confident walk. No weapon visible as without fear, he it was, certainly, encroaching into my space as I into his, yes, I saw his recognition. The information was to myself. I had known him since selection days, his, mine, boyhood. If there is hatred, what it may be. We speak of it. How that we do.

We continued, staring ahead only and the odour here was strong, sweet-smelling. My body ached, we all of us. Before me a woman tripped at the heels of the man to the front, catching onto the woman to her side, mumbling mumbling. In falling the mumbling did not cease, nor afterwards, rising onto her feet, clutching at her bag, glancing only one moment sideways and I saw her eyes, something there to myself. I listened to her mumbling, it was not prayers, I could not hear the words. Her voice was accented, if from way south southeast, it is possible. What it was of this woman, something for me, I could not think, yet something, I knew it, I had seen her before this period, where I had seen her, if I had. But we see faces, and this odour clouding, sweetish, thickly, it might choke me, also other voices, ravings, and children also were there. A rush of words now from the woman, the securitys hurrying us, she looking to one side and here I was and she frowned, if seeing someone, looking to me but not seeing me, perhaps into herself, how that she survived, marvelling that she did so, yes, and such a thing was possible. She looked again to myself, looking to my body. It is true that we see the bodies, we see sinews, muscles there, we see all strengths, if there are weakened parts, what futures may be. Now this woman, her arms as pencils, carrying her one bag only bag, staring ahead, lifting it lightly, bag of air. I saw she was older, her neck also thin, stalk of a flower, dancer, the skull shape, her head, forty years old I think. She kissed me, looking to my body, kissing me, felt for my genitals, moving from me, looking sideways.

Others would listen on behalf of them, and the one whom I was acquainted, dangerous man, I knew it well, I knew also he soon would be dead, and in the pit there all in maggots. Maggots may be good. He would meet maggots, hullo, how are you, he would meet them.

What.

All, yes, I hoped so. I was glad, so, if it may be, all of these lives, lifetimes.

I had entered the area of his vision. When he looked to me it was something, information so conveyed. What was it, wanting something. What I could give him, if something could be given him, what it could be.

This was a time, he did not acknowledge me. Now that he not done so it would not be done, the secret created by himself.

It was the interim period. The woman was at my side now. I placed my arm onto her shoulders, if she might have fallen. The security had watched this. His hands clasped behind, shoulders stiffly held and legs also at ease as at attention, security man who was military man.

Nothing may be said. I say this now as then, yes, as then, I have said it. It was into my memory, I had killed him. I do not know. If my acquaintance with him had been from childhood, infanthood, it is true. If he was a torturer, he was.

What is justify

Some were pushed on entry by securitys, they by the door, he and with the others, showing no malice but absently. Now he walked away from them and there was the confidence, what, swaggering, and seeing the dancer-woman, she was by myself, and her mumbling as we entered, her hand now clutching my clothes so that I had difficulty in walking, could not dislodge her, I tried to but she stayed by me and her mumbling mumbling if soon it would be raving until quietened, the securitys rendering her quiet as such people they do so, making silence as they do so. Another woman now in from the door. She was staring, to here, there, searching those to come and now making space. It was for myself, that I might sit by herself. I did not look to her but she saw that I understood and was waiting. She was bigger. I looked for the dancer-woman, sitting somewhere. The bigger woman allowed space beside her, I could not delay, so, now, sitting with her. Moments passed. The bigger woman placed her hand onto mine, pressing, she lifted it, she stared at it. I drew my knees up, rested my head there. Later night had fallen, she moved onto her side, she had a covering, pulling this over herself and later further space into her and allowing herself near to myself so that I lay by her and onto her, my front onto her, she pushing backwards that we rested, so, the covering to me and her hand reaching behind and I had arousal, raising her skirt and opening my trousers, pushing my penis in between her thighs, she settling there, pulling it, and I could move to inside her, her flesh enclosing me, tugging, and my ejaculation would come and my fingers were gripping her. I stayed inside her and was sleeping.

When I was awake the dancer-woman was there, not far from us, her face revealing nothing. Two elderly women were by her. Others also were there. Soon two securitys came, it was for this dancer-woman. One took her wrist, leading her. She was docile. The security I had known from boyhood days returned by the doorway but now followed these others who took the dancer-woman. I could recall his father many months ago living at one section, how he would look to others, terror, suspicion, what were their thoughts, those of him, towards him, father of him, now glancing this way that way, if we had seen into his mind, what was inside there, thoughts of himself. He knew of my earlier acquaintance with his son, casting it irrelevant. At the outset he spoke with me but becoming silent quite soon and I saw that talk of his old district brought thoughts of his son who now was known for a fashion of brutality, spasms in his head, I saw it, how his son was a torturer, if he might discard these thoughts but could not they so persisted until he embraced them, I saw it, yes, he was scared, but also I saw he gloated, if he himself so was respected. Of course. Why they should not, his son is a great butcher, sees all people, weighing them, seeing his own father also and weighs him, he cannot help this, is this skin rough, does it conceal meat, meat that is only knotted muscle.

What had happened to the father. Months had passed since my time in that section.

I knew that the security looked to myself. I wondered that he saw me, recognised me, of course, that I am one human being. The light was bad but I knew it. And what was for myself, what to come. The twisted brains of these people are into our heads. The children learn to hate. The boys become responsible but the mark of this is the extent of that hate. They become capable of greater violence, torture. The more responsible from adolescence is the extent of the torture they may carry out. In considering torture, what torture may be. Brains cannot scream.

I have brains. I only nod. I know what these people can do. The dancer-woman was returned walking to our room, the elderly women making space for her, she looking to the floor by her feet, neither left nor right until lowering herself down. I knew that the bigger woman also was watching, would know I was not sleeping.

36

"we have our positions"

What girl with me? She would not share with me. My bed.
I said that. She had shared my bed then no longer. I do not
know why. She

she is woman he is man, I am he, he is man, is not woman,
we differ one from another. I do not know. Yes. Continued as
intimate. Sharing confidences, secrets of herself. Myself not
myself, secrets are not easily shared. She would whisper to me
late in the evening. I watched her laughing. It was that night
with the others I left the room. She was laughing then, yes. The
foreign journalist saw me leave, he followed me. You are unlike
these others, he said.

Why is that? I said.

You are your own self, he said, own person.

Something, I cannot remember. I stopped then with him.
Why speak to me like this. I said, Are you a fool? Surely you
must be.

But he had the confidence. He smiled to me. I could have
killed him then I could have killed him, had to turn from him,
I could not have concealed it. I thought to tell him outright as
I had learned. Yes had been taught, as he said. But if so he
would have used it, for such a thing he would have waited and
waited, it is what he wanted. Yes he goaded, this was goading
from him. Friend, he said and I turned again to him, laughed
into his face, Am I your friend?

Yes, he said.

No.

But I am your friend.

You are not my friend.

I could be your friend, if I could be.

You are the fool, doing such injustice to us. You do not understand, cannot, will not learn. It is you.

Yes he was the fool and I could have killed him. Not then. I did not say then. But what account is this? I can return over everything. Tell me? What is the detail required? If I know I can speak of it, I state only the truth.

What else, what else is there?

Not now, not for myself, for us, speaking of we, all of we, or us.

The other girl also, I can speak of her. The conversation was then behind me, involving three securitys alongside the other, and the foreign journalist also present. It too turned upon the subjection of women, and of the three the one who spoke in whispers was the more forceful. And this was a surprise to other listeners, we outside the group. He said that each time he looked into the mirror and saw himself he grew an erection, and he repeated this with gesture, making gesture. Not secretly but for anyone in vision to see.

The three securitys were laughing, slapping his shoulder, he was a good fellow. The foreign journalist also. He was there but had moved that he might appear distanced from them. For our sake. That is how I see it. He was not shamed. He required a separation, themself himself, but was not shamed. I do not think so. Yet he it was should have been taken into consideration by us, marked as the object of our greater caution.

These securitys had not that regard for him. He was of them. Perhaps not of them, but not of us, certainly.

The space was confined, none having the option but to listen, and their gestures. Of course women, children, also elderly women. All. How could these men not know this. Yes arrogance that they should continue but what form, what form is this arrogance, surely the irony of such arrogance? This was not normal arrogance, securitys or men, I saw other forms. What was it, if something other, I do not know

There were these most evil incidents, horrific incidents. They had occurred most certainly. We all knew of them. And himself I had marked, yes, looking to myself

I can speak of dreams, presages. I dreamt of him as though of an old acquaintance, the one who spoke in whispers, I may identify him for we had become friends there, yes colleagues, within the dream. Now he is dead, not then. There was a closeness or loyalty, bringing a difference that is distinct. Not to dwell on old history we had a difference of opinion becoming a battle between us, prolonged warfare between us. It was not an amusement but I regarded him as one friend. Those who knew us were surprised we engaged upon this warfare. I myself was sickened. Our acquaintance now ended. I would hear stories of him. Not friendship, acquaintance, I said it.

A dream, it is only a dream. Some thought I would wish to know everything, they would tell me. There was the girl, others also, women, elderly women, I think not boys. But I did have the curiosity, expecting bad news. I was not given this information, I, we, none of us.

The foreign journalist spoke. He asked could I calm him. Yes could I calm him I could calm him.

This is as it was.

I could calm him. I do not know of others. He had colleagues, I do not know friends, also from early days his brothers, I know that he had them, two or three. Here in our section he spoke to none, I think only to me.

I cannot say what he said.

It was dreams. Then he too was dead. I was surprised. It is

simply I was so told. I had had no meeting with him, our acquaintance broken.

The foreign journalist said to me, How could it be that now he is dead? Surely such breaches are always healed, surely he could not have been dead prior to that?

I said, Prior to.

The foreign journalist stared at me. What it is you are saying, that it is prior, his death is prior, what is that?

The foreign journalist thought me deceitful. Why? There was no justification. He thought I had deceived him for some long period of time. I denied this to him. I said to him how his opinion of himself could not be so high if I could deceive him so simply, if this was as he thought. If he was not an astute man. People said so. How could it be? Surely it was not possible? He was embittered, I said it to him. Some wondered about his people, what had happened to them. I did not. I wondered about the one who spoke in whispers and the foreign journalist thinking to turn from him and his comrades, was that possible? I think not. He thought to remain distanced from them while in the company, the company also of ourselves, thinking we might trust him. Elderly women and men, children, boys and girls, all might be present.

I cannot believe such arrogance. Who is the fool? I said it to him. His death is prior. No, I cannot believe such arrogance

Of course we have our positions and we argue for them. If unasked I can say this and shall say this. What else must we do. I learned this as we all did. From our politics and our philosophy, we learned, some that we were taught, so they said. Some of us retained a belief in god, a god, and continue to retain that belief I think. If people are to be killed we rationalise. Who cannot. What is to rationalise? If it is to know the nature of the project. We know the nature of the project. Yes there are victims. Of course. We accept it, as do they themselves, their relatives and wider family circle. If they are dead they do not accept it, I am not foolish. When the foreign journalist was with us he attempted to speak to some among us on matters, sensitive matters. He thought to speak so to me. It was said of him that he was presumptuous, impudent, so others said.

Some, some said so. I heard it. He was thought to be impudent.

I have no opinion.

No opinion. I saw him, I heard him. He did not speak to me. Not fully. Of course chatting as conversation. He did not value me, such as me. He desired a core, to enter the core, seeking entry via myself, such as me

I say this as I can. I give my own thoughts on it, there is no line, designed so, there is none, we have our positions but not that these are/have been designed.

Yes.

The foreign journalist thought we all were of a persuasion, he said "persuasion". I have heard others say this also, "persuasion". What is "persuasion"? Is "persuasion" martian, for I have heard this. I have heard this said of others that they are martians. When the foreign journalist thought we all were of a persuasion our colleagues did not respond to him but some made a humorous face one to another, inter as between. Some laughed. Hullo comrade-colleague, here from planet Mars. I did not. I was younger. Yes angrier. Than who? Him? Who. Who else might it be? He said to me, Friend

Friend. I might have strangled him, I had no weapon.

You are the decoy, he said.

I am the decoy. You are the fool.

That was the foreign journalist. I have spoken of him, now also. And now the other fellow, his colleague, I am to talk of him and only of him. Yet I do not know him, only in dreams, images of future events. I said colleague, was he not colleague, I thought he was so. I am not sarcastic.

Thus of whom, of whom I am to talk if I do not know him, himself himself.

I said angrier, I was angrier. I said this.

Angrier than who?

Myself, angrier, angrier than myself. Yes, both, he and myself, anyone and myself.

I retain that anger, yes am angry now, these questions are through my brain and numbing me, numbing me I cannot think of what, think of what what am I thinking of

If I had scorned laughter. I scorned the journalist. For he scorned us. I did not laugh. The colleague, friend, he laughed. I scorned this, laughter. I had not laughed, did not laugh. For many months, yes, it is amusing, I am amused. All people are amused. The foreign journalist was amused. Now he is dead. Yes or what? I do not know. Perhaps he is resurrected. That is my joke. I have repugnance for religion. My childhood was of that, believing in god, gods and prophets and devils and thus are we resurrected, when we are dead we are not so we come then alive again in all our glory, sanctified as non-killers we become in the windows, glass stained by great artists and we children also in the mother, gods mothers, believing of gods and mothers, having the mother, god has the mother.

Personages are also gods. Are they, I do not know. There are devils.

These things are amusing. Not amusing.

Some have these positions also. I had no religion, not now but not then, no. I said I did have. People say that they do not believe, that which they do not believe. What are we to think? There is the truth, falsely stated.

These were not his people. They did not accept him. He wanted that they might but no, they did not "god", the all-powerful being, and in his son and other prophets, holy people

What? What I am to say
if I am to say, what

"such collusion"

I had not been so angry before. I considered this. If repercussions had resulted, retrograde movement, if for myself, retrogressive, if it was so. In front of the others I must remain calm. We did observe one another. It was our habit. Who could have had an objection. It had to be done. We searched out those not to be trusted. The man with whom I was sharing would acknowledge this by smiling, by raising his arm as though in surrender. Yes, you do not trust me but this is no personal matter as you acknowledge. I acknowledge also.

Something now of this matter became clear. I could resist these thoughts, entire notion, reality, of how it was. It was. It was being done to me willingly. It was collusion. It could not be denied. This point so striking, so blatant, yes, as that my hair standing on end. What did they do did they do a thing that might change for me. They refused. What this does signal to me. Their project has been to conceal a reality. These details that are obvious. These people think sometime in ignorance, things are to be moved along, inconsistencies consistencies, they move along that they might fall into place.

It was happening. Others did not comprehend. I was to inform them. I was to inform them of reality, as so, reality! Yes, this is reality. I was to tell them outright yet in considerate terms so not to upset them, explain to them the situation. I knew they would not hear what that I was saying. I would be speaking but would see they did not hear it. Why that would be if they were not deaf and what I was saying, it would not be heard, they did not suffer impairment. Beyond words, communication, humans, beings we are human. Basic principles of humans.

I do not believe in a separation between forms of understanding, I do not believe it.

These and other things are said to them, I also as part of them, said to us. I want to close my ears, screaming at them inside my head.

I know collusion, concerning silence, silences. It undoubtedly is true. Where potential separation does exist, where is it not acceptable.

I was angry with these thoughts for they were not my thoughts but thoughts held by others of me, thus being coerced into a situation, one that must be intolerable, I was so. I never could have admitted that, not to the others. And this was known to them, known to these others. Therefore why they would recount to me a story.

They recount a story to me. I would recount the story. Who could not.

Already I had explained that this was the case, obviously so, that this is the premise we begin from as humans, human beings, members of that family, building ourselves as a species on concepts such as these, material concepts I can say, beginning from the factual basis we are related therefore love one another, acknowledging yes that we too exist, we too simply it is what it is survival, yes, what may it be else, other than that.

But these older forms do not interest them. They would suppose me naive. I agree that it can be said I am so naive. I have no interest in forms of denial.

I do not feel threatened. If I am so threatened what then. If the question is to me, it is to me.

38

"thought"

But this then at that time was good for myself, and how my mind progresses I enter into the inner smile as I think it my brain. When these people are looking to me and this it is that I must be careful, if the smile will come outside too and the eyes are watching for any such sign thinking one might not sense what is to be sensed. If they are around me. Always. If they do things, are these things

the body is the body. I am not a woman. My own body

He had no hand. I did not ask more of it. We did not speak. There is contamination. Securitys believe so

They watch for such indicators. Eyes may signal, one flicker is attack, two flickers

what two flickers

these are sarcasm, he said his hand was lost for sarcasm. He said it to myself. I have no hand, they took it, severed it from here, look, showing me his wrist, stump of it, its end, where the skin is pulled so, and they put him into that room. I heard him asking, Where is my hand.

Things may be said. If I am to say them, I can say nothing, I say it to them, nothing

what is it? nothing

if they hurt bodies what the outcome may be, if they have patience no, nothing

if he has had a limb taken, people take more, taken, if these are severed, as this man simply chopped, taking his hand from his arm, nothing

39

"censure is not expulsion"

Suspicion again had been turned onto myself. Prior to these last days I had noticed the distancing to myself from these colleagues, colleagues who were my colleagues. And a woman I knew so well also, she was to lead this inquiry. How that I gathered such information? I did so. Perhaps by inference. Perhaps I cannot remember. I am not sarcastic. Tired, yes. But also the decoy, he would have noticed such a thing to himself. It came often in silence. One might enter a room, talk would cease, seeing also they would not meet one's eyes, could not. Such it was for myself as of other inquiries that I was familiar with, and I knew what was to come. As the decoy must also have known but that this was for myself he would not understand, that he was the decoy, he did not know it. If one is the decoy and advice is to be given of this, it will come later, if it will come prior, it could not be so, of course, advice must come later.

So, this evening that I speak, what I should say, "trial", not inquiry. I entered the building and upstairs to the room where the bedding lay, this that I had been allocated, discovering that a dozen colleagues were there in wait, waiting, including these three others who shared this room with myself, we four. And would I control my anger. Yes. But what was my anger. I knew it and did not know it, if truly it was anger. I was silent, greeting individuals by sign, moving to my bed and sitting there. Yes, no eyes upon myself, as that reality lay elsewhere. Minutes passed. Now came the decoy. I saw that he had removed from us, as within himself, his emotions. Yes myself, also, as one of this committee as he thought. We had not been friends but acquaintances, yes, he was not lacking in respect, not from myself. He was not the stronger, as individuals there among us, having our obligations.

It was the process. What process. Yes.

I found it a spectacle and did not care for it. This was from inculcation, bred into us, that we should trust none, in we ourselves, inculcated. But it was the process. It could not be trusted. I no longer did so. Elements were here. None might respect them, I did not. It was a drama we would enjoy in a theatre, a movie. Are we actors and singers, if we are dancers. No. I watched the decoy's face. He fought for his life. This was the struggle and was our struggle, struggles. His defiance was there. Mine also but that I was stronger, thought that I must be so, or knowledge that I had greater than his, strength than his, for I was in receipt of the knowledge. I knew the situation truly, as he did not, and it gave me a strength now for our colleague, the woman who was to assume leadership of the committee, and this was a woman who that had been close, she had been, myself herself.

She gave no indication of a truer situation, instead looking to all she gestured to the decoy and said to him, We now shall ask the questions.

Then I shall know what to say, said the decoy, what not to say.

You must speak, said our colleague, we have spoken to you.

You have spoken to me, what is that? I did not ask that you speak to me, what is the obligation, I have none. It is growing late, work is to be done. You say you know my position, further talk is unnecessary, yes, what may be done you are to do it, you hold that authority, supreme authority.

We are none in that position, she said.

223

Here in this group.

Here in this group, yes. She gestured to include all others yet neither to exclude the decoy himself. But I looked for the inclusion of myself and if it was so I did not see it. I could have smiled. If I did so.

The decoy stared to her.

She said to him, Yes you also are included for it remains we ourselves, all of us here ourselves, it does remain so. You say that we have heard your position and its circumstances. I say that I have heard you speak to yourself. We have been present when you speak to yourself. To describe something as your circumstances would not be proper. I do not have that intention. You spoke thoughts aloud, I was present. Our minds revolve, this is how we settle on things. You were engaging in that process.

What process?

Thought process, said our colleague.

Another present looked to me as for corroboration, and smiling, yes, to me. I also a conspirator, no, I do not think so, no, I could not care for this, so was not responding to him, only kneeling at my bedding by the wall. Nor could I care for our colleague, my companion who then was so.

I had thought that it was passing from between us, what was between us, male to female, now no longer. Most certainly those dreams of her, having had those. It had gone from myself. I heard how to these others she repeated her joke, what process thought process, and she also was smiling and I thought how I could not care for her. She said to him, You suppose to rid yourself of guilt you state its substance.

The decoy said, Yes, that is what it is, you know me by now.

We know you.

I have no guilt.

You have guilt, this work we do, who does not have guilt.

I have no guilt, the work is necessary. It is a cleansing process.

Always there is motion, if people are here, always already, in motion always, set as unto. All colleagues know this. I have no guilt. None.

All know this? I said.

The decoy looked to me, wondering, anxiety in him. Others looked to me with a fuller attention.

I said, Tell me how is it that colleagues know it.

An older fellow was by the doorway, smoking a cigarette, now raising his hand and he called, How do we know it?

The decoy said to our colleague. This is free to all?

It is not interrogation, said our colleague, nodding now to the older man.

The decoy said, I am to answer him?

Why not answer him?

The decoy looked to myself.

I said, Why look to me?

The decoy said, Who other than yourself. It is not anyone. You have said how colleagues will judge of our work, and that is necessary, as the work itself is necessary, cleansing process. But how do they know it, as you state, how do they do this? I try to do as yourself, myself yourself. I also try.

I did not use that word. "Judge" is not a word, I did not use it.

The decoy was wondering. I saw now in his eyes, something. Cunning, perhaps, who would not be so cunning. Of course, looking to our colleague, now to myself, not so anxiously. She said to him, Our people are experienced. They might so judge, or not, if as you say. But what if so, this word "judge", you are worried by it?

I am not worried. The decoy shrugged, looking to myself

You are afraid to judge, thus you do judge, judging those who judge.

No, said the decoy but now he frowned, and after some moments he stared to myself, coming to understand the situation.

And our colleague said, If so that you will not judge then it is a wish to offload your own burden, shifting that onto others. Some have their burdens, this would be in addition.

Yes, said the decoy. He smiled to her. It is for you, making use even of sexuality, you are a woman, it is not difficult to make of it against us. You display your power, personal power, but the power you have is authority, authority of such as myself, myself himself. You exercise that. You speak we listen.

This was nonsense. I said to our colleague, Your attempt now is to provoke me. This man is a fool, if he is a decoy what has he to do concerning myself, making use of him in this way, it is to say how that we share factors? Of course, he is a man, yes, also

But he is a father.

He is a father I am a father. Yes, I am a father.

Your child has a mother. How may I provoke you sexually? What do you say. I can be in authority over you? He says that I can.

Yes in power, I said, but it is representative only, I know it, power may be representative, I am not forgetful. If I could be forgetful, it is not possible.

Another woman was there and she called out, He has daughters.

He has one daughter, said the decoy, I have two. Also sons, two of them.

Our colleague held up her hand to him. Why are you speaking? You have nothing of this, no longer, it does not concern you. This is a new situation, surely you have understood it.

The decoy looked from our colleague to myself.

You are the decoy, I said

You are taking no part, said our colleague.

I am taking no part?

No.

If I am decoy?

If you are decoy it is not you, you are decoy.

Scapegoat?

Our colleague turned from him and said to myself, This is censure, not expulsion. You talk as though in hold of a mystery which itself is a position, as has been stated. Certainly it is a position, a position that we cannot condone, we cannot, ourselves and all colleagues, yes, with whom you are familiar, who have trusted in you, as I have, all that have accompanied yourself on these more hazardous occasions, awkward, dangerous, where decisions are to be made quickly, there never was reason that trust should not be placed in yourself, yet we may not condone such a position.

Therefore trust cannot continue to be so placed?

This issue is serious, regard it seriously, if it affects trust nothing is more serious

I feel that I am insulted.

Yes.

If it is something other, what.

It is nothing other.

I looked at the others. I said, It is during night meetings issues such as this are discussed, theoretics.

Our colleague smiled. Theoretics.

Yes.

But it has been argued and I have argued, as with yourself, that there is no mystery and can be no mystery, not unless contrived. I argued that this could never be a position held by such as ourself, we all, myself yourself, all other colleagues. I have argued this consistently.

As I also argue.

Yes.

Yes? If I am being charged with the opposite, not so, held guilty of such an article, that I have laid against others, having found others so guilty. Other of my colleagues must accept and agree with this.

227

The old man standing at the rear at the doorway called, You are bitter.

I am bitter. What else bitter. Things have happened and happened to myself and I am to be responsible for these, look, we have no wine, no cigarettes

I have cigarettes, said the old man.

Let him speak, said our colleague.

I am not God, I said. If I am by this place and such a thing is happening, do not blame me for it, it is no effect, I do not bring it into existence. Dust is in my food, if I am to blame that there is no rain, and if these individuals are there as I am then they are not there from myself, I do not invite them. I cannot understand why such as this may be necessary

You are in control, said our colleague.

I am excluded.

You think so? Moral things are also personal. What?

I am not speaking.

You looked to me.

I looked to you, yes, you are talking, I looked to you.

You are not speaking.

This is in operation, this now is proceeding, what I am to say, if you are in control. We have shared more difficult situations.

Yes, as others in this room.

And now this against myself, yes, and if I have done something, what, and none can say, and if none can say, why is it, if these proceedings are deserving, the situation giving rise to these proceedings, no, I do not think so, there is none, I have not been in control, it is no error, if I have been so tell me, but none may tell me, if it is not the case. Yes I may feel bitterness. Also irritation.

Anger, said our colleague.

Anger. Yes.

It is misplaced.

If it is misplaced, no, I do not think so. When my head is

there as now I am aware of myself, also physically, but not to rid myself of myself, it is not possible. I have anger, it is justified, what may come of it, it is the time of day, how that I am.

Not in this manner, she said.

In this manner. Say if your experience is longer.

It is longer, she said.

People die young, younger. We make no evaluation.

Some do.

Some cannot accept that a fact is stated.

You have stated a fact? she said.

Some cannot accept it. I had thought to explain it. You also. We said so, we spoke together, have done so many times, sharing.

Yes.

But the denial was quickly to me.

These are old matters.

Old matters?

What else they may be, nothing.

How is it you say it to me? If there was a choice.

If there was a choice, she said, but there is none. She gestured round the room at all who were there. This only is censure.

I cannot speak to you.

Now your anger.

You thought to lead me, I would quarrel with you.

Instead you give nothing of yourself

I have not remained silent.

Your hostility is great. I saw you spitting. Our presence was so sour for you, when you entered here and saw that here we were, we waited for you, yes, you spitting, I saw it.

If I was spitting.

I saw it.

My mouth is dry, what this is, spitting, I do not understand you, what it does signal, nothing. I am to speak, now I may speak and shall say of my position, if it is my position that you are to know from this censure of myself then it is not important to myself, I can say more and now shall say it. You have prepared for this

A woman at the side of the room raising her hand, she called, We were not prepared for you.

Yes prepared for me, for myself, censure of myself, when? among each of you one to another? speaking of myself, when? when I was not there, when I was sleeping, fulfilling obligations? when, when did you speak together?

Prepared for you, what do you mean, it is insulting.

You met with one another.

What does he mean? said the woman.

Before now you have discussed matters of myself, you have discussed these matters.

Of course, said our colleague, this position is your position.

We have heard you saying it, called the older man from the doorway.

Saying what?

So. That you do not have a position, but if that you did it would not be ours.

This is nonsense.

It is not nonsense, called another man, we have heard you.

You have heard me, yes, all have heard me. Good. You ask questions, these may be answered. I am powerless not to so answer, I am not dumb, therefore I spoke, but no further.

Censure is not expulsion, said the other woman, you are too angry.

I am angry.

Too angry.

There is no trust in me now, censure is not expulsion, but it leads to expulsion, which may be voluntary.

It was now that I saw a shift occur, one individual another individual, another had lighted a cigarette, another reaching to speak to another, and farther behind now I saw the decoy and he had moved to the exit, standing by the older fellow who whispered to him and if it could not be heard, not by myself, and now our colleague walked to them, the decoy stepping outside, she following, she followed him. If there is more, yes, of course

40

"demons, upon me"

No matter that we place little value on that segment of the planet, ours, the segment, it is that we prefer to remain in it, what is known to us. We go back as once we were, attempting to make use of what we have been through, as though our handling of previous experience will allow of a determinant. I am to say that the demons were upon me, say also I had had these demons before. I ignored them but they would fight through my defences. I heard their whisperings, rush of their breeze. There was the urgency. They gloated, so it seemed, yet rushing on. I would get to the window and out from the window, looking out from the window, using all of my resolve, yet what I did see only, a thick spiral of them. As I looked my eye drifted from bottom to top, until the horde had become invisible. Sunset? Thirty minutes on. The more I observed the spiral other factors clarified for me, that some thousands of these demons were not rising but flying in zig-zagging spheres. Areas of the air belonged to them. No birds would enter there, small bird, not ever.

So yes never, this then was my segment.

And now into my thoughts that one concerning only myself, that I was never an equal, never the elder of the younger, the elder among the younger, I was never that.

I could only be equal.

But I was always younger when the younger.

Yet I should have been elder. I could have been, easily, if so allowed. Women and men both. I saw the children and learned from them. This was necessary. So, I walked out. So, I did that. I saw how for all for them

and when they are moved to anger and lash out at friends it is because rules of play are not observed. They become angry when another has transgressed those rules. If irrelevant, the rules are not are known [unknown], if it is so. More than that, the knowledge of these rules is in common is not extant. It need not be said but also is requiring to be said that these rules neither are written nor are they discussed in advance. Children may begin play and there is the knowledge of these rules. It is true that one child can bully others. This is not to be denied, as other parent adults, I had been prepared, as they are. But also how we see they become perpetrators, that too was important then. Now it is not so important. Not for me. I do not worry about such things. Children also are in denial. Yes, they may be.

In my mind now I believe in only this one factor arising from the swarm. The swarm. And spiralling. I can finalise that. These demons cannot devour me. I may devour them.

I knew we were to become the perpetrators. The parents had prepared us, the men but not only the men. From such phenomena we draw inferences concerning our own behaviour, occasional conclusions. I could be an elder, would become so, it could not be avoided, as some thought.

Yes, cowards, those who will not look to reality. I say cowards

Women and men both. We say children, if what children are, if what they do, if they are not irresponsible

I was weaker then. Not physically, working on the stone and earthpits, my muscles in use, muscles of my body as a younger man, I was so.

They are now not in use. Our bodies are now not in use. I say it, that I say

"girl too close"

She moved closer to me, not against my leg but very close so that I felt the presence, blood into my veins, and looked again and the girl must not have been older than twelve years, younger older, I thought so. She was humming a song. This was close to the market, I was looking to buy tea and water, this stall had coffee, other items. Children are dangerous. I stepped aside if to let her pass but she only edged closer again and the woman of the stall here I looked at her I think to share confidence but she did not notice what happened. This is a girl, simply a child. I knew it, understood it, resisted, not encouraging sexual thoughts but her presence was physical, her body touching in some way, pressure of herself, perhaps her arm and the urge in me was real enough.

I paid for tea, other items as purchased, water, left this part of the market, but this girl came behind quickly and was walking more quickly and then she was on in front of me, now as that she was loitering, humming the song, no, not smiling, absorption in herself, projects, yes what projects of her own self, I looked to the side, other side, behind, in front, but not to attract attention to myself but if accomplices were there, people of her. Yes, perhaps older than twelve years but a little only, her legs so thin, childish, her skirt short, short. I knew that she slowed now so that I would reach her, turning her head, seeing back to myself and I could not stop my action that I did, staring into her eyes but how she managed this making it be that she had not looked to myself but only I looking to herself and she skipped on more quickly, then slowed again, touching her leg with her fingers, turning her head to one side.

I was not allowing this that this might happen but if an arousal was there, it was so, affecting my walk and there were many people, this was closer to the central market area, more tourist area and securitys of course dangerous places and moments, of course, it was this, I knew this but could not think what was taking place, if something more had begun, this girl slowing again, looking behind now to myself if my eyes were on her, did she look to my groin, I imagined this, she had done so, not smiling, yes, not so, fully in herself, now looking to the front direction and this moment I moved to the side and a portal there entranceway and if she saw me I do not think so, entering quickly, throughway, stepping ahead and by a corner and waited there by a wall, now seeing a vendor was here at my side, their stall here, I had not seen, materials, such articles, cloths, gauze-materials, the vendor was a woman, two women.

Yes they watched me, they did so. I was there moments, it was a pillar of stone bricks. I rested my head against there, cooling my head, eyes closing. If the women vendors watched me, if they might wonder that I was ill, fainting, steadying myself. I saw there to be no exit other than by return, other than entering premises within this yard. What I would do if this girl entered here. If the girl had led me to here. Or if she waited for myself and with others, accomplices, or securitys, pointing at me that I had followed her. What to say it was dangerous, of course. I stood there, moments. I had a cigarette, match for it, smoked some of it. The women vendors had no interest, seeming not so to have, two more women now were at this stall. I heard sounds, footsteps hurrying along as of outside, and the alleyway, if they would enter to here and if I was to move, quickly.

"homecoming stories"

by his absence, so much, by virtue of that. I have said he died younger than I now am, this colleague. So of course not moments, more such of slow periods, periods of time we can have that are of peace, we cannot deny that such moments as these are of peace, in that connection, when he was killed, my mind

when she was young, had not married his grandfather, her lover. My colleague talking so, his homecoming story to me

Lover, former lover, as he said to me, she met with him, speaking of his grandmother. This was before the first explosion.

His disappearance was posted.

I have said of it.

What is required. I am to tell this. What is it that it may be. What I am to tell. It is pain.

My body now is hurting it aches yes. What I am to say now, what account it is to be, I can speak if I should speak you can listen, I shall speak, speak now, let me speak, I wish to

when she was young

his grandmother, I think, mother, father's mother, and former lover, I think, wife may be.

These are histories, lives of our people, peoples

what are histories

we are to tell them I can recount them, listen to me of them. It was nothing from me. Only himself. He said he would tell me a story of his grandmother, it was in some hovel or other.

What could I do, listen. I did not want to listen. Homecoming stories. I cannot listen to them. He had one strange eye, so squinting one way now another. It was known of him as the identifying factor. Yes I listened, trying. Also I was exhausted, we both. Why we did not sleep. We could have. I said it to him, repeated, repeated. No, he said, we stay awake.

He said of his grandmother when she returned to her district she was met by an old friend, perhaps former lover. He was uncertain. Former lover of his grandmother.

So many stories of people returning, events that have taken place. These events lie in the past. Yet it is their future, it is what they see, over our mind, beyond. They tell old stories and they are of the future. They do not know what it is for, this that they hope. Their minds become occupied by it. Then too these images in this region where we were, spurring the story, any story, the light after heavy rain, the sky now so clear, entering into a reverie, anyone, away. I say beautiful. Something that I knew, from where I do not know, these things gone from my life, my own past, own stories. I looked to him, seeing his face and his eyes, worries there.

He said, Why do you smile?

I was smiling. I thought to smile again but could not. So, and he continued, his story set in some hovel in some village, or town, as he told it, small town, speaking of his grandmother. As also where we were at that moment, hovel in a village, and its ghosts, yes, it came to me of other old people, those who had lived where we now were, old people and their bygone relationships. I even could hear the noise of them, such it seemed. The dampness there in stone walls, old brickwork, its plaster crumbled and fungus growing, wooden beams, a whiteness. This had never been a good place. I am not superstitious more than others, not religious but I do not like these things, unnatural things. I could say it more strongly, immaterials, talk of spirits. Why had we stopped there, I do not know. I also had my map and saw nothing. But he knew the land, had thought to disguise this knowledge, leading me here to this village as though stumbling on the unknown. Now telling me stories. I could tell stories to him. This place would tell them, itself alone. Ghosts, old moments, ghost moments, everywhere around us, no people, broken buildings, silences. Of course there are these things. It is not in dispute. There were times I lay down to sleep and these filled my head. I could have said to him but no, instead loosening my boots.

I ask that you listen, he said, only that.

He reached to shake hands with me, sealing the trust, but what trust, how sealing

Humanity, humanity. Yes, we are human beings, I shake your hand. Thank you. Yes, not an animal, we none of us. On other occasions also he would do it, the strange eye to me, reaching suddenly, taking my hand, now relaxing.

Please, you can listen.

I am exhausted, we could sleep. We must sleep.

We cannot sleep.

I could be first, you second.

His eyes had closed. He did not wish to fight me. We cannot sleep. But also it was exhaustion, exhaustion, we both of us.

Now he spoke again, We cannot sleep, and his eyes were open, staring at me. I did not like it, both eyes red, black rimmed, the dried mud. I touched my chin and the mud there also, I picked at it. Now he gripped my wrist, but lightly, as the father holds the child, settling the child, and he said to me. I speak, you listen. He smiled again. Better than sleep. My stories to give you energy. You will sleep, later.

I will sleep later. Good. Thank you. I looked down to his hand and he took it from my wrist. The tale would be recounted. I sat with my shoulders straightened, the air into my lungs, deeply, breathing it, breathing it, blood will circulate I shall be strong. For now I stay awake, later I shall sleep.

Yes, he said, we two, good.

I listened to him, also wondering about him, many days now together. This story of his grandmother. I did not know my grandmothers, parents of my parents. I did not wonder about them. Nowadays yes, who they might be, how they fought, if they did so, perhaps never. Not my father, he did not fight, never. It did not dominate my mind. It is true that I wondered, about him, yes, wondering, of course, and becoming clear, it becomes so, these lucid moments, lengthening moments.

You are not listening, he said.

I am listening.

You are not, no. He stared at me. But I could also stare, his behaviour did not intimidate me. He continued staring. He could not intimidate me. Homecomings, I said, tales of family and community, yes, but a world now gone, a world now dead.

Not dead.

Yes, dead, as my own world is dead, my own grandmother. I could speak of her. Also grandfather, my mother, my father, uncles, I can speak of all them, my son also, what of him, you do not ask of him, listen to stories of him, he is alive, living and breathing, if he is, a little child, we see the children, what of my son.

Aah.

But that world is gone.

No, you are not listening.

I am listening, it is you who are not

Please, he said, and he stared at me.

Your eye traps me.

Yes. He smiled. This is the magician's eye. It was given to me by an angel of God.

Female angel, spirit-lady, you saw her?

He looked at me.

I am sorry. It is this place.

He now was silent.

239

I said, Continue the story.

Of my grandmother?

Yes, your grandmother, tell me why she is so distinct, unlike other grandmothers such a beautiful woman, ninety-nine years of age, and beautiful.

Beautiful, yes, beautiful woman, and also there was her lover, when she returned to her town after many many years

Lover?

Yes, this is why I tell you, why I want to tell you of her when at last she was coming home, after so many years.

Your grandmother's lover?

Former lover, yes, when she was not my grandmother, I was not yet born, a young healthy woman.

Aah

And now you interrupt

No I am listening I am listening

Yes you are listening, as you make comments listening, two things.

No, it is different now.

Sexual relationships are different.

Yes, young healthy woman, I am concentrating to hear this story, sexual relationships

And so you now laugh at my grandmother.

I am smiling. Tell me. What age was he, this lover

Former lover, a young man, thirty, thirty-five.

Thirty-five is not young. I had a grandfather, he was thirty-five.

Yes.

What age was she?

You are not listening.

I am asking her age, of when you speak.

I told you she was young, I said it. Now listen, listen to me, do not interrupt. Please.

I am tired

Yes, so you are telling me.

It is a homecoming story. I know homecoming stories. My life is full of homecoming stories

Your life, no, I do not think so. Listen to me, when my grandmother returned to her town she was met by her former lover. She had not seen him for a dozen years, more. She had returned by air and had come unannounced.

Of course, I said, this is what we do.

Yet also she had wanted to see what things for her own self, wanted to journey into town by bus, from there disembark, continue the journey by foot, through the streets, she wanted to be among her people and see how they were in this new way, especially so the people of her little district, the places, buildings that stood or not, she would see the absent ones, absent people, she knew this, wanted it, from among her own people, from where from when she had been. I was not yet born you see

And he continued with this story, family story, his beginnings. There was the strain in telling it to me, and resignation, all familiar to me, now speaking of how his grandmother walked through her little town, seeing her world made anew. It was dreams, dreams. I would have closed my ears. Dreams dreams dreams. Whose story was this, his father's, mother's. I was not wanting to hear him and his dreams, dreams. I also have my family, families, their lives and thoughts and their future to be, not to be, as this, as he had, him to become, dreams, dreams. I could not listen to him. Also to sleep, so sleep, I was exhausted he was exhausted why not sleep, none would be there, none would find us, we were safe there in that hovel for that time what was his worry, there was none, worrier, I saw it in him, magician's eye, give sleep to us, strength to us.

What is wrong?

Nothing is wrong.

Yes, tell me.

I cannot listen to you, I cannot, dreams, I cannot listen. Dreams are also in my head. I survive with them, but they are only for myself, I do not ask that you share them, that you receive them from me. I do not want to hear these dreams that are your dreams, family dreams. I want to sleep and must do so, you may watch I may sleep

What is wrong?

I cannot listen to you. Dreams of homecomings, I cannot listen. You wish to go back but there is no such going back it is not possible does not exist, dream world. Live in this world which is a real world, where we now are in this decay, destroyed building, destroyed lives and dreams of life, deaths of children, killings of children, live in this world, this is why we now exist continue to exist spiting spiting, this is why, not for dreams, lives as once they were, what of my son and his story my story, where is his mother is she dead where I do not know now for three years so tell to me and his family to come, where are his mountains and rivers

I was now onto my feet. I walked around, kicked at the old old plasterwork, the rubble, perhaps something was to be found. Hiding places. Articles secreted there from years gone by. A woman hiding these from her husband, treasures. For the coming family. Thus to astonish him years later, their first daughter now to marry, and from this secret place she would bring out these treasures, hand-me-down trinkets, jewellery of ancestors, the husband dumbfounded, looking on her with amazement. These are for our grandchildren.

Stories stories, ghosts

I had not known of this place, this place where we now were, hovel, hovel as I thought

I was to the other side of the room. He was by the hole where had been a window, seated there, looking to the sky. I would apologise to him. He did not understand me. I did not make myself known to him, thoughts that I had, we were not so far apart. If these stories were so upsetting to me, they were so, I could tell him. Perhaps to others he might tell them, not to me, I could not hear them.

I had respect for him. But in that place there can only be ghosts, as in all places where humans are, and we are our ghosts also, they are within us, it is within us, as also death to come, his death my death. My question to him

yes, I had such a question. Certainly I was no stranger to this region. I had come so and again. He had respect for this. And so my question, what of my death, did he see my death? I had questions for him. And why I was there. These are not dreams. Why there is continuation. So many questions. I could ask him. Also his own death, was this true, did he feel this before him. As I did. We all of us, all, ourselves, every one, who did not who did not

Where does this come from. Do ghosts exist. What questions, may we ask them, all such any such, I have no God, gods

What is wrong? he said.

Nothing is wrong.

Sit down.

I have to walk.

You are tired.

Exhausted, yes, we both

But you make my nerves on end

I do not enjoy your stories

My grandmother when a girl, I was telling you of her life, but you cannot hear, you are not able to hear, you cannot listen

I can listen

You do not

Yes, if it is your grandmother. You say you are telling me of her but no, it is another subject, she is become so. This is a story for you, a story for why you continue to exist, a story that must exclude myself, such as myself, it can only exclude.

I am sorry.

243

I have no grandmothers, grandfathers, mother of my child, I have none.

I am sorry.

Why. I am not. I do not seek reasons, it is not important to me. I do not want these stories.

It is a story yet you cannot listen.

Homecoming stories.

A story from my family, he said. You do not listen.

I can listen, I shall listen, speak.

You command me?

I command you.

Thus I am commanded. So, my grandmother came home. She came firstly to town

Not village?

Town, the streets of her district, this was as she wanted, she had arrived at the seaport and come through customs and also visa, worried, worried.

You said airport.

Airport, yes. But through she came. All the taxis! She walked along and passed them by. She came into town by bus. No fanfare played for her, no bands massed for her. So she told us, humour always with her you see. A large woman and robust, she wore town clothes. Many of the women dressed that way, when they were home also. She came into town as desired, she herself desired, disembarked from the bus, now began walking, walking through the streets. Carried only one bag for luggage.

Now this is a dream, everyone's dream, one bag for luggage, simple thing, everyone's dream, life as it had been to recapture, her family friends and lovers, a moment in time, the stillness, it is everyone's dream.

It is not everyone's dream.

Yes.

It is not everyone's dream, it is not my dream, it is life, it is life in this story, for there, as she came walking through the streets she saw that in the street, there as she walked, after these years, there he was, there standing, her former lover.

What standing who standing what is it, story, what story this is no story

This is a homecoming, he said, homecomings are not simple things.

Yes.

No.

Mine will be simple.

Your homecoming!

Yes my homecoming why not my homecoming, my home-coming can be real thing, material life and not make-believe.

You dream of homecoming?

Yes. Why not?

He smiled, waited for me to speak more, but I was tired. I could have smiled. He said, You do not have dreams?

He was attacking me. I did not reply but only looked at him, then away.

You have dreams! I do not think you have dreams.

Everyone has dreams.

Of your own place?

Of your own place. Of your own place in my own place, in this hovel-place, place of ghosts, wherever place, whatever country, where we are, we ourselves, any place, I have dreams, any place.

He laughed and then was silent.

Any place that I am.

My grandmother's dreams, he said, this was her village, her country. He stared at me and I saw the strain in him.

You speak of me as a foreigner, stranger to this region. I am not so, I said, I am not so. Why do you say it?

I am sorry.

It is not sorry, sorry is nothing, I ask you why. You speak of my country, it is my country, well and I do not speak of it.

That is your own make-believe, it is what you need, a necessity that you demand, you and some other of your people, always, to see it in front of your eyes. And you have me in front of your eyes, representative of my country, you have it here, but I am not representative.

What are you saying?

I said it.

But it is nonsense.

Well it is nonsense. You say to me of my country, that is nonsense, also your grandmother, more nonsense, make-believe story, but I am to listen to you. You demand it of me, using rank at me, that I listen to a justification, the struggle now is for what existed in the past. This is not dreams but make-believe lies. You are telling me lies, seeking reasons, there are no reasons.

What do you say to me?

You are telling me lies, seeking reasons, there are no reasons, I do not know reasons, they do not exist.

I do not tell you lies. He glanced off and out through the hole where had been a window.

You say my country is another country. You say this to me, call it my country but I do not call it so, I am not there but here, I am here, in your country, your country is my country and you must allow it, it is this, you must allow it. If it is not to be so allowed, if not by yourself, so I do not know, there cannot be such justification. There is not only your struggle, not only your struggle. Are you observing ourselves, engaged not engaged, lawyers from overseas, all observers from international sources, foreign journalists of media, who are you now become, tell me?

One who does not tell you lies.

You do not tell me lies?

No.

Where is the cigarette?

What?

The cigarette? You had it.

The cigarette is gone. It is gone now.

Through the hole I saw layers of dark cloud. Dusk. If there had been sunset we would not have seen it. I could be sleeping, only ten minutes. I could sleep then he could sleep. I thought to say so again and began to but stopped. What was I to say, what had I said to him. He sat with his shoulders held, elbows to his sides, not able to relax but he might sleep in that posture.

He was thinking of morning. He would be thinking now for longer, not talking but in his own head. I could sleep ten minutes, he could waken me.

What morning would bring. It was a useless concern. I wanted to have him understand this. We had been together now five days. I had respect for him. He took the role of leader. It was a natural thing to myself but I said nothing and thus he was the leader. Through that I regained strength, I shall say it, facing the time to come. He it was.

I laid old plasterwork down, covered it with crumpled newspapers, lay with it as a pillow. I said to him, Speak, otherwise I shall sleep

You command me?

I command you.

My grandmother?

And her lover, yes.

Yes, he said, so, in her district. She had arrived there, walking through her streets, in her town, as you know, enjoying what had been her desire, as you know, the smells and the sounds, shades and light, hustle and bustle of people, all as you know, busy busy busy, and children, daughters and sons who are to live lives of great beauty, such existences, famous artists and authors, musicians and philosophers, all, all who are there, peoples and peoples, around her, everywhere, and it was in her place, was her home, this was to where, and there now in front of her, as the years had vanished, her former lover was standing, yes, standing there.

He shook his head and stared at the hole in the wall. I saw his right hand, the knuckles clenching, the tension at his eyes.

So tell me. I reached to his hand, to the back of it, rubbing the veins there. He watched me doing this. Do not worry, I said, you are tired, I am tired, we both are tired.

I am not tired.

You are tired, I see your magician's eye, it is black now and sunken, it may fall out and I shall not catch it, I am tired, it shall fall to the insects thus we are to sleep, you first I shall be awake, alert, I shall watch these stars through this window.

I am not tired.

Yes.

I am thinking of another time. Still my grandmother, a friend of hers, from schoolchildren days. This had been a best friend, girls together

Sharing their dreams.

Sharing their dreams, yes.

This is a future for ourselves, sharing our dreams, only men together not girls. I am your grandmother's best friend.

He smiled. You are holding my hand, oh lover.

I am holding your hand. Now no, take it. You must sleep, your brain is exhausted.

First is the story. Later, when she had bathed

Who, spirit-lady, angel from god?

Young lady, she had freshened, changed her traveller's clothes, bathed and freshened, she made a telephone call to my grandmother's lover

You people had telephones? You people, you had telephones?

My family was wealthy, computers and pianos, all new technologies, telephone call to this lover, her friend made this call. It was at that time I tell you now that her former lover, I have to tell you now. This young man, thirty-five years

Grandfather, you are returning to him?

Her former lover, yes.

But about the girl, young lady?

Ah.

Tell me!

You are listening.

Tell me about her, how tall and what shape?

What?

What, tell me.

I do not know, tell you, tell you what?

Under her clothes, what shape? Loose clothes?

Loose clothes, yes.

What shape?

What?

Clinging? Clothes clinging, to her body, fresh-smelling?

Fresh-smelling.

Fresh-smelling!

Yes, scented.

What age?

As my grandmother, friends from schoolchildren days.

Yes but at that time I want to know, of when you speak.

She was not a girl, of the time I speak, it is you now, dreaming, it is you.

You said so.

No.

Yes.

No, it is you who is now worried, worrying. But you should not, these are stories, homecomings, leavetakings.

You are wrong.

I am not wrong. He smiled. There will be a time for you also. Yes, there will be.

Not for me.

Yes, for you.

No.

He now did not speak but instead clapped my shoulder and was shaking his head. I knew that turn in him, but as also in me, it was also in me. And this moment later when he had tensed, I too, we both, tensing. There were things he was to say to me but these times would not come into existence. He saw I was waiting and he waited also. I nodded he nodded, having heard simultaneously, knowing there was not sleep and what was to happen from this moment

but of course his judgment vindicated. And when he raised his arm we were moving from there so very quickly. Yes it was then, as we moved from that abandoned old place, that first explosion, I was behind him. We separated. If he said something further, I do not think so, if he did so, it is that I forget it, I had been tired, we both of us, I do not know, perhaps, I may not have heard it, I have said so, that I did not see him again.

43

"letter fragments"

I hoped all might be well with her. I do not know what to
say, nor then, to her. We should play together and I should
take you on long walks. Do you have your friends? It is good
to have friends. In the future this will be past and I shall be
home with you. Do you see mountains from the window? In
the mountains one can walk and see no one after miles. If
one

it is I that say it myself, myself, having walked in the mountains and there are streams throughout, down from the higher
peaks. This water is the purer, clear and cold, it is healthy
water, no living thing has touched this water. I can take you
there, if your mother is also home, where she is, if she will
be come home then. Do you have a letter from your mother?
If your grandmother hears of her, perhaps she does and has
had a letter from her, your mother, you can ask your grandmother of this. I shall be home soon.

Here is not so good as home. People here are strangers to me,
you would also think it. I work with funny men, they say
things that are funny but sometimes I do not like them. It is
necessary work. Until it is finished I shall be here but perhaps
it will finish sooner. Here it is flat and if there is a little hill

people say of it it is a mountain, you might laugh to hear them

If your mother has spoken to your grandparents, perhaps she has, you may ask them

I have written this letter to your mother. I do not know where you are. I have heard of our daughter, she is good, healthy, a friend has said it to me, he is trusted. What is wrong? How are you, if you are in good health, nothing has happened to you

I have written this to your mother. How are you? Are you in good health? I think here of yourself, and our daughter, how is our daughter, is she in good health. She should have friends. It is not so fine where I now am, people are not the same, they are not what to say I think trusted, I say that I do not trust them but what that is to say who is one to trust, in all this life, do we trust people, how many, if we have one person to trust then we trust him but how many might there be, if I complain, yes, I am the greater fool, and without you

"newcomer, I am the fool"

She had not found space by the wall for many others were there, also two babies, one who would not sleep. I had gone for something, now returning with it in one container, tea, also one cigarette. The space was to the centre of the floor, she was seated there, covering drawn to her waist. She was exhausted I was exhausted, more. So, in the darkness now, stepping over bodies, not spilling liquid, passing the container to her, sitting down close to her, now lying farther, farther, my head at her waist, we smoked the cigarette, later she was placing her hand to my forehead, closing my eyes as the child, as I would to a child, now feeling the covering, draught of it, she having drawn it over my body, once more her hand to my forehead, it becoming as a weight on me, until then I was hearing music from childhood days, religious times, yes in my head choral music, these low drums, also tapping hands, other sounds, and other sounds also there and I was coming awake, this fellow's voice, stranger's voice, he had arrived in our space, sitting here by my companion, and whispering to her. If he was a security, it was possible, where silence was the answer, who was not there and the room in darkness and the whining of the one baby, now moaning, it was its lungs, little thing, and not good. My eyelids were closed, it was thought I was sleeping, I did not open them, only listening listening but I could not make sense, I did not know this voice, who was he. And now my companion spoke, yes if there was agitation in her voice, yes, I heard it but that as I lay next to her and was to the other side from this newcomer, who spoke so quietly to her on the side other than myself. What she did say, nor what this other said to her, I do not know, sounds and not any sense, a droning. Anxiety was in her voice. Certainly.

I opened my eyes only a little, that I might not to be seen. Who else might be there. There only was he, that one. But this space was small, who else might have entered. But outside this area I could not say, if others, yes, perhaps waiting for this one beyond here.

He was speaking as forcing an issue onto her, that I was not present, addressing herself alone, so for him I was not in existence. If he was entirely a stranger to myself, he was not so to my companion. I understood this, he was familiar. Only something in her, lightness of tone in speaking, easy manner, I cannot say, perhaps as in movement how she stretched her legs, confidence also was there in her. Yes she knew this man. Intimately perhaps, it is possible. I worried so at these earlier moments and could not discard the thought. Yet also in my companion there was caution, knowing him she did not trust him, what it was there, personal impersonal, what it was, I sensed it there. A silence had come between them, and my throat now, irritation, my mouth dry my throat dry, yes, we had smoked the cigarette earlier. I would have reached for the container, perhaps tea remained there. Perhaps my companion had given it to this stranger. He was speaking again, whispering, so not to disturb people around, also for eavesdroppers, some always were awake, seeing things hearing things.

Who was he. I could suppose. If in former days political, they might say. I say security, then as now. But if these two had been in struggle together, why should she not say, afterwards she might say it to me. We would speak.

We did so together. Not for every thing. I did not say to her she was beautiful, I did not say to her how I loved to see her, only to see her. Our coming together was a recent thing.

Intimacy. What is meant by this. The sexual act, of course but also intimacy meaning moments together, safely, safety, if to relax and as then if asleep by her, safekeeping.

If she knew this stranger. She knew him, it is beyond doubt. I lay still, listening. In his voice was humour, irony, yes and also there I heard someone cynical, his quiet quiet voice oh do not trust this man.

Who could care for this. I did not. Oh yes, pretending analysis, international situations, worldly perspectives. I now could make sense and knew it, knew also it was not serious from him. Analysis of the situation, the political, all manoeuvres and movements, intervention from unlikely sources, foreign sources. No, he could not be trusted, even as he spoke. Surely my companion knew this. If she might listen to this in seriousness, no, I could not believe it. I made the movement as waking, opening my eyes, blinking, yawning, other detail, looking to herself but then to the newcomer, and puzzled. And my companion looked to me, gestured at him. I was yawning again and she whispered to me, He is repeating a lecture. Hear him, it is a lecture.

But you know different, I said.

I know different, yes.

But she had not liked that I spoke to her as I did. I looked to the newcomer, to her again. And in my look was my question but no, she did not introduce this man, neither himself, he did not do so.

What then I was to do, what, leave this place where we were. What was expected of myself. No. I did not know. I smiled but faltered and only I think was staring, I do not know. It was in darkness there and others were around, children also as I have said babies and not all were sleeping and if someone smoked the light also would affect us and all were conscious of others during this period and would not talk loudly and would be careful for others, how else, if there is continuation we must take such routes for other people, each of these days was survival, are we to survive I am to survive, and my neighbours, what are the children here may we look after them, the lungs of the baby, what, what anyone is to do, the mother or the father who were like myself, young people. Yes, I was young, if so, growing older.

The newcomer scratched his ear. I understood he was expecting of her that she might know this scratching as a sign, signifying an experience shared, as from a former period that they were together, knowledge one to another, intimacy of them, shared of them. I knew it. It was certain. But if he wanted her to recall this shared moment she did not, did not, nor any response to him.

He now was silent, waiting for some other thing, perhaps of myself, response of a different form, might I enter into this, if we were in competition. He would fight with me. Yes. If he was fighting for her, aggression certainly was in him, and subtlety of voice also, yes, he was a dangerous man. But I too, also, if he thought to intimidate myself then we might see, let us, we can see what would happen. But if he was a security. There was no sign from my companion, none to myself. Under the covering her leg lay against mine, she was not removing it, also now from her was a pressure, and I laid my hand onto her thigh, and in a moment her leg was into a new position and I moved my hand, from her. And he was speaking again now in his quiet quiet voice, conversing, it was simply that, he was here to be conversing, waking us from sleep that he might simply converse, his nonsense talk, international affairs and relations yes we do not know this, cannot understand this cannot comprehend this I am a poor peasant of the low low classes of people, lower classes of people. Who has power, yes not myself, not myself, not we. I listened to him

listened to him

What was happening. I was not in battle, not fighting. In warfare, what warfare. Certainly for himself, if this was fighting of we two, himself myself, what fighting had he done. I could not know yet in his manner there was surety, surety. Yes a dangerous man, I say so.

My companion did not make introductions. Why. It was courtesy. What else would she have done. She had allowed intimacy between them, a familiarity. If a courtesy to myself also the newcomer, we having no knowledge, one to the other. I knew nothing but that he coveted her, yes, of course, what is to say here there is nothing he coveted her and her body was from mine, removed herself, her leg from my leg. Yes it is foolish, these things are foolish, as if life, if life is serious, I cannot discover when it is so, perhaps never.

I know it. If I did not say it. Of course. The container of tea was with him and so I reached for it. I held the tea to my lips. But she watched, frowning. I acted not to notice, folding my arms after drinking. Now I was not so exhausted, not so tired, and withdrew from the covering, my legs up now to be squatting, yes, I could have sprung, power from there, yes. I said to her, Yes, it would be good for a cigarette now. Also for wine, brandy, if we had something.

Ssh

Ssh

People are sleeping.

Yes, people are sleeping, you say it for myself not to him, when I am speaking, you say it only for myself.

Now she looked to me and I saw in her eyes the sparking, it was in her eyes, sparking. Shining, in darkness but I did see it, a light from some other place reflected there, perhaps her spirit. Also as a child. She had one photograph in her box, keeping it there, and she showed it to me, this of herself, ten years old. Certainly she was beautiful, I can see her, bright eyes, limbs, laughing, playful. If I then was thinking of my own family, and thinking of these old days when my own wife had not disappeared I did so also with this woman who now was my companion, had become so, I thought that she was.

But this newcomer, what he had said, I did not respect it and thought surely she did not, how she could believe it it was falsity, falsity, if she did so believe it. But what he was saying to her, listening and I heard and was understanding that also it was the analysis of our situation from higher level of command, as he had access, had had access. Yet I did not doubt such was or had been his access. If she listened. She did listen. I do not say *believed*, listening only, but with greater attention. I know it. International perspectives, international corporations, co-operations, peacetime wartime co-operations. Concerns of these powers, obligations also, charitable to such as us, duties, yes, to such as, all to such as us, so he said, what is such as us, if shareholders he said it is security he said you know security, what is security.

He looked to me. I did not answer. What is warfare. I would not answer him, argue, not answer. Did he know I had the weapon, he must have. He said it again to me. What is security. I looked at her and she said to the newcomer. We are alive, we three.

I said, Yes, we are alive.

You are too loud.

I am too loud.

There are children here.

What

You are too angry, she whispered.

These statements he makes, I am too angry, this rhetoric that is nonsense for whose ears, to whose ears, to ours, to mine, not to mine, to yours perhaps, not to mine, it is falsity. Yes he would anger myself. Yes.

I saw now he was looking to myself and directly, in no fear, I did not think so, not physically, not as intellectual, in thoughts, arguments, conjectures and beliefs, that we may have had, any of it none of it, it was of no account to him, neither myself as a man, I was of no account, only I was stupid.

To him anything, I did not care. What he had for me, nothing. But he would be here and think anything was for him. Who was he, what to this woman who was my companion, what was he, and now he was looking to me and he spoke, quietly, calmly. He addressed my companion as before but now was looking to me also, so not to exclude, not excluding myself.

We cannot effect change, he said, also it is our preference. Our people should not dispel energy, not needlessly, as in discussion of these matters. If decisions are made elsewhere and our energy is crucial, as it is, your energy our energy my energy, for all of us, we accept this as adult beings, mature beings, we cannot challenge as from no basis it becomes nonsense strategy, reflection of fools, suited to youthful years.

Listen to him, whispered my companion.

Yes I listen to him but it is his behaviour, I recognise it, and as without respect, yes without respect, certainly it is patronising. Youthful years. What this does mean, if he knows anything, anything or nothing.

The newcomer looked to my companion, a smile was on his face. She said, He is a colleague, friend also, we have been in situations of complexity, issues of greater importance, superiors and others, all were present, foreign people, authoritys.

Thus I am to obey this man, obedience to him? No. What is this obligation? He is older man, oh, I must be respectful!

Sarcasm, she said.

Sarcasm, yes.

Foolish, she said, now turning from me, turning also from this newcomer, looking to other people there. She always would say what was the case, what that she believed it to be, never rising to such as this, if wasting her breath, she would not, and her irritability, I saw it and might have laughed but that what had happened before was again happening, and her irritability was against myself.

259

I could not believe it. It was not to this other one, only myself. How could I believe it. Yet it was true. She did not disguise her perception of a situation, not from myself, I would see it, I would know it. It was this newcomer having his influence, affecting her behaviour. Of course it was puzzling to me, of course. Now where my anger was it was other factors, emotions. I thought to drink the tea, it would have nauseated me, my stomach.

Now this one spoke across her so that she stopped talking, staring at the floor. He was talking to myself, looking to myself. I did not know. I said nothing. I was not talking to him. Energy for nothing. What was he talking, why we were to allow it, talking in this manner. I said, Why are you here? What is happening?

The newcomer would have spoken but was stopped by my companion who whispered to me. You must listen to him, it is important.

What is important, what he says, of course it is important, if you say it, I shall concede it.

You are bitter, said the newcomer.

I am bitter.

Matters are acute to us.

Matters that cannot be aired are acute to us, matters that we require none to inform us, of what exists in our midst, we do not require such information thrust down our throats, I said, not from colleagues. Neither lectures, we do not require lectures, not from such as yourself.

He looked to my companion, It is contempt, he said, contempt from him.

Then how do you respond? If you are to respond.

He smiled. I shall respond.

In what way?

Again he smiled.

I thought how easily I could strike him. My companion was

unsmiling, and her agitation, I saw it. Now she looked to myself. I was a puzzle to her. The newcomer whispered, You are returning?

Yes, if it is possible, sooner or later.

Your companion has his own plans, perhaps strategies. He smiled again to her, and not to me, now taking from his coat a pack of cigarettes, matches, passing the cigarette to me. I did not accept it. He looked to her. Now I did accept and he had the match, striking it for me. I did not lean to him, he now moved his hand with the lighted match so that I could take the light, not moving too much for it. I did not see at his eyes in that glare. I smoked the cigarette for more than two draws, and did not look to them, until returning it to him. He smoked one draw and gave it to her.

Yes you are irritable, she said to me. It was not spoken as to goad you. It is a philosophy he outlines to you, allow him to further advance his argument.

We have all the time, I said.

We have time, she said.

Yes. I whispered to the newcomer, What will you tell me now, of foreign lawyers and theoreticians, yes, very moral people, talk to us of them, members of the human species, tell me of securitys, how they also are people, we may respect humanity, they may answer back to us, answering questions firstly, the killing will follow, nothing will change, only speakers.

The newcomer passed the cigarette on to me.

This is not sarcasm, I said, only tell me. He made a gesture, not as to antagonise. Now there was silence. I smoked the cigarette. Only a little was left, I ground it out. I thought now of all that I could say, and said it to her, You do not wish me here.

I saw her exhaustion, knees drawn up, arms folded on them, chin resting. I could see her eyes. We had been in awkward circumstances, situations. Who had not been. I also was exhausted, body aching, food.

She said, What do you mean. You are speaking nonsense, I do not want to hear nonsense.

What is wrong?

Nothing is wrong. I am tired of you. You are irritable, your bitterness, we cannot talk, you will not allow it, I see your face, he says things and you must deny you must deny you cannot listen.

I cannot listen.

No.

No, I said, I cannot. You are tired of me, he is here and you say it. No, not to me, you will not do it. It is not justifiable.

Nothing is justifiable.

Yes, I am wrong, I am sorry for it. I got onto my feet quickly, looking not to her, neither to him never to him. Nearby I heard movement and further stirring from others, some listening, they could not do other, I could not blame them, and I said again to her, No, this is not justifiable. And I left her, striding from her, the bitterness in me and what reason what reason.

And now happened that most unexpected thing, a security was in the doorway out from our building and I knocked into him, and off balance he falling. My impulse was to strike at him I was angry, to hurt him, and overpowered him could have struck at him easily but did not or would have been dead at once. He lay a moment then twisting and rolling immediately off from myself as expecting blows from myself. Now he saw it, knew what it had been, an accident, and he was onto his feet and he moved now towards me, as I also backwards. He gripping my arm and up under my shoulder turning my body, knocking me sideways and down and I was on the ground, himself on top, astride my shoulders now, and angry so very angry I thought to see his knife now to cut my throat. You fool. If I had had strength, I had none, I could not have unseated him. More securitys now behind and to the side. You fool, he said, and looking into my eyes as I also. Our eyes, myself himself.

About him I do not know, staring down but I also to him, and he saw that and I saw his face, expressive. He was older, heavy on me, now that I could see him. He shook his head. You are a fool.

As you also I said but into my mind, but why insult him, this was my own self to blame for this, striking into him so that he was foolish, looking so, if his other colleagues were there. My mind then went to my child. I thought I am dying they must kill me now, she will not know. Instead he slapped my face, and greater force, feeling at the corner of my eye if it was the skin tore, as though my eye would hit into my nose and fall out. One security laughed. One other said, A slapping for him, he is a naughty boy.

Instead if they had killed me, I thought it then, if death was to come it would be peace, if none was to know, not anything.

I remained on the ground. My eyes were open. The securitys had gone. Voices now also gone. Nothing. But the night, it also had gone. If I had lost consciousness, perhaps I did do so. How long I was there lying, if I did glimpse her, perhaps. There was good light, moonlight, sunlight, towards dawn. I thought I did see her in the doorway, a shape there. I could see a person, someone there observing. Now as in a dream what she was doing, images crowded of my companion and the newcomer, these two now together, and the voice now that I heard it, strongly, this voice talking, These people want from me what is it they want from me.

Later it was dawn. I walked by the perimeter, securitys were there, one challenged me. I acted as though not hearing that he might ignore me. None else may have heard, there was no necessity that a confrontation should take place. But he stepped sideways into my path and raised his arm and I stopped and his eyes stared into myself, a moment there standing until he thought not to bring matters further. What is there to die for. I can die for it, not as others had done, if others had done, my own death might be for anything, nothing. I walked to the outer area, others were here. If there is the wish to die it is nothing to talk about.

The moon was not part of it, the moon was above another part of it, someone's world where children were and smells of old people, people near to death, now from the other section smells also. Later I would return to mine, securitys by the door, barring entry, now seeing myself, raising the weapon, I was no threat. Of course she would have gone, nothing there in the space, also clothings that I had, these also gone.

The security was in my path.

How long it had been here in this place. Some detailed the days and the weeks.

45

"letter to widow, unfinished"

Unfortunately no one told me of his death. I would have wanted to know. I would have thought of him. At the farewell-gathering I could have sat by myself, ensuring some solitary time. This is the ritual. I could have performed it. I know about rituals that they may allow us an understanding and in this will lie their worth. Ritual is far from a bad thing, if under the fore-going, if it is so.

Then during the periods of repose these moments where nothing is demanded of us, reflection on the individual now deceased often will transform itself into lived-experience and we are remembering scenes of our youth, feelings that we shared, our various leanings, political, sporting, other, also love, loves, early ideas of love. I here am referring to the deepmost experi-ences of our youth. We re-encounter the most vivid images of greatness, future greatness, for the species, of which we are a part, gloriously. We think then of tragedy, for we consider humanity itself. We consider individual human beings, we regard them as tragedies and ponder on meaning, their significance for us. We are aware these are not the experience of youth, that we have no true knowledge of such a thing, as a tragedy, its reality, which is for adults, and we are able to glorify in that, as in our youth, we glorify in this now, this present, this

communing,

that we are here in the face of a form of greatness, for what else is death?

This is how we think. Yet too we would know it as erroneous. When we become older we are aware that tragedy is an experience, deeply, another experience, another reality, this is what it has become, that we encounter it throughout our lives, individuals whom we have enjoyed, who have become no longer with us, and we are to experience this.

In these most difficult moments such as that now before us we think how would it be if our children were present. I also think this. I cannot halt the thought, my own child. And could such a thing be possible? Have children, dependent children, been present? Of course they have. What did the father do? Did he cope? If it is not possible to cope. Myself to think so, for to what is it akin, or may it be so? War situations, where one has to have one's children? Be at war but take care of them. Yes. And to go further, we must recognise that this is as it is for all parents, as we are and have been, and for all time. If I may think of Egyptian peasants of 7000 years ago in the knowledge that this is not ruled out as a form of hell, that drawing an exception to this rule indicates only the nature of generality, that a rule may enclose any number of general indicators, only they are a guide to behaviour, behaviour that is difficult in situations grasped as socially awkward. But from the earliest time we both set out to show the positive aspect to this, that these insurmountable burdens superficially are so, only so, that they do much to alleviate the unbearable, unbearable action, the nature, of our present environment.

I become weary of the extension, it becomes further descent, my own inability, and lack

Movement, confined space, always that presupposition. Examples?

I received word of his death too late. No one advised me earlier. I regret this. It is awkward, is to be so expressed.

Yet such as this cannot be helped, these are the thoughts,

there is a time for such thoughts, it is during the grieving, perhaps at the outset, of the grieving period, and no one told me of his death, no one told me, I write to you

I write to you

46

"this comes back"

If I could not move my body if it was not broken. You have him, he said, voice coming from where. It was not, I was not, this was a floor, floor, pallet and covering, and the hand at my groin and I moved, shifting onto my side and it over me the arm over me the hand gripping me. The heat great and sweat, old layers. If my head was beneath the covering I would not breathe, I knew it, could not, suffocating, I knew it. Drifting again into sleep, something like sleep, a pain dissipated. If I would awaken, if it was a dream passing, an event past, from earlier in life or if it had been happening how long a long time, and the erection now, thinking it happening, it was happening, as endless thing, as dreams are, cyclic. And I was awake again, and the hand having me there gripping me, I felt the heat also from her body. I barely could move, stretch only my limbs. What was it asked, things asked. If things were asked I heard them then the next moment had arrived, I would not know until the moment to follow, or longer, how long, hours. What these questions were. The hand gripped me, tight in, strength there squeezing, yet I would open my legs, wishing I might do so but what the dread was, or dreading that I was, but was not it was not,

Also in my memory, and with that the dread, and the body behind, somebody known to me, I thought, known to me, and a sickening feeling. Had I seen this woman I thought I had seen this woman. Something of my life now was ended and this other thing that I knew, also finished, that I cared about, this other thing, it too, it was beyond, what

And if resisting. I was resisting. It was passive and had to be passive, not to move that I was known to be conscious. It was to loosen myself, in preparation. I would relax, but in preparation, try for that. Her hand big round me my penis small, gripping my testicles, big round me her hand, and clutching, my eyes shut, my chest constricted, needing properly to breathe but not that power, I wanted a strength so to accomplish this, and my lungs, I was gulping, not to gasp, spits of light behind my eyes, sparking, pin-points, behind my eyes now suffocating. My chest.

It comes in saliva, we tell these things. I just was to lie. I could not fight my way clear. They could not know I was conscious. I would die. I am saying that. I knew it, it was not possible, speaking of escape, it was to control the nerves in my stomach, that I may control the nerves in my stomach or the oxygen leaving my lungs but beyond this not controlling any thing and my chest such heaving if my lungs exploded, if it is happening to myself

My memory, thinking of past moments, these things of home. My child, her mother, dead or alive, parents, brothers, sisters. Who was dead now? Disappearances, who could say. Later I might see her, my colleague my love perhaps much later but I would see them. Perhaps tomorrow, it might be tomorrow. Of how things would be then, tomorrow, my child was smiling as also my father, he too was smiling, my father. A time in the future, not so far away, he does not see us yet we are there, I with his daughter-in-law and granddaughter, he does not see that we approach the house, we are coming to our home. He is at the window, gazing where, as from afar, as into a past, not seeing me, not seeing me, I walk with my wife and my daughter, I walk with them, are we upon him, he does not see us. And suddenly that moment, and I am to the rear watching this way that way, while my child skips ahead, that we are safe, we are alive, his son and his grand-daughter, daughter-in-law, my colleague, my lover, he sees us, yes, they are coming, they are coming, he shouts to my mother, here they are coming, who do you think it is your son and granddaughter, they are coming home! My father smiling. I could hear no breathing and the body was not pressing against me yet behind once more and I was drifting, aware of the body was to me seeming hard even muscular yet in places flabby, or soft. I wondered what of *her* who this might be. I saw a woman, her arms were folded beneath her breasts, no eyes were in her face. And I was concentrating, and distinguishing a smell, sensing it, I would know it. Now a sensation into my toes, bones. The hand now massaging my testicles, I was grateful, my breathing regulated, then too, at peace, it too, I might settle like that, it was possible, the weight of the arm across me on my side, no, it was ended now and would not resume. I accepted that if it was over that it might yet have been dreams, or temporary, if it would end soon, would end soon, and I was to have a freedom, freedom coming to me. But for myself then it was how to get from this, it was a plight, and dangerous, I always had recognised this as a situation with greater danger for myself, the figure, who had me here, this power, more powerful than myself, much more. If I could not escape I would have been in these throes, death throes

displacement, displacement

if who I was, whom I was, identity, who was I, in my space now shifting. Where. And I was drifting, and tingling, behind my eyes, listening I might hear, hearing a rumbling, a groan, all sensations, and laughter. I could move, moving onto my back and the body as a dead weight moving with me, but what pain now using my wrist this pain so pain, edging along the blanket, the head and body there at me, my wrists, breathing into me, and on my other side the other body, now backed into me, woman now, was this it, feeling against me, I thought so it was, then heavy at me, on my testicles now gripping me, my wrists. The covering was heavy, I could barely shift it, now raised from me, hanging, wrapping itself down on me. I was having to burrow down and out from the bottom, covering, pushing my way out, how the caterpillar might do it, front or backwards, to burrow down. But down only so far, so far. I stopped, fearful and heat, becoming trapped, I would, heat, heat there.

This gripping of my shoulders begun again I experienced the jolting, sparks thudding pain, and into within my bones what pain pain where I do not know having no control forcing into me I had no control none could be had this pain agonising gasping from me thinking that thought of myself, thought of myself, always the mediator, I was, always, what did my father do, or for me, betrayal, community leaders and elders, betrayal, voices can scream from within me, smile and scream from within me it was happening, what, if it was pain it was pain. I see my own woman, colleague, my lover, she is smiling, the sun in her eyes and she shades them. I see her wipe at the dryness at the corner of her mouth, wiping at the dryness, she has that dryness always. It does not worry her but myself what is it such a dryness. The sparking comes and goes, spits of light, pin-points, turning over, where my legs. The other body, I knew who this was, this person now here, I knew, who this was, had led me to here, to this, I knew, and now the weight onto me. Do not move, he said. And if I could I can not move, could not have moved, it was not possible. He forced me forwards, his hand to my neck, I heard a grunting but not him I think, not him it was the other with him. You have him, now grunting and amusement. I do not want him I want you and laughter you cannot have me but you can have him so too yes, if it was, what womans, my head is to the side, turning and my neck stiffly as to snap they would snap my neck, bone there backbone my legs from the covering what pressure these points pin-pricks stabbing

"sea dreams"

Such a freedom. The calmness of the water. The seabirds had vanished.

I was again in the depth of the dream, boyish, favoured book from childhood, discovering the secret world, how the waves concealed a myriad of things. Swimming far down, far far down, there in the sea, or ocean, the greatest of depth, the coldness and dark dark waters, searching, yes, secret passageway, in search of the secret passageway, security by three octopi I had to fight for the right of entry and swim with great difficulty through the narrowest of chambers, tight twists and turns, claustrophobic, ever-pressing, now fighting for breath my lungs swelling to burst, pricks of light, blue sharp electric voltage gasping gasping, last gasping, kicking hard and the walls of the chamber into a tunnel, would I stick fast here, tunnel, decreasing and with its twists and turns then finally the brightening, sun rays lined through the water, above that light, safety light, kicking for it this last upsurge towards the end of the tunnel, and into another chamber when breaking the surface but now the new world and an individual there, a colleague, he handed me a container, it was of tea, inside it was green tea, lemon juice, refreshing drink. It was a sea estuary of greater size, we had entered a greater sea estuary, the engine chugging, the pilot savouring the approach. There was his respect for this place, I sensed it. Of its three shores the one to which we sailed took shape distinctly, a cluster of buildings. We were entering a canal system and with wooden footbridges arching at unexpected angles, impressing that here was no theoretical work but a world, its countless generations of human endeavour, occupying different positions, erected in all different periods down through the past, way way far-off.

These buildings were unique one to another.

A large boat was moving towards us, two employees inside. The boat glided past, the men rowing, neither looked in our direction and were soon out of view. My father. He was there and his younger brother. I thought of them as the employees, they disappeared for now we were at the jetty, a security having prepared for landing and when he showed me up onto a passageway he returned thereafter to the launch. I was to wait. Soon came one other security, gesturing to my bag. What of my bag, but I did not wait, only lifting it onto my shoulder, carefully. So to the other side of the jetty, moored there was a skiff, he was indicating this and then from inside he rowed me a distance, it was to a single-storey structure on one of the outer bands on the eastern perimeter. When I was onto the passageway there the skiff had vanished and there was a peace

aspects of myself

and for the whole of that evening I remained in my room. By the window, shutters half drawn. The sky was keeping alive

and closeby the moon

and in these patches the water yellowish, not black, not translucent, where it was not black the water, not yellowish, only translucent, the shimmering effect seeming to give a yellow towards the outer sections

translucence

Other buildings and structures within view were dense, dense objects, strange objects. This place also, now it was strange to me, that it might cease to exist by virtue of my having become part of it. But I could never truly be part of it. No matter what transpired it would lie always outside of myself. Certain things, they are thought to change but merely recharge, in appearance dormant

It was very late when I went to sleep and in that last moment of wakefulness forcing myself to utter words. These words shame me now. I pulled the covering over my head in order to say them aloud, the blood rushing to my face, roaring in my eardrums. What were these words, they are gone from my memory, humiliations, shamed by these things, essences, I cannot say, such humiliations occurring only when the individual is alone

And on the parapet a bird looking at me while the music of the wind

these are dreams

witnessing the clarity, freshening, the freedom we can desire, we can

dreams

the wooden spars in the wind, boards of the passageways, creaking

Next morning I saw that the shutters had been left as they were and I was up from the floor, my bed, out from my bed, and across and trying to pull open the window, it opening in such a way that if I could squeeze through my head I could not, only with difficulty, greater difficulty, then could see out, shouting into the morning, not able to stop myself, yes shouting, and the echoes!

And when I managed to close over the shutters

vastness, something of the spirit, godlike

yes, closing over the shutters and remembering my parents, why thoughts of them, I cannot say, I had had to close over the shutters, close over my eyelids, hoping not to think, not to be aware of any thing, any thing, yes, it was no dream here, no dreamworld, here were these others, here was danger, we would move carefully here, was it a haven, no, no haven, boyish dreams, haven for these, and there also I saw the tourists, foreign people, vendors and strangers, if what they were looking for, if they were here why were they, I looked for the elderly, and where were the children, if our children

But it too was a dream, sea dreams here too. Why we do heal, we do heal

48

"it is said that I did"

I did not kill him. It is said that I did, I did not. I wonder when these things are said. Who says it. Why. All have aims and objectives, targets they must achieve. We can say goals, we have goals. I played football. I was in midfield, football player as we say fed to strikers, broke down attacks, attacks by opponents, yes, strikers of the opponents, I was to win the ball, such was my job, security job, the objective from my role. Break down these attacks, my coach would advise me. How you do it, this is your own self. Think of football, passing play, these Germans or English, from France, what they do, or from South America what they do, Uruguay, the Argentine, also Spain, they break down attacks. It is what I do. Others perform to a standard that is greater, Brazil, Italy, Netherlands. It is good, I would not say bad, why? We recognise good play, good players also, of course we must. My coach would say those things, advising myself, his advice was proper.

What we say do we say

I did not kill him. Why? It then was finished. If it was finished. It was finished, so if he was the problem to myself then it was finished, what

Who says it? People say things. What people? I ask that.

These men would play football. Football is manly, we do not break legs. Legs are broken but it is not as in design, the purpose. This purpose, no purpose. It happens as peripheral, always peripheral bones do break, they are brittle. Some bones are brittle. Mine are not brittle, nor ever were they brittle, not weakened. Some are weakened. These men look of the strongest but are not. It is no pretence. They do not know that they are weak. They believe themselves strong, of the stronger and enter the tackle to see only that their legs are broken, pelvis fractured, collar bone also broken, necks also, they are broken, skulls shatter. People do not know, these men who are strong, thinking themselves so, and we who are their opponents, entering into these tackles that we might win the ball, the breakdown of attacks by our opponents.

Defenders are also strikers, striking down our opponents.

What do our coaches say?

I would play for my country. It is we who play and play it our own selves. If we are to refrain in tackling we cannot do so that then damage may be done us ourselves. Footballers know it, if one footballer is one own self, one own self, one person, then one does know it

what

Damage has not been done to myself. My body is strong. In tackles I did not depart in injury, I did not acquire injury, my bones are not brittle. I was in many tackles, I was midfield player, fed to strikers, broke down opponents.

I did not kill him. Yes I saw this man. I did not know him. I saw him, had seen him, yes, many times, some times, he liked women, girls. He would wait there by the entrance to that place, others also, what was that place, club, I do not know, for tourists. Women went to there girls went to there. Money exchanged. Of course money exchanged, all goods, cash goods, tourist quarter, if tourists would go then of course money, tourists are money. He too would know it and he would go to there. He of whom we speak. He is dead. I did not kill him. I knew him but barely, a little. If he was husband, father, if he was married, I think so. In his own place. People come to here from distant districts, different areas, small towns, village life. And here into here, this is a city, it is very big, it is a greater change to people's lives. They have lives in their own places and then into this city and there is so much now that is different for them, they give up their lives and have new lives, men with family now become single and are with new women.

I like women. I see women, they are the strong ones, we humans, it is women who lead onward, onward, there is the new future and the women give birth to the new people and they go onward. Girls, if they are young. Younger women, girls. What I am to say. If I so like women, women are good. Girls. Of course girls what age are girls, if they are women, they go to these clubs. Girls. And men go to these clubs, tourists will go, they are not fools, they bring money, cash goods, they are strangers to this country and bring money, strangers who may be tourists. He waited for them. This one of whom it is said, said that I did kill him, I did not. It is said that. It is so. Yes I could have, I could have, if I was to kill him, yes. He went to that place, it is a club, he went to there. I knew this of him as he also knew of tourist men, strangers, that they take the dangerous route, these men, some may be fools, tourist men, their money, cash goods, there is darkness, they see this for cover, as the cat moves, seeking cover, it moves stealthily, as these men also, they go where darkness is the greater, moving in cover, knowing not who lies in wait, if one lies in wait, as also we who are in midfield as we are there and the opponent is coming and we brace ourselves and our bodies for impact and force of impact, discovering of ourselves are we of the stronger or weakened, may we not be weakened please to God, it is our prayer. We could not then survive. Humans are to survive. It is not the weak. People are invalids. In war they are become invalids, but they are not said to be weak. I would not say this of them. They would have been of the stronger but then in battle or by what means any means who would say, but these people are then injured, injured badly and thus become invalids, their limbs are gone, blown from them, bombs and mines beneath road surface, designated areas, who does know, none, the cat does not see through layers of soil and stone and these people do not. Neither, they do not. But this is that they become invalids, they are not weakened people, as others may be. I say that others can be weakened, it is nothing to say. Human beings are of all kinds different, one to another, no one the same, one to another, we can say twin children identical children but one differs from the other. How so. Not in visual things. Identical children. Identical adults. These are different one to another. Some are dancers, musicians and poets, others again enjoy games to play, as chess, as cards, they may gamble, some enjoy to play games of physical feats, so sports, as we can play football, I have said. We are different. But men have same things, yes, women, thinking of women, all men

I have said it. Strangers come. I do not fear strangers. These people are in this country, I am not in their country. People can be foreign, to us foreign, they may be. This country is my home. I may go to other countries. I never have been to the other country, any one. To what other country? I can go to Brazil, see football. Eetalee, Engaland, Nederland, Braseeleea, Braseeleea.

Strangers are in all countries. They may give money to myself, myself, that I may visit their countries, thank you.

Amereeca, give me passport and visa card that I may board a ship.

From our own city there is such a ship, give me money I can go, give me visa card passport

What.

I can play football, handball, bodyball, what is bodyball, I do not know bodyball. If I would kill then with the pistol, such a weapon. If this man was kicked. If he is dead, by kicking, I did not kill him. He was kicked in the body, I did not kick him in the body, in the head, everywhere. Football player, not bodyball.

Strangers are tourists. All times not all times. But also strangers can be strong men, if they are, who thinks that, yet some can be. If he who is dead thought to rob some one, if he did, who can say, the tourist is a big man and strong and too a fighter, who is to say, heavy heavy man, tourist man, some are dangerous to others, to ourselves.

He who is dead, skin and bone, what age he was, twenty-seven years and weight, skin and bone, if he could fight, I do not think so.

I did not say political. Some are political, he was not. I did not know him, if that he was, perhaps so, some may be, not political political, if he was. Some also are robbers, yes they are political and also they are robbers. All of we ourselves, we are human beings. He too was human being, waiting at this club where women and girls will be, and for tourists.

If he was there why was he there. Yes, he who is dead. If he was younger, if he was older, older than who younger than who. He liked women, yes, girls too, and was waiting for tourist men, why he was so waiting, taking their money, robbing it from them. And if tourist men wanted him, if then. Some say women but it is men, they say women but if it is women it is to men they look, if these tourist men wanted him, perhaps they did so, he was young man, if he was, I do not know

all things

People say to me political, what is that, I say football, yes, we know football. I walked over the hill, I followed the road, I crossed to the street, I followed it down, I went to there. Here is the club, there is the football, stadium, grass for it. I have played football and [k]now football what of football. Here is the girls here is the women, the tourists

I do not know. Political not political. I do not know.

What is political? Some one will come and take your money, will take your property, raping your women. I do not know. If he was angry with tourist men, he might be. What is to happen.

Some are in power, some in authority, holding this over others. Yes there is security, there is also terrorists, as he who is dead, as is known. He was no problem to me, mister skin and bone, if he might be, what, what problem? Political robber terrorist robber, mister brittle bone, what might he be? He is not to be there at that club, club is for tourist men, what is he there for, to rob these men, strangers to our country, bringing cash goods to our country, who are fools, these men are not fools, if he thought they might be

49

"where, how"

Anywhere, it was just to anywhere, needing that I had, yes escape from this territory. I could not understand my fellows. I was an adult. I did not ask for children's things. Offerings for children. We had our children, own children, looking to us for guidance. How were they to mature, they required to develop. They would become adults. What sort of adults would they become. They required our presence. But human beings as responsible, as adults, individuals, not images of themselves.

And we were as children. And if we were, yes, why was that. We had become so. How had this happened, what had we done, had it been done to us.

Yes it is true. We were not regarded as full beings. And we were not. It could not be said of us. None enjoys humiliation.

(I had to be going, to be anywhere, just so, as so.)

They spoke of us within our hearing. Yes, we then were present, we did not deter them. If the plight of a people is not recognised.

Our plight was lacking respect. Much would be asked of us, that we take part in our own subjection.

It was asked of us. What does it mean. This was asked of us. I had to be going. Not now, not then. Thus not respected and now I can say as human beings. I understand that. Nor could it have been other, yes, also, I understand it. But I had to be going.

How are we to accomplish that.

How are we to agree our subjection.

But what is the form that it takes. We are to become peasants, children, infant children, in the play-area, servants in a kitchen, waiters waiting, waiting.

I ask now, asked then, tomorrow. We can be asked. Neither indefinitely. I am one who will wield a weapon, any weapon, what is there, if I may reach let me reach, I can. It is something that can be said of me, also

not also, I would be anywhere

I may wish that it had been the case. I have a child.

But I was battered and could not make any movement, not to make any movement. My ankles and wrists, and shoulders too, unable to become free, or to sleep, even that, I could have wished. Before I could sleep, the spirit refreshening, strengthening, and bruises can heal, the body is beautiful. In sleep we recuperate.

All had ceased to be. In that way, it was how

That I may choose.

Each morning to drag myself into consciousness. I could be dead and would have wanted so to be, many many occasions and the continuation, existing through hatred, a perversion. Is this for children. Children kill, lacking in sensibility.

I can say it that none wished our survival. Finding this difficult to accept!

I could be anywhere

nor that to accept it was necessary, also, I knew that. I looked at our children, did they too understand, did they accept it. I think that they did. All children. What age are children, three years, twelve years. This difference may not be in the intellect.

We saw our children. Yes, again yes, yes yes yes yes. And girls, of course women, our town your town any town.

Some did not have women. They were not with us, but then later.

Neither beside us.

What difference.

My body felt that way, it was as though dragging myself, I knew not what to do.

No.

I knew nothing, except that to be anywhere, being anywhere what do we say

50

"it is possible"

I had been walking steadily, for how long I do not know. Of course in my own thoughts. Also there is a bend in the track, it is slight but enough. I thought the shape was of an animal, a large hare, motionless, by the centre of the way. This was when first I could see it. Not until fairly close did I understand that it was a person. It was a male, a small man. I took him to be in a seated position. It did not seem abnormal. Closer and almost upon him I heard and spied the insects buzzing, flies, varieties of them, also their sizes.

And his eyelids were closed. I did not inspect fully. I had my own business. If the man was dead there was nothing could be done for him. Later I would think of it. I would return short of two hours.

It was simply that I was easing my head. I had been under great stress in that recent period. I was coping. It was such as then that allowed me that I can state I was coping, now.

His legs and arms were bare, a form of covering about his feet, this man on the track. Not shoes, I would say not. I cannot remember clearly. A form of covering. I do not know.

His hair straggled, thinning and grey, dirty in appearance. Perhaps only this was the colour, this grey. I have the strong impression of dust on his head, I would say there was. The flies buzzed here and around exploratory. There was no smell. I walked on walked on.

Yes, I had put it from my mind. I can put things from my

mind. Of course such a thing is disturbing and certainly I was disturbed.

It did not spoil my time. I have become adept, it is no insult to me. I have acquired this. Resolve, it is resolve, my own will that I have developed, I am contented with it.

I walked on by the side track, by the edge of the forest. The branches are overhanging. I do not know enough about that country, the kinds of tree there, but of course varied. The track here never meets the sunlight so that if rain has fallen days previously then the mud lingers, even many days.

It was then a common outing for me, that place. I would go there by the same route, rarely deviating. The sameness of things was no drawback, I would say a pleasurable thing.

But that country always can be changing. From the autumn period, which was then at its beginning, the colours shift daily, and for me always enjoyable. I did detect here once odours. It might have been sickening. I do not know, I did not breathe through my nose.

Things that we learn, they come instinctively to us. Often they do, resulting from experience.

In what I do I am experienced, yes. I should notice changes. I do notice them. It is right that I do. On the other occasion in this vicinity it was by the shore I recall and that it was a catch had been dumped.

It is my recollection that it was a catch.

Shellfish, whelks, this is what it was. A dry-spell, rotting in the sun. The stench then was a sweetness. These odours at the edge of the forest differed. I would have known if otherwise.

I said this day was hot, humid, sweat poured from me. It was beyond the path that I stripped off my shirt, coming out from the undergrowth and ahead stretched the mountains and already my spirits had lifted so greatly. Always when there is the sense of freedom. And the air too, the whole of it, everything. The freedom may be a real thing. Achievable. Of course achievable.

I carried no burden. I had tied my shirt about my waist. I might have left it by the track but did not. I might have done that, I did not. My return through here was not a thing that was conclusive, not in advance, advance of it.

Blue sky above the mountains, white clouds.

Emotions, we ourselves, we have them.

I was gone only fifty minutes, one hour. No more. I saw no other human being, no animals, squirrels, rabbits, deer, none. But birds, different birds. Yes at another time two whole hours, easily, I say that, but this occasion only one hour and it came time. Time that I return, thinking now of the man, the body of the man, the carcass. What I would do. Of course I would report on it, a corpse, offer an account. But in the meantime, what. I had no blanket nor coat that I might use to shield it, if concealment, I could drag it onto the verge, from the track, into the bushes. But what then. It would have become the more available to prey, simply that. Others can say what they could have done, what they could have done, if, they can say that. They are entitled to say as much. I only say what I did, what thoughts occurred that now I remember.

Returning along the track I saw ahead the carcass as before. And many more flies now buzzing, many many more, and settled now on it, a horde of them, all over, face and neck, bare limbs, all over, everything, bare skin and in the hair, buzzing in the hair. Yes it was horrible, as a human being, one to another, to see this happening. Of course my stomach turned, of course.

Having to pass it by, I had to, and so I approached. Now to have left the track and gone at a distance, no, I could not have done so, not that. I approached and was passing, keeping my eyes to the earth before my feet. Soft here, always soft. I could not look I could not, as another human being, a fellow, this was a man, yes, of course and this horrible deafening, this buzzing such a great loudness, I could not stop my ears hearing it, the buzzing. What else. It was deafening, deafening, I have to say it, how strongly, deafening. Many many flies, tiny tiny, yes mosquitoes and larger, heavy, bloated they looked to me and this oh just the noise of them. Then I roared. I roared. It came out from me. I did not think to do it, neither to stop myself, I could not. To frighten and scatter them. These fly hordes, vultures, they prey on us, they will survive when we have gone.

Yes I roared.

No I am not a religious man. I can say this in my way, that I have no religion, I believe in no god, no gods, these give me irritation. I become angry by such notions. I am not ashamed. Why. I become angry. Yes I become angry, I will never be ashamed. These others should be ashamed. Yes I call myself socialist. I am socialist, a socialist.

How should I say this. Is there a way. No, I do not think so. I do not know what is wanted. I do not.

But that the insects are not the enemy. Of me. Of anyone. They are not the enemy. I say that.

Yes my stomach was heaving, I said so. I said so. Turning, it was. But I saw that scarcely were they affected.

The insects.

I had passed on.

I said that scarcely were they affected. A voice is a weapon. As human beings we have different weapons, many weapons. Yet such had been the depth of my roar I felt something of it might linger, captured there. I do not know. A sound is material. A sound causes vibration. Thunder can shake a house. A woman whose child is dead, her scream. These things are material, things in the world. The sound I made, that roar. I cannot say but that there seemed no impact, scarcely were these flies affected. I thought that. But now from behind me, not less than ten paces on from the body, there was the disturbance, I heard it, horrible disturbance. And looking back seeing the carcass, that it moved, I saw it, the body of the dead man moving, it did, moved. From the seated position. The seated position, where it was. The carcass crumpling. But the legs then kicking out. They certainly kicked out. Then a second time. The flies had scattered. But not far, then returning. And the body lying still. The body now lying still. A carcass, corpse, yes. I saw also that the eyes were open. Sometime they had opened. I cannot say anything more and nor could something have been done, if life had been there. Some life had been there, certainly I would say that it was possible certainly possible, but not now.

I am saying that life might have been there. It is me who says that.

I am not ashamed. Of what. There is nothing I need be ashamed. I adapt, also. I adapt. We adapt. We all adapt, you and I, there are many of us. No, I do not feel guilty.

It is me who says that, I said that. That moment. When I saw the moving, the body moving. So from that, the impact, when I roared so so loudly, so very loudly I do not know how loudly but I yes screamed, it was screaming. We are humans together. The eyes open. Nothing further could be done.

Yes I say that. The period when nothing can be done, there is that period.

Yes I walked on. I said that.

51

"her arms folded"

The name of an individual is important, I know that it is, but also that what is to do, I know, from myself not from myself, what to do, what I can do, what that I am to do, if I can do it then I shall do it, that I am not obstructing movement, we move ahead, we are to progress, how that is to be doubted, not by myself.

When she spoke to me she tried always not to smile, her arms folded beneath her bosom. I had to look from her, away from her, her from my mind. Yes, it was herself and her smile to me. It is sentiment. I do not know if she is dead. The sentiment comes not from that. She may be dead, it is a memory of her smile. I may lie awake through the night and the noises of the others and in my mind her smile is to me. Who she was, arms folded there and her smile. Yes to me. I have said. What could be denied, by whom is it.

It is possible, I do not think so. If it is so not by myself.

People do seek that they will know it, they will not know it by myself, myself myself. There is no matter other. I do not charge people other. They have their lives we have our lives, having these lives individually one another one to another,

what, if I am to say, what it is.

The image now recedes, if it is this required of me, yes, I no longer see her clearly, her smile is sad was sad is sad. I did not recognise the sadness, if it was earlier, seeing only the smile, arms folded, beneath her bosom, character of women, making smiles from we ourselves, detail of character, details, those of women, we men smile.

If I knew who that she was, I am to say it, no, I do not think so, I do not think it is possible, if she slips from my mind. I am one man. Others have seen her, men have seen her. They may be asked, not asked

If she slips from my mind.

What it is required, I am not to lie awake, I am to guard even my mind, she must not gain entry, what is this woman, who she is, what we men must do must not do, if her name is important why that can be, what the outcome, if some one end is there. I said her smile was there always. It is my memory. What we may mean by memory, I do not say what that is, all know what it is, I am one yes one of all I am not god, there are children, men, women, we ourselves, who we can be, and simply I am one of those, if her name is important what I am to say, her name is denouncing her, I am to denounce her, it is not possible. I am to die, kill me.

Yes I smile. I am safe, thus it is, she is in me. It is not ended. I do not care if so not so. If its importance is to myself, what it may be. It is man from woman.

When she spoke to me. I said that she did so, yes.

If she said things I do not know what those might be.

I can speak, speak not speak, I have no power. I can sleep, if I can sleep I shall sleep.

And if she comes to me, she may come to me, amid noise of others that also may sleep, in sleep, sleeping noise.

I smile, in her memory, memory of her, memory gives to me the image of her, I smile now, her memory is not with me it is she who is with me and her arms folded there, she always is so, alive, smiling to me, present there, also now, now.

52

"spectral body"

I could not. I did not know. Or if he was not human, perhaps if he is not human. Some are dead things, if he too was such a thing. Yes I thought that he might be, if it was a boy. What hand laid against my back if this was its hand, spectral body, laid as gently, this wisp of breeze, where life is and departing, this was a spirit, if of relatives, dead people, this was such a spirit. I thought through it but there was none, perhaps older, ancestor, closer to my grandfather, watching for me

darkness in the doorway

He is not dead but living, as spirits may do, living and breathing staring to myself. But I knew nothing of such a boy, or if a girl, if she had been a living thing and now was dead. What? This spirit was as nothing. I am a human being, neither blind nor deaf, not dumb, able to listen, touch or smell, I do all things. I am no killer of children. We may expect of security. If they are protectors, whose. In the club downside the bridge I saw her. This is the girl, she is the same, also watching us then, but boys and girls may vanish quickly, they go and return, not seen, we do not see them unless they make us so, also spectral.

53

"who asks the question"

And for how many languages? One may know all languages thus inferior to all peoples. I know all languages, I am inferior to all peoples. It is not sarcasm. I am capable of sarcasm, this is not it. They spoke a dialect that rendered them inferior but they were not inferior, they did not allow of it. But myself, yes. If it mattered, it did not.

This woman was familiar with their dialect, I have said, that language. They knew nothing of hers. Thus she had become the inferior. This is as it was, it remains so, for myself also, individuals inferiorised, myself herself.

She had become the inferior as I also became at the prior time. These matters were occurring.

All periods are significant. And effected through the one factor. It is asked of the one factor, can it exist.

Who asks the question.

They come in the night. They drag us from sleep, from sleep into sleep, as unto death. Myself herself.

They supposed I had my own pleasures, as we two. What these might be.

They looked to myself. Others. Who and what were this being, man creature. I am a man I am a creature. Human being.

Who looks at me!

This was the look, that the question. I would say it, man as human. There are iniquities.

These are iniquities. Iniquities were practised. I say it now.

If you can hear. I am to be heard.

For the other also, this would have been the address. The method of address as practised. I have no doubt.

We were different. What is identity, one to one, to the other, one another. If he thinks it is myself it is not, he has no knowledge

I can be in error she can be in error, could have been.

I am in error now. I am not in error now.

I can be in error. I can say it. But it was in that country on their behalf, that is why that I was there, she also. I do not say it is not my own behalf, also, I do not say that

I then was capable of error.

Of course. I was in error. What can be admitted. Error. Of course error, we all are in error I was in error. People have thoughts he had thoughts. He was a man. Men have thoughts. I know no other reason.

Humanity is a reason. Tell me.

There is something, it can be said, as of her people. What of her. One may say also of their children, say it as of them
as of them.

Everything I was to know was known to me. Had I so desired, I might know more. I would have been enabled to learn.

There was the other colleague of whom the subject of inquiry. If I am to speak, it cannot be so to speak, I cannot.

What I am to say, how it may be said, what form, that it may be effected, brought about

The operations of my mind

if I am to speak of my mind and its capacity, full capacity, my mind and its operations.

What is good capacity. Full capacity.

We had been encouraged to become familiar with the concept.

We two, myself herself. Also is there pain we speak of. It was spoken of. When? Myself to herself. Pain to myself and herself

I see now that in order to succeed fully they would have us believe that a ground was in common, it did exist.

A ground this ground.

This ground may be called land. Some call it so. I cannot, cannot say of this ground how it may be land. For how many lands! One may know all lands. Ours is the inferior, always, and for all. I know all languages, I said it, thus am I inferior. And to all peoples, if it matters, then mattered, it did not, does not.

Ourselves and these people. This other, subject of inquiry.

Bodies. Who says carcass, carcasses.

Myself or us. I would see them, I looked at them one by one, I saw that one and that one, that one. I would think yes, children, I also am a father and to these people.

We have become fathers [mothers]. Fathers not parents. I can be a father. I am a father [mother]. And I am no parent, not a parent. Myself, killer of children.

I am a killer. I am a killer of children.

These are questions, we state these, asking ourselves

Such a belief is an imperative. We accept it now. I also accept it. Now. And as it had been. If then as now, for it would have been. We are logicians, we killers

And too I was aware of these others. She too was one such. It began from their talking, how that they accomplished this. They thought of we ourselves of our familiarity with them, their own people, how it must please them. Also of their familiarity with my people.

This is as they thought it,

they knew my people, so they thought, intimate familiarity, so they thought. But in this these people are fools, then as now.

I bore them no ill feeling yet it was hypocrisy. This hypocrisy was not amusing, neither hurtful. Their manners a description of my actions into the face of our peers, heralding the freedom and its price, and to acquire it I had become an accomplice.

If they thought to attack by this, how they could, I do not understand. Yet they did attack. I would be on the margin, kept there. Communication circled me. I was on that perimeter, as though dwelling there. They had articles they might lose, communication with such as myself might lead them unto that pass. It is understood how they were to resist holding trust in me. Who would lay blame, who would lay the charge.

Heart-sorry.

I did not love these people. I might have become bitter. They did not love me. They had no regard for me. They saw the mountains I saw the mountains, they saw the mountains of home as I also, yes, I saw home, as they say "their", their mountains I might say "mine", my mountains, our mountains, they say land I said ground. They knew nothing of my language yet believed that they did, believed from that ignorance. They were taught that they knew, their familiarity with that language, yet I was the inferior, become so as also she did

and later

I did not love these people.

Heart-sorry, I heard it so.

What abuse may be, violation. We may know all words, words from all languages. What then is signified, we judge that.

I was the inferior she was the inferior

54

"it is true"

I cannot say about a beginning, or beginnings, if there is to be the cause of all, I do not see this. There are events, I speak of them, if I am to speak then it is these, if I may speak.